The Longest Road…

Brendan Edwards

Acknowledgments

I'm very much thrilled and amazed having finally made it this far, but I also acknowledge that I didn't make it here on my own. The following thanks go out to these amazing individuals. Chanel, my light and love, thank you for being the most wonderful daughter a father could have ever asked for. My mother Kathryn Massey, thank you for all your undying love and support, without which none of this would have been possible. Thank you for always believing in me. My (step) father Derek Massey, thank you for being the rock behind the scenes, and thank you for making my mother happy all these years. My brother Chris "Eddie," someone I've always looked up to for your hard work and relentless determination. I'd also like to thank Nathan and Tegan Jones, as well as Martin Haydock for the many years of great friendship. A special thank you to Chris Chambers for your support during some of my most challenging times. My editor Kat Betts, thank you for your knowledge, help and expertise, I learnt many things working with you. Alesha Saliba for your help and knowledge in design and Kelli Grandiek for your wonderful art. Of course, there are many other people I've met along my journey here, and to you all I say thank you. Wishing you all nothing but love and good fortune.

About the Author

Brendan Edwards was born in Melbourne, having moved at a young age, he has spent the majority of his life in sunny Queensland. As a first-time author, he took a rather large leap of faith into the world of writing. The young father of one left his full-time job in cash-in-transit security section in the pursuit of a more fulfilling and creative career. Brendan has always had a wildly vivid imagination, and after some rather unexpected and difficult times decided to dig deep and follow what came naturally to him. As an avid explorer and adventurer, he now spends the majority of his daylight hours wandering the gorgeous Australian landscape with a passion for nature and photography.

Brendan would love to connect, you can contact him by email, b_edwards_@hotmail.com or you can connect with him and share in his happy moments on Instagram at @brendanedwards88

The Longest Road

BRENDAN EDWARDS

Art by Kelly Grandiek

*The only impossible journey
is the one you never begin . . .*
-Tony Robbins

Chapter 1

'Beep! Beep! Beep!' The sound of an alarm brings a jolting start to the day for Broady. He rolls over in his bed; a slit of sunlight traces across the bed and right into his eyes. Broady squints as he reaches out for his phone vibrating on the bedside table. The brassy sound of the alarm is painful; fumbling, he knocks the phone onto the floor. Broady grunts as he sits up on the side of his bed, reaching down to turn it off. *5:55 am.* Annoyed about having been robbed of his precious snooze minutes. Seeing no point in laying back down again, he rubs his hands hard across his eyes and around the stubble on his face. Reluctantly he peers through one half-open eye looking onto the floor. His phone lay between his feet, the screen illuminated with a background image, a picture of a little blond girl in a yellow dress cheekily smiling ear to ear on a tree swing. The pretty little girl is Charlotte, his daughter. He closes his eyes and briefly reminisces about that time he took that picture. The thought brings a smirk to his tired face. She turns five next weekend. Broady sits, visualising the weekend trip away he has planned for her to the

Australia Zoo. She's a passionate animal lover, and it's the perfect gift he thinks.

The thoughts generate enough energy for him to propel himself up and out of bed, dragging his feet along the wooden floor and into the kitchen.

He flicks the coffee machine on and begins his first brew. The grinding of the fresh coffee beans is deafly loud this time of the morning; Broady screws his face up, turning his head away as he holds the grinder. The thought of the sweetly bitter brown liquid keeps his focus in check.

He stands quietly, leaning over the edge of the cold stone-top kitchen bench. He looks around at his tiny two-bedroom apartment. Somewhat of a minimalist with furnishings, his little apartment is quite warm and homely. A small green cactus sits on a small circular wooden coffee table with thin black metal legs beside his brown mid-century couch. A rather plain grey shaggy rug lay in front. A small square wooden dining table with white chairs sits only a few short metres from the living room.

He's meticulously clean, although he hasn't always been; since the arrival of Charlotte, his standards for himself jumped considerably. He spends the majority of his day prepping Charlotte's room, giving her fresh linen, positioning the obscene number of stuffed animals on her bed perfectly in line. Broady likes his little abode, with just Charlotte and himself.

With the arrival of his little girl this week, he likes to have everything perfect and in place for her. His close friends often give him a bit of a hard time about it, they're what you would generally describe as typical working-class males, no real sense in style or homewares, most leaving their partners to put in the effort around the house. Broady can't afford the luxury of having someone clean up after him but still wants to instil good values in Charlotte so he usually just laughs it off, not one to fire back. He's generally quiet and reserved.

That's until of course, Charlotte came to be. Broady was only twenty-one when her mother, Abby, fell pregnant with her. The two dated in high school. They split when Broady moved away from their little hometown in search of a different life. Abby followed him a year after dropping out of college. The two were happy for a few years, but just before the arrival of Charlotte, Broady lost his job in construction. With the arrival of a newborn and periods of unemployment, the stress in the relationship became detrimental. Broady struggled to find any long-term employment with the sudden economic downturn. Even when he secured a casual job, it was barely enough to support the three of them. After months of arguing he managed to obtain a high-paying mining job on a fly-in fly-out basis. Broady was excited and hoped that this would fix the couple's issues. With Abby's family too far away to help the young couple out with Charlotte, Abby became ever more dependent on Broady. Every time Broady left on another stint, she became unhappy. Abby sunk into a depression relying on Broady to pick up the pieces around the house when he flew back in. After a few trips back and forth he began to look forward to leaving just to get away from the tension in the household. Mining was hard work, but the physical part was not nearly as draining as the mental anguish he experienced at home. The two pushed on for two years like this before Abby decided to end the relationship after offering Broady an ultimatum.

"Quit your job and come home to your family or I'm leaving," were her words. Broady was torn, he was the sole financial supporter for the couple, and he saw no other means at the time, at least not anything stable. Seeing it as a backward step, he resented her for it. After all, he took the job in the first place to support the two. He couldn't understand this, seeing the situation a lose-lose. Coupled with the constant fighting, frustration and anger, Broady knew deep down that it was no place to raise a child. He didn't put up much of a fight when she left. She moved back to her parents' place having no other way of supporting herself.

Unfortunately, this now meant a four-hour drive south of the border for Broady to see Charlotte. Stuck between that and working away, he and Abby continued to fight for months after the split until Abby agreed she would drive up with Charlotte during the holidays and Broady would drive down and stay in town every other month. It wasn't the outcome that the hard-working miner had envisioned, but with no other foreseeable option he could think of, he settled with it, and at least for now, the fighting has stopped. Besides, Abby's family were good hard-working people; her parents would provide a stable family environment giving Abby the support she needed. A good place for Charlotte to grow up in.

Having spent the majority of his day still in his underwear he quickly threw on a plain black shirt from his wardrobe, pulling on some blue skinny jeans laying on the floor beside his bed from yesterday. Needing to get outside into some fresh air he decides to go to the shopping mall and get some groceries, wanting to be prepared for when Charlotte arrives. He much prefers going on a late Sunday afternoon to avoid the crowds. He picks his phone up off the floor and heads out the front door, almost forgetting his keys sitting on the counter beside the door.

His apartment sits in the centre of a long corridor with apartment doors beside and adjacent to his. Sensor lights light up the corridor as he enters. There're large glass windows at either end that let in the natural light from outside. It's a generally quiet building which suits him perfectly. He moseys on to the end of the corridor. There is a wide staircase at the end that heads down into the basement car park. Looking up out the window at the end of the corridor he notices a lot of cloud cover outside. He pauses at the top of the stairs and grabs his phone from inside his jeans pocket, checking the weather app to see if he needs to head back in to grab a jacket. As he unlocks his phone, he hears some voices from behind unit forty-eight's door. It's too muffled to make out what is being said. The voices become louder as the person on the other side approaches the door. He watches the handle on the door as it begins to open. As it does, the voice from behind the door begins to loudly bellow into the hallway.

"I'll be home when I'm walking back in the door!" a female voice yells.

As the door swings open a skinny little teenage girl walks out. Her hair dyed black, parted perfectly down the middle and dead straight. Wearing a black crop top and ripped jeans, she swings her small glittery purse up over her shoulder.

"For fuck's sake," she mutters quietly to herself as she rolls her eyes. Failing to see Broady standing there at first, she brushes her hair from her face.

"Hey there, Allison," Broady announces himself, feeling awkward in the middle of the family feud going on. He slides his phone back into his pocket to engage with her.

"Oh, hey Broads!" she chirps excitedly. Her tone and body language change considerably, a full 180 from her closed-off attitude only moments ago.

Allison has always had a little crush on Broady ever since Charlotte and he moved into the building last September. She's lived with her mum Jen, and Ray her mother's boyfriend since not long after her father passed away. She long suspected the two began seeing each other while her father was ill and has resented her mother ever since. Ray is a very controlling alcoholic, so when Broady moved in she greatly admired the fact that he seemed like a devoted and loving father to Charlotte. They met by the pool one morning, it wasn't hard for Broady to see and hear what was happening in her home, inviting her over quite often for dinner or to play video games with him and Charlotte, or just to hang out. He sees her as a sort of little sister and seeing the tough times she's been having he likes to think he's helping her out.

As the two continue down the staircase, Broady asks, "So, what's new, mate?" Knowing full well nothing good.

"Same old shit, Broads, you know how it is in there." She points over her shoulder with her thumb to her front door.

"Asshole won't leave me the fuck alone," she grunts.

"I hear ya!" he says, nodding his head. "Where are you off to?"

"Anywhere but here," she says, rolling her eyes again with a sour look on her face.

"Hey when's Charlotte coming?" she asks, changing the subject. "I've bought her something for her birthday."

"She comes on Monday. I'm heading to the mall now to pick up some things ready for when she comes," he replies.

"Aww, awesome. Can I come bowling with you guys again?" she asks.

"No dramas," he replies, lightening her mood.

"Hey, you think I could get a lift to the mall with you?" she asks.

"Maybe," he says. "But only if you keep that filthy potty mouth of yours at bay." Broady looks out of the corner of his eye, trying to keep a stern face.

"Fuck off!" She laughs, shoving him in the shoulder.

"When are you going to get your licence anyway? You could have gotten is ages ago, right?" Broady asks.

"When you let me drive your car and teach me," she says as she gives him a subtle wink.

"Haha, fat chance on that one, honey!" Broady says.

The two head down into the basement, Broady opening the basement door as Allison slips through. They head over to Broady's black jeep parked below. Allison's phone tings as they walk over to his car. Pulling out her phone from her purse she looks at the phone in disgust.

"Eh." She grunts before throwing it back in.

"Everything alright?" Broady asks.

"Not even one minute out of the house and this fucker is on my case!"

Broady jokingly glares at her swearing as he opens the passenger door for her.

Allison cheekily looks back at him. "Why thank you, kind sir." She stirs him up putting on a posh English accent. "Such a gentleman, Broady, how is it you're still single?" She winks, trying to flirt with him.

Broady picks up on her innocent advances and is quick to shut her down. "By choice, my dear!" he says. "Between looking after Charlotte and looking out for you I've got enough female drama in my life at the moment, thank you."

Allison slumps back into her seat.

Broady begins to drive out toward the ramp up onto the street.

Ray is standing at the top of the driveway looking down the street, obviously looking where Allison has taken off to.

"Quick, duck!" Broady pushes down on Allison's shoulder.

Seeing her stepfather, she quickly shuffles down into the bottom of the car floor. Broady casually waves at Ray as he drives out. Ray doesn't wave back, instead, he glares at him with a pissed-off look on his face.

"You're a legend!" Allison shouts with enthusiasm, jumping back up into her seat.

She sits up and laughs as she peeks through the gap between the headrest and the seat, giving Ray the finger as they drive off

Turning back around, Broady can see the huge grin on her face and feel the utter relief. He smirks to himself as they drive the short few kilometres to the shopping mall.

Broady parks in the bottom of the multi-level car park marked Level A with green paint on the concrete pillars. Not many cars are parked at the shopping centre, which is why he always chooses to go shopping in the late afternoon. The majority of the retail outlets are closed, leaving the place much quieter, suiting him perfectly. He generally tries to avoid the crowds and likes to park right near the entrance.

He parks and the two hop out, heading toward the entrance. Broady stops and checks his back pockets.

"Damn it!"

"What's wrong, precious?" Allison asks.

"I forgot my bloody shopping list, I'm hopeless without it."

"Well, that's one thing we can agree on." She smirks. "Lucky I'm here, I'll just come with you, and I'll probably get Charlotte way better stuff anyway. She'll be much happier."

"Ok, thanks," Broady says.

"You'll have the poor girl eating curried sausages again if I don't," she says, screwing up her face.

"Nothing wrong with them." Broady holds his head up proudly.

Allison sticks her finger down her throat and makes an awful gagging sound.

"That's gross," Broady says disapprovingly. "If my cooking is so bad then why are you always rocking up at my house for dinner? Maybe you can start to take care of yourself instead of having me look after you," Broady says, having a little dig at her.

Allison just brushes off the comment. "You can thank me later." She smirks as she runs off in front of him, jumping along the painted lines on the concrete driveway.

"Bloody child!" he yells out to her.

The two walk together through the aisles; Broady pushes the trolley and scratches his head trying to remember what's on the list. Meanwhile, Allison begins throwing all sorts of junk into

Broady's trolley like a basketball into a hoop. Broady just shakes his head, trying not to laugh and further encourage her. He pulls out the items and puts them back on the shelf when she's not watching.

They continue to walk through the aisles, into the female hygiene section.

"You know, won't be long before you're in here, Broads, having to manoeuvre your way through these items!" She giggles as she picks up a packet of tampons.

Broady just stares with a blank look on his face.

"Don't worry." She winks. "I'll look after you!"

"OH, wow. Thanks, Allison, you're so AMAZING!" he replies sarcastically.

"I know, right!" She keeps walking, picking up a packet of condoms from the shelf.

A strange ringing sound begins to buzz through Broady's head. Slightly disorientating him, he shakes his head and looks at Allison.

"These too," she says, cheekily holding the packet up over her face.

Broady's face drops immediately.

"Don't you even f—"

Broady is cut short by a thunderous *BOOM*, the vibrations ripping right the way through the entire store.

The ground shakes as the fluorescent lights flicker and sway in their hanging fittings.

Allison squeals, jumping close to Broady.

"What the fuck was that?" Allison nervously asks

Startled, Broady replies, "I have no idea."

The two hold each other, briefly cowering their heads and wondering if it's going to happen again.

The store has gone completely quiet. A minute goes by before anyone says anything.

"Holy shit!" Broady says.

"What the fuck was that?" Allison repeats.

"You all good?" Broady holds Allison close, nervously looking around.

Allison peeks up at Broady's face. "I'm good," she replies, secretly enjoying the embrace. "That's the first time I've heard you swear!" she adds.

"Come on, let's see what's going on." Broady lets go and begins to walk slowly toward the entrance. Allison quickly grabs onto the back of his shirt, following in tow.

As the two approach the end of the aisle, a blood-curdling scream echoes out through the store. The echo makes it difficult to hear where it's coming from.

It sounds like a woman's scream, so hideous the sound is that it sends chills down Broady's spine, every hair on his arms and the back of his neck stand up. There's no mistaking something awful has happened to the woman. Slowly creeping forward making it to the end of the aisle, Broady looks back to see Allison's petrified face; the unforgettable scream has momentarily paralysed her. Whispering, he calls out to her.

"Come on." He waves his hands up over her face, snapping her out of it.

She runs up right behind him tightly gripping his shirt and the belt at the back of his pants as she peers over his shoulder. Crouching down, Broady leans forward, stretching out his neck as he peeps around the corner. He props himself straight up for a moment before ducking back down. Allison, too scared to surface, quivers pulling down on his shirt. In the far distance, Broady can see figures running away down through the mall. The grocery store appears deserted until he spots a checkout girl. She's cowering on the floor below her cash register. Broady can see she's frightened, her skin is ghostly white and she's shivering. Her long red hair sits messily around her face. Whatever she's seen must have frightened her tremendously as she stares blankly at the ground.

He moves out into the open and behind the checkout. The checkout girl barely moves as the two crouch down in the tight space.

"Are you alright?" Broady gently touches the girl on the arm; her skin ice-cold, she doesn't respond. Allison looks at the girl bizarrely, having never seen anybody so visibly traumatised and in a state of shock, she is both intrigued and concerned by what could have caused it. A growing sense of fear begins bubbling up inside her stomach the longer her thoughts linger on it.

Now being closer to the large entrance to the rest of the shopping centre, Broady hears a peculiar sound. A crunching and grinding sound he can't quite make sense of, along with a growling gnawing sound, like a pig eating its feed.

Allison, seeing just how frightened the girl is, begins to console her, rubbing her on the back. "Are you ok, honey?" she asks.

The girl stops shaking, she tilts her head up to look at Allison with a glazed, cold look on her face.

"What is that?" she says with a flat voice.

Both Broady and Allison look at each other puzzled.

"I need to get a better look," Broady whispers. He slowly begins to stand up. Broady peers over the counter, he can see the top half of an older woman lying flat on her back. The rest of her body is behind a large concrete pillar obscuring Broady's view. The woman is too ghostly white, and at first, Broady thinks she is dead, however after a few moments, he notices her body jerk and shake slightly from side to side. Her eyes are closed, and she's making no sounds; he wonders if she's having a seizure. As he peers farther over to get a better glimpse, he begins to step around the counter, feeling the need to assist the woman. Before he can even move more than a step Allison panics, jumps up onto him and pulls him back down to the floor.

"What the heck are you doing?" Broady says, annoyed.

"I don't have a good feeling—"

"Shhh!" Broady cuts her off. "The sound has stopped," he whispers.

Allison goes quiet as the three listen carefully.

He picks himself up, crouching down behind the counter he lifts himself again, this time making a quick jump up and looking farther over. This time he can see the lower half of the woman's torso. Her clothes are covered in blood and it looks as though her insides are skewered all over the polished concrete floor. Getting a glimpse of a long dark-coloured arm, the rest still obscured by the pole, there's a dark shadow lurking over her body. Broady gasps and he pops back down to the floor.

Allison can see the startled look on his face and begins to fret. "What did you see?" she nervously asks.

Broady shushes her again, stunned as to what he's seen, frantically trying to make sense of it. "Listen," he says, placing his finger up to his ear. There's a light pitter-patter sound that can only be described as footsteps on a wet floor moving in front of them. Broady's stomach drops. His eyes widen and his heartbeat quickens as he stares toward Allison.

The pitter-patter sound comes in short bursts, moving quickly then stopping. The sound moves side to side, right in front of the register. "What do we do?" Allison mimes.

He puts his hand up, gesturing for her to stay still. Lowing himself down, Broady peers through the gap in the bottom of the register cabinet and the floor. Resting his cheek against the cold concrete, he sees bony-looking feet briefly stop a few metres from him on the other side. Only getting a quick glimpse of the very bottom, its skin is dark-grey-looking with dirty black smudges. Not the regular size and shape of a person, Broady is unsure if they are human or not. Its toes appear curled up and shrivelled, its toenails pale and cracked. With only a limited view from the gap under the counter, he's unable to see if the ball of the foot extends up into a heel as a person's on tiptoe would. The wet pitter-pattering sound of the footsteps is from its blood-soaked feet, leaving little bloody footprints along the floor. Becoming ever more frightening the closer the footsteps come, the checkout girl starts to cry, letting out faint squeals. Allison quickly tries to hush the girl pulling her head into her chest. For a moment there is nothing, not a sound.

The cabinet then begins to creak as weight is being placed upon it. A clicking sound echoes right above their heads as the cabinet creaks again as more weight bears down. Whatever was on the other side is now on top of the register. The three cower in as close as they can. Broady knows it's only a few moments before they're discovered. He clenches his hand and makes a fist. *I'm not going down without a fight*, he thinks. The air is tense, only broken by the frightening clicking sound from above on the counter. As Broady begins the idea of surprising whatever it is, there is a sound of shutter doors banging open and shut, followed by the sound of running boots and jingling keys.

"HEY, YOU!" a deep voice bellows.

"Get on the ground now!"

Broady's relieved at the voice, believing it to be a police officer.

The officer yells again for compliance, and as he does an ear-piercing squeal rings out from above the counter, hurting Broady's eardrums, followed by three loud bangs, one after the other. Gunshots ring out as the three still huddle under the counter, blocking their ears from the sounds. The cabinet creaks again as the weight jumps off, followed by fast-paced striding footsteps heading away from them.

A few moments of silence go by before Broady announces their presence.

"Don't shoot!" he yells from underneath the counter, slowly beginning to raise his hands high in the air. Broady makes eye contact with the officer, he can see that the officer's every bit as frightened and confused as he is. He wipes the sweat below his thick dark hair still firmly holding his firearm at Broady. Broady looks down, gesturing for the girls to slowly get up, thinking that if the officer sees two scared females it will lower his angst. It goes to plan perfectly, and the officer lowers his weapon.

"We're all good?" Broady enquires, not sure of the spooked officer's mental state.

He ignores him, grabbing the radio attached to the top of his police jacket.

"Two-four-two, shots fired, Robina Shopping Centre, Woolworths entrance."

"Hey!" Broady calls out again.

The officer turns away, repeating his words into the radio. Broady can hear there is no response, only static.

"Shit!" he says under his breath looking toward the floor, discovering the elderly lady's body. He jumps back, looking straight up at the trio. Attempting to compose himself with not much luck, Broady sees the officer's eyeballs just about popping out of his skull with astonishment.

"Officer! HELLO!" Broady yells.

"Excuse me," Allison pipes up, managing to grab the officer's attention. "What the heck is going on?" she yells to him. "And what were you shooting at?"

The officer pauses for a moment in a state of shock. His eyes dart back and forward, trying to understand what's just transpired.

"I . . . I don't know," he says.

Broady rolls his eyes hoping for a better answer. He leads the girls around from the counter as the officer steps toward them.

"I thought it was a person, a skinny fellow, then I saw something protruding out its upper back, skin dark-grey coloured, all dirty and charred looking," the officer says, rubbing his hands around the skin on his face.

"I'm sorry, what do you mean something protruding out its back?" Allison barks at the officer. "What the fuck are you talking about!" she says, agitated. "What the fuck is going on?"

Seeing she's working herself up, Broady tries to comfort her, holding her shoulder and rubbing her back.

Broady composes himself and takes charge of the questions.

"Where's the rest of your squad? Or your partner? Do you have a partner?" he asks.

"I'm a motorcycle cop, I only stopped here to get something from the supermarket, I wasn't called here. I heard the blast as I was walking in, I ran back outside to take a look. That's when I heard a woman screaming so I headed back inside," he explains.

"I need to call my mum," the checkout girl says softly; she's shaking, her arms wrapped around herself. Allison comforts her, wrapping her arms around her while Broady continues to find out more.

"What was that gigantic booming sound?" he asks. "Are we under attack?"

"I'm not certain, there was a huge fireball coming from the direction of the service station right on the corner of the promenade," the officer explains, pointing in the general direction.

"My handheld radio is down; I have another on my motorcycle," he explains. "I'm going to call for backup, everyone stay put, and I'll need to get statements from everybody. Don't touch anything," he demands, beginning to walk away.

"Wait wait wait . . . Hold on a second. You want us to stay here after *that*?" Broady says, dumbfounded. "You don't even know what was attacking us, and you want us to wait here . . . With *that*!" Broady points to the woman's mutilated body, glimpsing at it for only a moment before his stomach turns.

The checkout girl's teeth begin to chatter as she bites her nails. She too looks down at the bloody corpse. Immediately beginning to hyperventilate she begins to cough, then choke before throwing her lunch up onto the floor. Allison steps over to help and holds her hair back. She spits the vomit taste out of her mouth and stands back up. "I'm staying with you." Covering her eyes from the woman's body she moves toward the officer.

Seeing how distressed the girl is he agrees. "Right!" he says. "Ok then, everyone follow me; we'll head out to my motorcycle together and get more help. Let's go!" He gestures waving his firearm, walking toward the shutter doors. The girls begin to fall in line.

"Hang on, mate!" Broady stops him. "That's the same direction whatever you fired on went, there's no way in hell I'm going out there."

Allison stops, considering what Broady's just said. "He's right," she agrees, moving a step back toward Broady.

"Besides you said the explosion came from out that way as well, it just doesn't seem like the best idea?" Broady says.

The officer, clearly irritated by Broady's questioning, shuts him down. "My motorcycle is out there, that's the only option we have to get any assistance, but you guys do whatever you want," he says dismissively.

"I'm staying with you, Broads," Allison says, stepping behind Broady.

"You guys are making a huge mistake." The officer sighs placing his hand on the lower back of the checkout girl and helps to usher her outside. The checkout girl looks back toward them sheepishly as the two run off through the large swinging doors.

Broady shakes his head.

"What do we do now, Broads?" Allison asks.

"We'll duck out this way," he says, pointing to the opposite side of the entrance.

Grabbing Allison by the arm, he moves quickly toward the long corridor to the left of the supermarket entrance.

The two neighbours begin to pick up the pace; their footsteps echoing through the corridor. As they run, Broady starts to become slightly disoriented as his vision becomes blurry. No longer able to focus on the doors at the end of the corridor, he looks toward Allison.

"Where are we going?" she asks him.

Broady doesn't respond, shaking his head as a ringing starts in his ears again. His vision begins to tunnel, and Broady's heart begins to race—he's worried he's about to pass out.

Just as his vision is almost blackened, he feels a strange sensation, like his head is floating away from his body. He blinks hard to straighten himself out.

He opens them only to see a blurred picture of the officer and the checkout girl running down what he believes is the opposite corridor like he's looking over their shoulders. They stop; the officer draws his weapon in almost a slow-motion manner. A dreary sound of the officer's voice yelling, "Don't move!"

He fires a shot. Broady can see the flame shoot out of the muzzle, the spent cartridge ejects and the ting of the brass hitting the concrete floor. The shots keep ringing out.

Broady can see a dark figure in the background pouncing toward them, far too blurry to make out what it is exactly. An ear-piercing squeal echoes through the corridor. His vision moves to the checkout girl who's on the floor with her fingers in her ears, her eyes shut tightly, with her mouth wide open, screaming. Broady tries to look up to what's approaching. His vision shifts back as the dark figure pounces on top of the officer pushing him back into Broady's view. Startled, Broady jolts, shutting his eyes.

When he opens them again, Allison is staring at him.

"Where are we going?" she asks.

Puzzled, Broady looks around in a moment of deja vu.

"Broady! Where are we going?" she yells, attempting to snap him out of it.

Multiple loud bangs manage to bring Broady back to his senses, startling Allison and followed again by that high-pitched squealing sound topped with the sound of a girl screaming.

"What the fuck is that?" Allison quivers

"That's the cop and the checkout girl," Broady whispers to himself. "They're dead."

"Wait . . . How do you know that?" Allison says, confused.

Broady stares at the floor for a moment, unsure about what's just transpired.

"Come on, we have to get out of here," he says, ushering Allison along, unsure of how to answer. No time for that. "We can head out the end, through the loading dock at the end of the corridor then double back around to the car park. There will be less people this way," he says. Broady approaches the door first. "Whoa whoa, hold up," he says holding up his arm. The duo stop, noses inches from the metal door.

Broady pauses, gently placing his fingertips on the door, hesitating briefly and anxious as to what awaits them on the other side. He gently pushes it open a few inches, peeking through the gap.

It's dark, and apart from the flicker of the fluorescent bulbs, it's completely quiet.

"Come on," Broady says, pushing the door wide open. The door creaks and squeals on its hinges. The sound makes them both cringe. However, the coast seems clear.

They make their way to the end of the dock and standing at the top of the truck delivery bay Broady peers out into the open. The sky is overcast and grey. In the distance, the clouds glow red and orange, with billows of smoke spots in all directions.

"What is going on?" Broady whispers to himself again, jumping down from the loading dock. Helping Allison down, the two scamper quickly behind a green industrial-sized garbage bin. Moving farther outside they can see a few cars speed past in the distance.

Broady squats for a moment thinking about the best way back to his vehicle.

The dock is eerily quiet with every little sound echoing down through the corridor putting Allison on edge.

Her alarm on her phone rings. Loudly.

"Fuck!" she yells, frantically pulling her phone out of her back pocket to silence it.

Broady glares at her, irritated.

"It's an alarm to take my pill!" she says.

Broady just rolls his eyes and starts looking around again.

"What?" she says, throwing her arms up.

The doors of the loading dock bang and shudder. Followed by the clicking sound, then a high-pitched screech. The sound echoes out into the loading dock.

They both turn to face the corridor. Chills run down

Broady's spine as the hairs on the back of his neck stand up.

"We have to move, now," he whispers firmly.

Broady leads first, crouching down hugging the concrete wall out into the open. Allison right behind him.

To the far left there's a large open grassed area, with the multi-level car park at the end. Broady holds up his arm, stopping Allison from stepping out into the open. He cautiously looks around the bend, still crouched behind the concrete wall.

"Come on, let's go!" she pushes him, urging to move.

"We don't know what's out there," Broady replies, holding her back.

Echoing down the corridor the screeching sound gets louder as it seemingly gets closer to the dock.

Allison freaks, pushing past Broady's arm and frantically sprinting out into the grassy field.

"Allison, wait!" Broady whispers.

Allison is moving too quickly and is too far to hear Broady's plea.

Broady takes after her, running madly out into the field. The dash is long, but with the help of the adrenaline pumping, they make it to the car-park entrance relatively quickly.

Allison pauses behind a pillar at the entrance as Broady catches up.

"That was stupid, Allison," Broady says, panting heavily.

"Fuck that!" she says, dismissing him. "We needed to get the fuck out of there!"

Broady can see his car, sitting desolate in the middle of the car park.

Taking a quick look around the vacant car park they sprint

for it. Making the hundred or so metre dash they duck down beside the passenger-side door. Broady fumbles to get his keys out of his pocket from his crouched position.

"HURRY UP!" Allison urges.

Unlocking the door, Allison jumps straight in, climbing over into the driver's seat. Broady, too, climbs in the passenger side after her.

"Keys, keys, keys!" Allison says, still in a panic.

"There's no way you're driving, you're a lunatic, we'll crash!"

Unimpressed by her neighbour's lack of faith, Allison awkwardly swaps positions jumping into the back allowing Broady to shuffle over before she moves into the passenger seat.

Broady struggles to keep it together, making the task of putting the key in the ignition all the more difficult, shaking and scratching the key around the car's ignition.

Another loud screech echoes through the car park.

"Broady!" Allison yells, panicking.

"I know, I know!" he says, looking down at what he's doing. Managing to get the key in the ignition, he quickly turns it, firing up the engine. "YESSS!" he proclaims a small victory.

"LOOK OUT!" Allison screams.

Startled, Broady looks up as a dark figure hurtles through the air toward the front windshield.

Locking eyes only briefly at the dark figure's frightening bright yellow eyes, momentarily paralyse him.

The crack of machine gunfire blasts through the car park hitting whatever was about to rain down on them. It falls onto the bonnet with a loud bang and slides down the side. Through the window, Broady can't see exactly what has fallen down next to his car. Looking back up he sees a squad of heavily armed police moving through the car park spread out in tactical formation. The two frightened neighbours sit like stunned mullets, watching the officers move toward the shopping centre. Seconds seem like hours before a bang on the bonnet gathers their attention. One of the heavily armed police has his hand on the bonnet of his vehicle. The two make eye contact. The man's face is covered by a black bandana and a police helmet. He makes no sound, instead placing his thumb up and gesturing with his head toward the exit.

Broady wastes no time, shifting the car into reverse stepping on the gas and hightailing it out of there; the tires screech and squeal on the sealed concrete floor as they take off. Turning onto the main road the two know, they need to make it home, somewhere where they are safe.

Chapter 2

Driving onto the main road away from the shopping centre, an emergency services crew speed hastily in the opposing direction, lights and sirens on. The few cars that remain on the road drive fanatically, speeding and running right through red lights, up over curbs and around other vehicles.

Broady's eyes widen in disbelief, paying close attention to the chaos that's seemingly enveloping him. Driving cautiously, Broady shakes his head. "What the fuck," he mutters under his breath.

"Look over there," Allison yells out, pointing her finger and tapping it on the glass.

"The whole place is alight," she says. A factory warehouse is completely ablaze.

That's not the only fire. Distant clouds glow red and orange from distant fires.

Continuing through the chaotic streets, they pass a car that's crashed head-on into a light pole, the pole slightly bent over onto the buckled vehicle. Allison twists around in her seat as they pass by, seeing the front windshield smashed and the car smoking. The driver is spread out, flung out of his seat and over the bonnet of the car. Blood pours down the side of the vehicle. Allison shrieks, quickly turning back around in her seat, holding her hand over her face and mouth.

"What?" Broady asks, curious as to what she's seen.

Allison shakes her head, unable to relay what she's just witnessed.

Broady slows the car down as they approach a steep hill with an intersection with traffic lights at the top. Creeping up the hill, he can see the traffic lights are inoperable and flashing yellow.

Broady can't quite see over the crest. Allison sits up in her seat stretching out her neck to see over the crest as they slowly creep over the white lines.

"We're good, just go!" she says.

As Broady releases his foot off the brake a little red Toyota flies over the top of the crest from the opposite direction with such speed its tyres almost leave the road. Reaching the middle of the intersection, a large concrete pumping truck speeds downhill into the intersection from the adjacent direction slamming into the side of the little red car. With a loud bang all the windows shatter and explode pieces of glass throughout the intersection, some pieces catapult into the air and ting on the bonnet of Broady's Jeep as they rain down like hail. The Toyota flips onto its side before rolling down the hill in the same direction the truck is travelling, before coming to rest against the traffic light. The collision barely phases the concrete truck, relatively undamaged with its large steel bullbar. The truck barely even appears to slow down. The large vehicle sways side to side over the road, its heavy body tipping its weight onto each side before the driver regains control and continues on. Broady pulls up the handbrake, putting the car into park. As he goes to unbuckle his seatbelt Allison's hands stop him.

"Don't you even think about getting out of this car, Broady Fitzgerald!" she yells frantically at him. Broady, seeing the concern on his neighbour's face, looks toward the mangled Toyota, still wanting to help. Fighting his urge, he stares at the wreck, smoke billows out from the bonnet before a small flame sparks from under the chassis. There is nothing he can do; even if they survived the horrific crash there was no way he could get them out safely.

Reluctantly peering again into the intersection, Broady steps on the accelerator; the two hang tight as they speed through, praying they too aren't taken out.

He exhales a large breath of relief as they exit the intersection. A loud explosion erupts and Broady looks back through his rear-view mirror seeing a billow of smoke raise from the other side of the crest where the car lay.

"This is insane," he mutters to himself.

They speed down their driveway into the basement car park. The suspension bottoms out, the car scrapes along the concrete, and the tyres bang in the wheel well.

"Erg," Allison mutters, bouncing and jerking in her seat. The basement car park is a long straight corridor with car spaces on either side. It's dimly lit from only a single row of fluorescent bulbs in the centre of the basement. Staircases up into each of the three stages of the apartment complex are spread evenly along the walls on the right side. Broady drives all the way to the end, and pulling up the handbrake quickly he doesn't bother to park in his allocated space. He opts instead for the car space closest to his building entrance.

Running up the stairs heavy-footed, Allison's front door opens. Ray comes out from his apartment to see what all the noise is from; he closes the door behind him.

"Where have you been?"

Allison's in no mood for his lectures, rolls her eyes snatching Broady's keys from his hands and brushes past Ray toward Broady's apartment without even acknowledging him.

Ray steps forward to go after her. Broady quickly butts in, taking the heat away from her.

"Hey Ray!" he says, stepping in front of him. Ray stares toward Allison and doesn't respond.

"Ray!" Broady yells again, getting up on his tiptoes, eye level with Ray; his breath is fruity from the pungent smell of booze. Broady manages to get his attention.

"Where's she going?" Ray frowns. "We've been watching the news, there's some sort of terrorist attack at the mall, and a few bombs went off in the surrounding industrial areas," he continues. "We've been worried sick."

Broady can see his pissed-off neighbour's attitude has changed to a concerned parent, albeit step-parent. The door opens again and Allison's mum, Jen, stands in the door.

"Was that Allison?" she asks.

Broady can see she's upset, her eyes red and glassy from crying. She's holding a handkerchief up over her mouth.

"Yes, that was her, she was with Broady at the mall!" Ray explains.

"The mall?" Jen shakes. "That's been all over the news with SERT police. Police helicopters filming the whole thing from above. People have been killed!"

Seeing Jen beginning to work herself up, Broady interrupts. "We're alright. She's fine, a little shaken but we're good."

"She needs to listen and come home now!" Ray demands.

Broady can see Ray's blood pressure rising, his face turning bright red as the vein on the side of his head begins to pulsate.

Ray begins to step forward. Broady steps back as Ray tries to use his size to push past him.

Jen reaches out, grabbing the back of his elbow. "Let her be." She sighs. "She's safe, that's all that matters."

Ray pauses, snarling, a bead of sweat pours down his brow sweating out the alcohol from his body. Too hard, he can't be bothered dealing with her. Seemingly pissed off he turns around and shoves the door open marching back inside his place. The door begins to self-close, before it does he pops his head back out, pointing his finger at Broady. "She's not to leave the building!" he demands in an attempt to have the last word of authority. The door shuts.

The corridor goes quiet. Jen is visibly upset; Broady can't help but feel sorry for her.

"She'll be safe with you, won't she?" she asks, looking to Broady for reassurance.

"Yeah, Jen. I'll keep a close eye on her for you."

She gently smiles at him before sheepishly heading back inside.

Before Broady even makes it to his front door he can hear the sound of the television. Opening the door, he's bombarded with a wave of noise, almost pushing him back out the door.

"Allison! Is it really necessary to have that up so loud?" he yells, heading into the lounge room.

His neighbour is standing in front of the TV, her jaw almost hitting the floor, her eyes wide open. "What the fuck!" she says, watching the news unfold on the TV. "The whole city is in chaos!"

Broady moves to sit on the couch, glued to what's being shown. Multiple reports of civil unrest, buildings on fire. Flashing to a news crew on the ground, positioned out the front of the mall. In the background, they can see the whole area cordoned off by police, roadblocks and emergency vehicles. The rolling comments on the bottom of the screen read *Possible terrorist attack*. Multiple people are running through the streets away from the shopping centre. Another news reporter on the ground catches up to one as the jerky camera angle films an interview with a man walking swiftly.

"It's crazy in there, people getting attacked, everyone's running, frantic," he puffs, wiping the sweat from his face.

"Running from what?" the reporter asks.

Unable to hold the microphone properly to the man's mouth the sound is faint and patchy.

"I'm not sure, I didn't get a good look," he pants.

"Did you see any terrorists?" she asks

"No, all I saw was a ruckus in the food court. People going crazy, bashing and clawing at each other, I thought it was a gang war, I got out of there as soon as I could."

"Wait, wait!" the reporter yells. "Just one more question." Before she can finish, unable to keep up with the man in her high-heel shoes, he's gone.

She pauses for a moment and composes herself.

"Well, more reports coming to you now, indicating more than just a terrorist attack. Something more sinister perhaps? We'll bring you more updates as they come in, for now, it's back to you in the studio."

Broady mutes the TV.

"Hey!" Allison complains.

"I need to call Abby, see if Charlotte is ok."

Allison sits down watching the TV on mute.

Broady paces back and forth in the kitchen. The phone rings out before going to Abby's message bank. Broady's anxiety rises as his heart beats hard in his chest.

Walking back to the couch, he sits down pushing the phone against his mouth anxiously, watching the headlines.

The headlines become more alarming, reports come in that it's not an isolated incident, helicopter footage shows civil unrest and multiple suburbs in chaos, buildings on fire, heavily armed riot police blockading entire streets.

Thunderous noise bellows from above Broady's apartment, he looks out his balcony window as the flashing lights of helicopters whiz over in the skies.

His phone begins to vibrate against his lips; Broady answers the call in record time.

"Hey sorry, we were swimming, what's up?" Abby's calm voice answers, seemingly unaware of what's going on.

Broady, sounding anxious and agitated almost shouts down the phone.

"Are you and Charlotte ok?"

Abby sounds concerned and confused. "Uh . . . What's wrong with you?"

"Are you both ok?" he shouts again.

"Yeah, chill. We're fine. What's going on?" she asks.

"Turn the news on," he says.

"I can't right now, we are down at the creek. My battery's about to die."

"Look!" Broady says. "Get Charlotte and stay inside." Before he can finish, the line goes dead. He throws the phone at the couch.

"Chill, Broady, it sounds like they're all good. It doesn't look like it's anywhere near where they are." Allison tries to comfort him as a map appears on the TV with red shading over multiple Gold Coast suburbs. She lays down on the couch with her head in his lap and pulls the throw rug over herself.

Happy to hear that they're ok, he sits back in his chair and stares at the TV. With so much going on the two completely forget it's on mute.

Hours go by, the same reports keep replaying over and over.

"Can you believe this," he says, nudging Allison.

She doesn't respond, he looks down, her eyes are shut and she's fast asleep. All the adrenaline from the chaos that's unfolded has left her body and she's crashed, hard.

Still far too worked up to relax, he continues to flick through the TV stations.

Switching on the television's Teletext he reads through the headlines, lying back on the couch getting into a semi-comfortable position—he tries not to move too much. He doesn't want to wake Allison, deciding it's better to let the poor kid sleep.

His eyes become heavy as he tires from reading. The time between blinking increases before closing his eyes to rest. Before long he too drifts into a light slumber.

A light tapping sound enters the unit. In a half-dazed state Broady takes no notice. The tapping sound continues before stopping. Broady opens his eyes—nothing.

Then it starts again. Exhausted, it takes him a moment to realise it's knocking on his front door. Rubbing his eyes in a half-asleep state, he grabs a cushion off the couch, placing it under Allison's head in place of his lap.

He stumbles to the door. Looking under the gap in the front door he can see someone's there. Immediately his heartbeat jumps, still jittery and unsettled, he anxiously places his eye up to the peephole.

It's Jen.

Unlocking the door, Broady greets his neighbour. "Hey, Jen. Is everything alright?" he asks, rubbing his face.

"Is she here?" she asks quietly.

"Yes, she's asleep on the couch, would you like me to wake her?" he replies, opening the door wider and beginning to turn around.

"Oh no, that's ok," she replies, reaching out to grab him.

Jen stands there awkwardly.

Broady pauses for a moment, giving her space to come out with whatever else she has to say. She remains silent. Seeing the worried look on her face, Broady attempts to reassure her again.

"She can sleep in Charlotte's bed, don't worry she's safe here," he says.

"You're really good to her, Broady; she speaks so highly of you."

"Thanks, Jen," he says, not knowing what else to say. Jen stands there for a few moments before saying goodnight. Broady shuts the door and locks the deadbolt.

He walks quietly back to the lounge room. Having watched

enough reruns, he stares down at Allison curled up on the couch. Not looking too comfortable, Broady scoops his arms under her and carries her to Charlotte's room. Reminding him of Charlotte and his bedtime routine, although much heavier, he gently places her on the bed pulling back the covers and tucking her in. He turns on the lava lamp Charlotte uses as a night light. Allison mutters something in her sleep before rolling back over. He heads out of the room, looking back in he whispers, "Goodnight kiddo," before closing the door almost all the way. Picking up the remote to turn the television off, there is a map marked with emergency evacuation points. Broady doesn't take much notice, turning it off, as well as all the lights, he heads into his room.

Standing by the window he stares out. The light from the streetlights illuminate his room. It's eerily quiet, and in an anxious state Broady's becomes hypervigilant. Able to hear even the slightest noise from the crickets outside buzzing away, besides the distant glow of fire, it almost looks like a regular evening.

Broady stands for a while, anticipating some movement. Several minutes pass and Broady begins to tire. He lies on his back on his mattress, staring at the ceiling. His mind begins to wander as he replays the day's events over and over in his head. His mind begins to race, unsure of what the following day will bring. The only comforting thoughts he can muster is that Charlotte is safe, for the meantime anyway. He unlocks his phone staring at the picture of her on his wallpaper for several minutes.

Resting his phone on his chest he drifts into sleep,

Believing he is having a dream, Broady's mind carries him outside, underneath a streetlight outside his apartment. Somewhat confused by his lucid dreaming state, the streetlights begin to flicker as dark shadowy bodies move around the building. His mind drifts up outside his window. Seeing himself sleeping, the street lights flicker again before going out completely. The moonlight becomes obstructed by the dark clouds rolling in. Now pitch black, Broady hears the distant sound of Charlotte's voice yell, "Daddy!"

Broady tosses and turns in his bed as the voice cries out louder. "Daddy!" He frantically moves around in the darkness. In the distance, Charlotte comes into focus, crouched down with her arms around herself wearing her bright yellow flower dress.

He is now unsure whether he is awake or still dreaming.

Broady cautiously approaches her as Charlotte crouches, sobbing and crying. Placing his hand on her back he comforts her. "It's ok, honey."

As he places his hands on her she turns around, and yells inches from his face, sending chills racing down his spine.

"They're coming!" she yells with a ghostly look on her face. "Wake UP!"

Her voice penetrates his whole body as tingles run down his arms and legs, jumping up out of his bed gasping for air.

His room is now almost completely black only a dim light emanates from the screen on his phone that's flipped face down on the end of the bed. It takes him a few moments to compose himself, his heart ferociously pounding from inside his chest. The red charge light from his phone charging pad has gone out. Peering outside he realises the streetlights are out too. Only faint light from the moon as it peeks out from behind the clouds.

Feeling uneasy, frightened and disorientated, he grabs his phone off the bed, turning on the flashlight. Was his dream really a dream?

Through the corner of his eye, a dark body moves quickly in the park across from his apartment. Paranoid, he's unsure whether he's just imagining things. However, after his experience in the shopping mall, he takes no chances, running out and bursting into Charlotte's room.

"Allison, Allison! Wake up!" he whispers, shaking her gently.

Startled, she jerks her body as she wakes.

"What the fuck, Broady," she groans in a daze.

"We have to get up, now!" he says. Leaving no time for her to get her senses back he grabs her arm, dragging her from the bed.

She fights back. "Broady, what's going on?"

"They're coming," he says coldly.

Allison's eyes widen, from the seriousness in his voice and the worried look on his face Allison doesn't question him further.

Grabbing his keys from the entry table he slowly pulls down on the handle of the front door, opening it slowly, he pops his head out the door. The sound of pots and pans banging together accompanied by the smashing sound of crockery. Broady freezes as he peers down the dark corridor. The emergency lights in the hallway flash and flicker, one eye around the door jamb he sees a dark shadowy figure outside Jen and Ray's apartments, their door is wide open. The dark figure stands slightly crouched over, its arms tucked up close its body like a bird, clicking and screeching.

Screams billow out of the apartment.

Allison, recognising the cry, calls out, "MUM?", trying to push through the door to find out.

"Allison, no," Broady turns his head and whispers, pushing

his body against hers as she tries to squeeze through.

Turning his head back, the dark figure's eyes cast in his direction. Bright yellow eyes glow in the darkness. Broady freezes for a moment, the sight of those eyes takes his breath away in a moment of sheer terror. The familiar high-pitched scream from the mall echoes through the hallway, every hair on Broady's body stands up. Making a leap toward them, Broady tucks his head back in, slamming the door shut. Stepping backward, he stumbles, his legs intertwined with Allison who is still trying to squeeze through. The two fall to the ground. Their eyes fixated on the door as a shadow casts from the emergency lighting underneath the door. The two remain silent, unsure if they've been discovered. The clicking sound is more distinct than ever, coming from the other side of the door. The door lock begins to shake, and the door vibrates loudly up and through the ceiling as the creature bashes on Broady's door, screeching and clicking.

The two scramble up off the floor. Running back into the lounge room, Allison skids along the wooden floor with her socks, sliding into the glass dining-room table knocking over the chairs. With the sound of the furniture crashing down, there's no way their presence has gone unnoticed. The high-pitched screaming intensifies, as does the booming sound of the door.

"What do we do?" Allison screams, standing by the balcony window.

Broady peers out the balcony door. It's a big drop, too far to jump without a rope. Not certain about what else may lurk outside, Broady thinks of somewhere to hide inside his tiny apartment.

"The laundry!" he says, grabbing Allison's hand. In the

laundry, there's a dropped ceiling with a manhole cover used for plumping and electrical maintenance.

Broady leaps on top of his washing machine and removes the plaster manhole cover, revealing a tiny cramped cavity in the roof. Holding out his hand he pulls Allison up onto the sink beside him and boosts her up into the roof. She shuffles around awkwardly making space before signalling Broady up after her.

The two uncomfortably crouch with their backs touching the concrete roof. It smells stuffy and damp. Broady tries to awkwardly balance on the timber beams not wanting to fall through the plastered ceiling. As he fumbles in the pitch-black bulkhead to find the cover, a tremendous bang billows out through the apartment. Something breaks off, it tings as it bounces, hitting the bottom of the kitchen cabinet and rolling into the laundry. The shiny aluminium door handle reflects a small amount of light in the room. Broady freezes, holding the cover. With the door now wide open, Broady realises it's now too late to put the cover on without making noise and giving away their hiding spot. Broady looks over to Allison, who's also crouched awkwardly on all fours. She gestures with her eyes looking at the cover. Broady shakes his head and holds it steady.

There's the pitter-patter sound of feet on the timber floors as the creature enters the apartment. The creature screeches and clicks as it moves farther in.

His heart is pounding as the cover becomes heavier and hard to hold steady. His arm begins to fatigue. The creature clicks and screeches as it moves around the apartment. He can hear it scratching, knocking over things in the kitchen, right next to the laundry. The footsteps move quickly then stop, quickly then stop. Broady can hear Allison breathing heavily and he looks over to her, gesturing with his lips for her to be quiet. She holds her hand over her mouth, knowing full well what awaits them if they're discovered.

The creature's pitter-pattering footsteps start again, and Broady sees its glowing yellow eyes from up above as it enters the laundry, stopping right below them. The poorly lit room makes it difficult to see clearly. Its skin appears black and grey with two odd-looking growths protruding out of its upper back, like a bird with clipped wings. It clicks, jerking its head side to side, looking around. The manhole cover becomes increasingly heavier the longer he holds it, his arm now aching. A bead of sweat rolls down Broady's forehead onto the tip of his nose. Broady fixates on the droplet as it stops, beginning to wobble. Holding his breath and trying to remain as still as possible.

They are trapped in a cramped space with nowhere to go. Broady begins to think this could be their last moments. Allison sees more droplets shimmer on Broady's forehead. Both watching as another bead of sweat trickles from his head pooling on his nose before escaping his body as if in slow motion. The pair stare as it glistens, encasing the light from the dim moonlit apartment. Jerking its head side to side the droplet passes right beside the creature and slams into the ground. In the absolute silence of the room, the sound of the droplet hitting the hard tiles is as loud as a dripping tap. Broady's eyes widen with their impending discovery. The creature looks down as the droplet shines on the tiled surface, jerking its head side to side. As it begins to straighten back up, the chairs that Allison knocked over from the dining room clash together and slide along the floor, more sounds of pitter-pattering footsteps enter the room. There's more than one, Broady realises, hearing more clicking and scratching coming from the lounge room. The creature below darts out of the laundry toward the other as another droplet of sweat leaves his face and falls to the tiled floor. Broady exhales in relief, wiping his forehead against his shirt.

Not out of trouble yet, Broady listens intensely to the sounds that emanate from the creatures. *Are they communicating with each other?* Broady wonders.

The pitter-pattering of footsteps move farther away as they seem to explore the apartment. Broady makes haste and gently places the cover over the manhole.

Banging, crashing and rummaging around with no prevail, the creatures continue to click and screech.

Feeling somewhat out of immediate danger, Broady reaches into his pocket. Grabbing his phone, he uses the screen as a dim light. The two quietly shuffle around, lying down on top of the timber beams.

"What do we do now?" Allison whispers. Broady just holds up his hand, placing his finger up to his mouth. Hoping the creatures will tire and eventually lose interest, Broady decides it's best to wait it out.

Only moments go by before a loud bellowing siren howls through the night sky. It sounds similar to a tornado warning siren he's heard before on American television. The horn's howl sends the creatures into a frenzy. Their screeching sounds become deafening, even through the roof cavity behind the plasterboard. Broady wonders where on Earth the sirens are coming from. Attributing it to the possibility of the building's fire alarm, yet having never heard it, he begins to worry whether the building is on fire, trapped in the ceiling with the creatures in his apartment below sends his thoughts into peril. The siren sounds a total of seven times, after such time everything goes quiet. It seems as though the creatures have left.

Several minutes pass. The two listening intently.

Shuffling around onto his back, he attempts to find a more comfortable position, with no luck. The beams dig into his spine and hip, his legs curled up to the side.

"What do we do now?" Allison whispers.

Broady responds this time. "We'll wait till daylight, make sure those things don't come back." The two lay uncomfortably, both frightened but relieved.

Chapter 3

A paper-thin strip of light shines up through a tiny gap in the manhole cover—a perfectly straight strip of yellow sunlight shines up onto the concrete ceiling, slightly illuminating the space. Broady looks around at the tight space, electrical cables and pipes going every which way. Dazed and tired it takes him almost a full two minutes to realise that it must be morning. Groggy and confused, Broady wonders whether he managed to doze off at all.

He grabs on to one of the pipes, helping himself up. His back and hip ache tremendously from the uncomfortable position on the hard timber beams. Grunting and groaning, Allison pushes herself upright, looking as though she's having similar complaints.

"My arm is dead!" she groans, screwing up her face.

Gently removing the cover, bright sunlight beams into the cavity. Both shield their eyes as they adjust. Broady pokes his head down out of the roof. Only able to see into the kitchen, his apartment sounds quiet and empty.

"I'm going down," he says. Lowering himself down, he hangs his hands from the cavity, his body swings gently a few inches from the ground, letting go of the beam he falls the few inches onto the floor, landing on top of the front door handle that's blasted its way through the new apartment. It clinks and tings as it rolls across the tiled floor, slamming into the wall. The sound first thing in the morning is ghastly. Allison freaks, gasping, cupping her hand over her mouth as Broady freezes in anticipation.

"Come on!" Broady says, irritated at himself.

He peers around the corner, his apartment is a mess, his furniture and décor scattered about the apartment. Boggled at his now-trashed apartment, he tiptoes his way around, peeking his head around every corner.

Allison waits anxiously. After checking the last bedroom, he yells out, "All clear!"

Walking back into the laundry, he helps his neighbour down, onto the washing machine then onto the floor. He grips his hands firmly around her waist. After lowering her down the two briefly make eye contact, her hands on top of his shoulders. Pausing for a moment she gazes at him with a sparkle in her eye. "Thanks, Broads," she says with a little smirk.

Becoming slightly uncomfortable with Allison's lingering gaze, Broady breaks eye contact and proceeds to walk off.

The front door is wide open; Broady walks over, swinging it shut. With no door handle and the self-close mechanism broken from the creatures barging through, the door slams shut and swings right back open. He stares at the door for a moment, bewildered.

"It's not safe here," he calls out as he storms into his bedroom.

The creatures have made a mess of his room, his belongings scattered all over the floor. Broady rummages around, picking up his duffle bag from the floor and moves into the kitchen throwing the bag onto the bench.

Allison stands in the middle of the room circling. Tired, confused and completely shocked at the state of things.

"What are you doing?" she asks.

"There are emergency checkpoints in the centre of town somewhere, we should head there," he says, vaguely remembering the images from the television last night.

"Ok, but WHAT are YOU doing?" She stares, puzzled.

"Non-perishable foods, it's not a good idea to rely on the emergency services for everything. Besides I doubt this is something they would have been prepared for, you never know," he says, grabbing canned tuna and rice cups and packets of biscuits.

He grabs the bag by its handles and slides it off the kitchen bench.

"I'll just grab a change of clothes and we'll head out," he says, heading into his room.

Broady reaches down to grab a few t-shirts and pants off the floor, noticing a sweaty funky smell coming from himself. All that sweating, running and hiding in hot cramped spaces has him smelling a little worse for wear. He rips off his t-shirt throwing it against the wall. It's unlike Broady to have his room in such a state, but he barely bats an eyelid, grabbing a shirt from his wardrobe and sliding in over his head. He heads into the ensuite, grabbing some deodorant from behind the mirrored cabinet, giving himself a shower from a can.

"I'll go grab clothes, too," Allison yells out. Broady shuts the cabinet and stares at his tired red eyes in the reflection.

"I'll see if Ray and Mum have any food as well!" she adds.

Taking a few moments for what's she said to sink in, he suddenly remembers the creature outside Ray and Jen's apartment. "Allison, wait!" He grabs the duffle bag and runs out after her, the front door still swinging. He stops in the hallway, seeing Allison standing outside her apartment. His stomach drops as he sees her frozen in shock. Tears begin to stream down her face as she covers her nose and mouth.

Broady races up to her and quickly peers inside. It's not a pretty sight, there's a bloodstained trail down the hallway and, shocked, he quickly turns away. He stands in front of the door, blocking Allison's view and embraces her, pulling her in tightly.

Unable to hold back she cries out. Broady pulls her head down into his shoulder, rocking gently side to side as he turns her away from the door. "Don't look, honey," he whispers into the top of her head.

Moving around, Broady gets a better glimpse inside.

Huge blood splatter spays up the wall, a few dots up on the ceiling. A large pool of blood sits just inside the door, trailing right down the hallway entrance as if something or somebody has been dragged through.

Oddly shaped bloody footprints cover the floor; the bloody footprints sit close together as if they were shuffling almost.

By the amount of blood present, Broady doubts it would be possible for anyone to have survived.

"We have to go," he whispers again, grabbing her wrist.

"No! I need to see if they're in there!" She struggles, determined to break Broady's grip. "Let me go!" she wails, tears pouring from her face. "I need to know!"

Believing he's protecting her, Broady gets hold of her arm.

"Allison, stop, you don't want to see that." He yanks her arm hard, pulling her off balance.

Using the momentum, he pulls her away and begins to run down the corridor. Allison's too distraught to fight back.

Broady pulls his neighbour's arm up over his shoulders. Supporting her as they run frantically down the stairs into the car park, Broady looks around. It's quiet and deserted. Only a few cars remain in their spaces. The car's blinkers flash as he unlocks the doors, ushering Allison into the passenger side. She turns pale and begins to shake in a state of shock; Broady reaches over to buckle her seatbelt.

As he leans over, the sound of the car-park door slamming echoes thought the concrete walls. Startled, Broady jumps and tenses up. Peeping up out the front windscreen he sees a couple appear, the man is holding a washing basket full of belongings, a woman follows him closely holding two big plastic bags. Broady recognises them from the building, living down on the opposite end of the corridor. Broady just stares, watching them. They quickly put their stuff in the boot of their car. The couple, fixated on getting out as quick as possible, fail to even see Broady or Allison sitting opposite them. They hop in the car and the man backs out of the car park. As he shifts the car out of reverse, Broady makes brief eye contact with the women in the passenger seat. She looks white as a ghost, her eyes glazed over. Whatever they've encountered the women looks traumatised. The car clunks into drive and the man steps on the accelerator, skidding the front wheels on the slippery sealed concrete surface. The woman just stares out the window blankly as they drive away.

He pauses for a moment looking over at Ray's car. There's an 'SPIPC' sticker on the side windshield.

"I need you to wait here," he says.

"Wait, what?" Allison exclaims, grabbing hold of his arm as he moves it away from her belt buckle.

Ray was a shooter and a member of the Southport Indoor Pistol Club.

"I'm going up to find Ray's pistol, we may need it," he says.

"But it's locked in his safe," she replies.

"He may have taken it out last night with everything going on, I'm going to check."

"I'm coming with you," Allison insists, attempting to unbuckle herself

"NO, ALLISON! Wait here," Broady says sternly.

Having never heard Broady raise his voice she's a little startled in her fragile state and sits back in her seat.

Broady feels awful—he's clearly frightened her.

She sinks into the seat so no one can see her.

As he heads back up the stairs, he hugs the wall tightly, crouching down; he quickly pops his head up, looking down the corridor. Neither a movement nor a sound.

Creeping down the hallway his heartbeat begins to increase, getting a sickly feeling in the back of his throat.

Taking a few deep breaths before heading toward the door, he braces himself for what he may find.

He pushes on the front door opening it up all the way. The air is tense, the smell of blood pours out of the apartment. The door squeaks very faintly as it hits the doorstop.

He tiptoes through the door, walking against the wall, attempting to avoid stepping in the blood that trails down the hallway.

The farther in he goes the more the smell of blood saturates the air. As he moves in, he feels his shoes become tacky. Lifting his foot off the floor he looks down at the bottom of his shoe; it's covered in blood. He's leaving bloody footprints on the floor. His hands begin to shake as his heart rate quickens, and he starts to breathe deeply, but the pungent smell envelops him. Tasting it in his mouth and down into the back of his throat, he chokes on the air; bending over he throws up onto the floor. The sight of blood and vomit mixed together is awful. He shuts his eyes tightly and tries to compose himself.

"Shit!" he says out loud. "Harden up," he adds, talking to himself.

Wiping his face on his sleeve, he props himself up against the wall, his eyes still watering. The trail leads around the corner into the open living and dining area. Light from the balcony doors streams through. Peeping around the corner, Broady's stunned to see that there are no bodies. The trail ends in the centre of the room, with bloody footprints all around. Their place too, looks completely ransacked. The balcony doors next to the living room are slightly open, bloody smudge marks smeared across the glass doors. He wonders if Ray or Jen went over the edge. He moves toward the door and out onto the balcony, preparing to find a gruesome discovery, he reluctantly peers over . . . Nothing.

Confused, he walks back inside, through into the main bedroom. It's not a pretty sight, the white bed sheets are torn and tattered, pillows have deep gashes through them, the fluffy contents spread around the floor, blood splatters cover the quilt and mattress.

"Where are they?" Broady whispers under his breath. The sheer amount of blood present makes it highly unlikely they are still alive. Nevertheless, he walks through into the wardrobe. The clothes are separated and Ray's safe is wide open. Broady takes a closer look. A few boxes of ammunition, Ray's, Jen's and Allison's passports as well as a few bundles of cash, but no gun. He stares at the cash, reluctant to take it. He shoves Allison's passport into his pants pocket and stands up to walk out. Having second thoughts he goes back and grabs the cash. He feels guilty, promising himself he'll pay them back once this is all over. He heads out into the main living area, with a large pool of blood congregated in the centre of the room. Broady wonders if this was where one of their bodies lay; he crouches down to see if Ray's gun is anywhere to be seen. Far up under the couch Broady spots it.

The gun must have been dropped and skidded under the couch. He reaches under and grabs it, tucking into the back of his pants. He wastes no time getting out of there, he doesn't bother to look for any more supplies or any of Allison's belongings.

Rushing back down to the car he opens the door and jumps in. Allison, anxiously waiting for him, immediately asks, "Did you see them?"

"No, I didn't," he replies, starting the car.

"Don't you lie to me, Broady Fitzgerald!" she pushes, not believing him.

Broady turns to her, looking her dead in the eye. "No, Allison, there was no one there. No bodies, nothing!" he confesses. He neglects to mention the blood-soaked mattress or the pools in the lounge room.

"Maybe they got out and went for help?" Allison says, thinking out loud as she sits back in her seat.

Not wanting to further upset her he remains silent, putting the car into drive and heading out. Sunlight beams through the front windshield partially obscuring Broady's view as he drives up from the basement car park, he pulls down the sun visor, revealing a quiet street with no one around.

Broady looks over at Allison slumped down in her seat.

"I'm sorry I yelled at you," he says softly. "I was afraid of what you might see in there. No one wants to see their parents like that."

"It's fine," she replies, staring out the window. "I understand."

Broady doesn't push the point farther. Pulling out his phone, he quickly searches the internet.

A news headline pops up in his search feed; scrolling quickly through he sees the same map from last night, the address on the bottom of the page instructs people to head to the Football stadium in Carrara.

"There's an emergency meeting point at the stadium. We'll head there."

"Maybe Mum and Ray are there?" Allison sits up in her seat.

"Yeah . . . Maybe," he says, trying to sound hopeful.

Heading toward the end of the street is a very different story.

The corner store at the end of the street has had its windows smashed in, shattered glass has spilled out into the short car park along with empty boxes and rubbish. The traffic lights have completely gone black, no longer flashing yellow. A large metal roller door that covers the entrance to the liquor market has been smashed in; the corrugated iron is all twisted bent. Possibly by a car backing into it, Broady thinks.

He cautiously drives out through the intersection making a right turn, luckily for him the stadium is only a five-minute drive along two main roads, and Broady is optimistic they'll make it there with little drama.

Farther onto the main road, people start to emerge. A family are pushing a pram down the street, Allison peers back as they pass. No baby, just piles of belongings. More people down the street, some pushing trolleys full of things as well. A few cars speed by.

In the distance he sees a sign from the local BP, prompting him to check his fuel gauge.

A quarter of a tank left.

Allison, seeing the fuel station, props herself up and over to check the fuel level.

"You need diesel," she says.

The closer they come to the service station the more unlikely it becomes. With no power, the service station lights are out. There is a string of cars lined up at the entrance. Stranded motorists stand around the pumps looking desperate and agitated, some holding jerry cans. As they pass by Allison spots a man using a hand pump out of one of the nozzles on the ground.

"We can get fuel, look," she says, pointing to the man with the pump.

Broady shakes his head, not liking the look and feel of the

situation. "We'll make it there; besides, it looks like things could get nasty," he says, cautious of the looting and unrest.

They continue down the road. A few cars turn on, heading in the same direction. A police car with its lights on is the only car heading in the opposite direction. Looking in his rear-view mirror he can see it pulling into the service station. Allison, following the car with her head, turns back around.

"Huh, good idea, Broady. The fuzz might have got ya." She winks.

The end of the main road is a big roundabout intersection with crossover bridges. More vehicles now enter the intersection from all direction, seemingly heading for the stadium. Making a left turn, the long-standing stadium lights that reach high into the sky come into view.

"Look, there it is!" Allison yells out, somewhat relieved and hoping to find her parents there.

The stadium sits about two kilometres down the road. As they merge into the road the traffic starts to mount. Brake lights as far as Broady can see litter the road with no view of the road surface. The car slows to a crawling pace for a few hundred metres before coming to a complete stop.

"Erggh." Allison sighs, putting her foot up on the dashboard. "Great."

Peering farther ahead, it seems as if some people have abandoned their cars on the side of the road and are walking, carrying backpacks and small children.

Broady turns around to look behind him, by now they are completely boxed in. He sees a woman in the car beside him equally frustrated, banging on the steering wheel. He looks around for a side street with no luck.

"Looks like we may have to walk from here, mate," he says.

"What?" she says, unimpressed. "You're not serious, are you?"

"We're jammed in with nowhere to go, there's not much of a choice."

"Erggh, fine." She groans again sliding her foot back off the dash. Broady hops out, reaching into the back and getting out his duffle bag, lifting his shirt and revealing the firearm down his pants. Beginning to walk off, Allison yells out to him.

"Broady!"

He reads her lips as she mimes the word gun silently, holding up her forefinger and thumb.

He quickly rearranges himself, looking around to see if anyone saw. Luckily, everyone else is too preoccupied.

Walking toward the stadium two low-flying military helicopters zoom past. They're deafly loud, flying so low they churn up dust and dirt off the road. They both squint their eyes, covering their faces, avoiding breathing in the debris. They peer into other people's vehicles as they walk by. A Japanese lady fans her crying baby in the back seat. A man and women argue about what to do.

"You're an idiot!" the woman yells, getting out and slamming the door. The male driver shakes his head but doesn't bother to pursue her.

The closer they get to the stadium the larger the group of people who are out of their cars and walking. Approaching the car park, they can see the entire perimeter is fenced, more than one layer. Broady is amazed at how quickly they must have worked, suspicious to whether they know something the general public doesn't. Razor wire sits between the two fences. People begin to bump into Broady as they're funnelled through into the main car-park entrance.

Military vehicles and Humvees are positioned at each side of the entrance. The tops of the vehicles are mounted with turret machine guns and soldiers sitting on the roofs of the vehicles. A megaphone attached to a Humvee roars out, "Everyone, please walk calmly through the gates."

Similar messages ramble on and on repeatedly. Broady sees one of the soldiers standing outside a Humvee door, resting one leg up talking into a handheld radio microphone.

There are further instructions for people to move through the gates to register themselves as they enter the stadium. Upon walking through the outer car-park area, past the double-lined fences and razor wire, the car park opens up, giving Broady and Allison more breathing room. Having forgotten his sunglasses, Broady squints heavily as the sun beams down on the concrete car park. There's a smell of diesel emissions in the air from large military vehicles offloading troops, as well as supplies and equipment. Walking across the few hundred metres of car spaces the crowd begins to funnel down again in a number of locations on the outside of the stadium. As they move closer, Broady can see soldiers patting people down as they move forward to the ticket booths.

"Broady, they're searching people," Allison whispers to him.

"Yeah, I can see," he says, spinning around on the spot, looking at his surroundings.

"What are you going to do?" she asks.

Spotting a bin on the left not too far in front of them, chained to a light pole, Broady grabs her arm and directs her to walk in the direction of the bin.

They scurry along weaving through the crowd of people.

"DADDY!" a loud voice cries out coming from behind him. The voice instantly sends shivers down Broady's spine and he immediately stops. Looking around behind him he steps back toward the entrance, weaving in and around the crowd holding up his hands as he gently manoeuvres people around him in search of the origin of the voice. People continue to brush past him without stopping, seemingly taking no notice. The voice sounded uncannily like Charlotte.

"Broady, what are you doing?" Allison calls out among the sea of people, still holding the lid of the bin open.

"Did you hear that?" he calls out, a few feet away.

"Hear what?" Allison looks at him confused.

Broady turns around again, searching the people as they walk by. The more he looks, the more panic begins to set in as a sickly feeling plummets to his stomach.

Allison abandons her position and walks over to him. She places her hands on his shoulders from behind, gently shaking him.

"Broady," she says, pulling his attention back.

He turns around facing Allison, his face is long. "I have to go and get Charlotte," he announces with a cold emotionless look. In somewhat of a trance, he turns back around and immediately begins walking away, leaving Allison stunned.

"Wait, what?" she yells, chasing off after him. He doesn't stop. "Broady, stop!" she yells again, grabbing his wrist. A sudden feeling of determination washes over him, a feeling he can't quite explain as he pulls his arm away.

With the sickly feeling still lingering in his stomach, Broady is convinced something awful is going to happen to Charlotte, the urge is so powerful that he's unable to shake it.

Allison runs around, stopping right in front of him. "Fucking stop!" she yells right in his face, shoving him backward, frustrated he's ignoring her.

Somewhat pulling him out of his trance, he stops and looks at her, grabbing both her hands. "Allison," he says softly looking her dead in the eye. "I NEED to go find Charlotte; I can't explain it."

Allison shakes her head confused.

"But I need to go NOW!" he says and begins to walk off.

"Fine," she says, confused but accepting. "I'm coming with you."

Broady turns around. "No, it's not safe for you."

"I'm sticking with you, Broady, the same as before," she says.

This time Broady won't have a bar of it. "You don't understand, I need to go and get Charlotte, I have a really awful feeling and with everything we have seen the safest place for you is here."

"But—"

"No!" he says, turning her around toward the stadium. "Just go. Please," he pleads with her.

Allison begins to cry.

Having never upset her before, now twice in one day, he begins to feel awful, walking up behind her he wraps his arm around her.

His embrace does little to soothe her.

"You have to stay here. This is the safest possible place for you," he whispers in her ear. With the awful feeling he has, he'll never forgive himself if she leaves with him and something happens to her. "I'll come find you, I promise."

She holds his finger, squeezing it tightly as he lets go of her. Tears stream down her face as she stands now scared and feeling very much alone.

Broady turns, walking back through the car park. He pauses for a moment. With a heavy heart, he turns around seeing Allison standing with her head slumped down. Wiping tears away from her eyes and shaking her hands, she jogs off toward the stadium.

Watching her hurry off, his conscious begins to plague him. Broady takes a deep breath, believing he's making the best decision for everyone. He turns back around and marches on.

Broady becomes fixated on the voice he heard cry out. *Was it really Charlotte?* he wonders. Is this all connected to the strange dreams he's been having? As well as the bizarre incident at the mall? He can't help but feel like this is all connected in some way. How? He rattles his brain.

Moving closer to the outer gates he begins to weave and bump into frightened and anxious people as they funnel in from outside. He manages to squeeze back through the open gates.

Broady stands at the outskirts of the gates and looks around as frightened and panicked people descend upon the stadium. The roads heading toward the stadium are all blocked, cars banked up for as far as the eye can see in either direction. The road heading away from the stadium toward the highway is clear with not a single car. With his car blocked some distance away, he tries to think of how he's going to make it to Charlotte some four hours away.

Hearing what sounds like people yelling, his attention is drawn back to the gate entrance. A Middle Eastern-looking man is arguing and yelling loudly at one of the soldiers standing on the back of a Humvee, manning a machine gun. Unable to hear what's being said, Broady curiously walks by.

"My car needs to go through!" the man yells in broken English, throwing up his hands pointing in the direction of the stadium. The man is wearing a long light-brown robe and a white Islamic cap.

"No, sir. Military vehicles only!" the soldier says rather abruptly.

The man points to the back seat of his car, clearly becoming frustrated. "Look! My wife is pregnant. I must get through."

As Broady wanders closer, he looks into the back of the old white dual-cab ute. He sees a lady lying along the back seat sprawled out as he moves up alongside the vehicle.

The woman is sweating and clearly distressed.

"She can't walk all this way; we have many supplies," the man continues to insist.

Broady watches as the soldiers become irritated and lash out at the man. "Get this heap of shit out of the way!" the soldier yells, jumping down from the back of the Humvee.

The man is quick to jump back in his car. Clearly not understanding the gravity of the situation, he starts the vehicle and begins to rev the engine hard, gathering the attention of more soldiers who jog over toward the ute.

The soldiers, now having no patience left, raise their rifles and aim at the man sitting in the car. They scream commands at him, instructing him to get out of the car.

Before the situation escalates any further the man throws up his hands. One of the soldiers opens the driver's door and pulls the man from the car. His wife screams from the back seat.

"I'm sorry, I'm sorry," he pleads.

His wife is hysterical at the sight of her husband being detained.

Broady can't understand the women as she yells what sound like obscenities, not in English.

Seeing an opportunity, he runs over to the man lying face down. A soldier's knee in his back as he pulls a zip tie from his back pants pocket.

"Excuse me!" Broady says, trying to appear non-threatening.

Before he can get within a few feet the soldier's comrades step forward pointing their rifles at Broady, screaming at him to stop.

"Whoa, whoa, whoa!" Broady backs up, holding up his hands.

"I just want to ask this man a question," Broady says, bending down toward the man.

"Q&A time is over, move along," the soldier says abruptly. Broady ignores him, focusing on the man as he lay still, facedown on the floor, a look of pain on his face.

"I can take your car for you!" Broady says.

The man looks at him puzzled.

"I can pay you," he continues, pulling out the wad of cash from Ray's safe from his pocket.

The man's eyes light up as if having flicked a switch.

The soldiers drag the man to his feet, his hands bound behind his back.

"Do you have gas?" Broady enquires.

"Yes, yes," he says. "Lots, and more in the back."

Walking to the back of the ute, the tray is jam-packed; Broady can see the car loaded with two jerry cans, an esky and a big plastic container full of food, as well as some Middle Eastern-looking furniture, rugs and blankets.

Broady wonders what the man was thinking.

"So how much you have?" the man asks, looking somewhat gleefully at the cash.

Looking over the car again, the old ute is battered and worn, with rust on the roof and down the side. No wonder the man is keen to offload it.

"About three to four Gs," Broady says, twisting the cash in his wrist, slightly overestimating.

"Ok, ok," the man says.

"See? I'm going to take the car away and this man will leave with his wife, no hassle for anyone," Broady reasons with the solider, who stands thinking for a moment.

The soldier pulls out a knife and cuts the zip ties that bound the man's hands.

"Get this heap of shit and FUCK OFF!" the soldier yells, fed up with the situation.

The man frightened and shaking nods and complies. "Ok, ok." He opens the back door of the vehicle and Broady helps the man get his wife out.

He runs around grabbing a bag and a few items out of the back seat, and placing his wife's arm over his shoulder, they walk away.

"I will report this car stolen after this is over," the man says as he walks off carrying his pregnant wife.

Broady shakes his head at the man. "Dick," Broady says under his breath, stunned at the arrogance of the man.

One of the other soldiers becomes impatient.

"Is this swap meeting over now, fellas?" he says sarcastically.

"Turn this heap of shit around, you're blocking aid supplies getting through."

Hopping in the driver's seat, a plume of dust and dirt spray into the cabin. The car is filthy, bits of rubbish and empty fast-food wrappers litter the floor. The car smells musty and damp, the man was clearly not very organised. Peering back through the rear window into the tray, two jerry cans are strapped to the side with an elastic strap. Broady gets a sinking feeling that they may be empty. Turning back around, noticing the fuel gauge is full at least.

The soldier bangs on the bonnet hard. "Move it!" he yells.

The car's gearbox grinds into first gear.

"What a heap," Broady says to himself, beginning to worry whether the old junk box will make the journey.

He swiftly turns the vehicle around and heads out the exit lane. Moving out into the main road he sees police vehicles blocking the entrance to another service station. Slowing down as he approaches, he notices a large fuel tanker. The tanker is unlike most, having no branded decals on the side. Two soldiers are unravelling large hoses as another kneels, unscrewing something on the ground.

The military must be pumping out fuel for their vehicles, he presumes. With a full state of emergency declared it appears they can take whatever they want. Having never seen anything like this before Broady continues to snoop. As he passes by the entrance, he notices an overweight police officer staring him down. Not wanting to create any suspicion, he pulls his eyes back to the road and continues driving away.

Broady can only drive at a crawling pace with people now littering the streets walking to the safe zone. He heads toward the main highway, with another large roundabout ahead. Cars block the intersection, and Broady stops short, deciding instead to mount the square gutter and drive onto the median strip. The ute bounces up and down, the junk in the back crashes and pounds against the metal. He turns to make sure he hasn't lost anything.

People yell and curse as they are forced to move out of his way. The suspension bottoms out as he drops off the gutter slamming the chassis into the road, then straight up onto the roundabout. Hitting it straight on the back end, the ute jolts up ferociously making the large rug in the back bounce out. Broady keeps driving through the grassy centre back down and through a gap in the traffic before heading away.

Cars on the opposite side of the road are bumper to bumper for as far as he can see. Strangely enough, no one has thought to drive down the wrong lane, making it a smooth drive out for Broady.

Approaching the highway overpass, things take a turn for the worse. The traffic bottlenecks onto the on-ramp and driving up over the bridge he's amazed at what he sees. Stopping in the middle of the overpass he pulls the ute over to the side and jumps out of the car. Walking onto the footpath he leans against the cold metal railing. Both directions are completely jammed. Hordes of people have seemingly abandoned their vehicles.

"What the fuck," he says, looking down in amazement. He pulls his phone from his pocket hoping to find an alternate route. *SOS only*, it reads.

"Shit!" he yells smacking his hand on his phone, unwittingly hoping to get signal. Broady's head begins to spin as his thoughts of getting to Charlotte seem impossible.

Feeling hopeless, he slumps down onto his knees. Ten minutes go by as he looks around watching the chaos on the highway. He turns around and sits down, his back pressed against the cold steel. He feels a cool breeze blow by, stirring at the hairs on his arm.

The wind carries rubbish and paper along the road. A pamphlet stops on his leg. Broady picks it up and unfolds it. As he unfolds it, he looks back toward the car and is hit with an idea.

He jumps up hastily, opening the passenger door of the car. He begins rummaging through the car door pockets and the centre console looking for a map, or even an old phone book.

By the state of the car, Broady's certain the ute's owner isn't one to throw anything away. Throwing wrappers and rubbish out onto the road, he searches for anything useful. Optimistically opening the glove compartment, there are only bills and receipts and the car's original service manual from 1991. Sifting further he becomes more desperate and irritated as bits of gooey paper from takeaway wrappers stick to his hands.

After a thorough search, he jumps up out of the car, slamming the door shut in anger and slumps down on the curb, bent over with his hand on his head. He closes his eyes. There is another way south down and through the mountain range out west, however not being certain of the route and under the current circumstances, he worries about getting lost and stranded without any fuel.

As the piles of rubbish begin to slowly blow over the road, he opens his eyes and sees a picture of Mount Warning and the Great Dividing Range on a small tourist booklet that he must have thrown out the door. It's covered in what looks like old sauce stains. Nevertheless, he flicks through the pages to the middle and the centre folds out into a little map, outlining the mountain ranges, tourist destinations and nature walks.

While roads aren't well mapped, showing only the main roads, its accurate enough to get him through the ranges. Broady traces his finger along the lines until he reaches a road intersection at the beginning of the map. *Tudors Road.*

"I know that road!" he says to himself, searching his rusty memory.

He gets up and jumps back in the car. He takes one last look through the railing and onto the highway before taking off. The rubbish on the road is left to blow in the wind as the exhaust smoke churns it up into the air.

Broady drives along toward an intersection he recognises on the tourist map. He comes around a bend and down a small gully where a large Seventh-day Adventist church sits. Cars begin to mount, parked up on the side of the road; people begin to amass walking hastily toward the church's entrance. Driving closer, an elderly woman holds up a sign reading *SAFETY,* possibly telling another passer-by. Another person holds a sign farther up. *Jesus will save US.* However, the man just glares unwelcomingly at Broady as he slowly drives by. Just outside the church driveway, a pale-looking man in a black suit is holding a megaphone. Broady is unsure if it's the church's priest, unable to see his white collar as it's obstructed by his hand.

Wearing a black hat, the pale man appears rather creepy as he speaks over the megaphone.

"Come in, children of God," he preaches. "We have shelter, food and we have all the answers to all the questions. Most importantly we have the LORD," he bellows, pointing his black bible up toward the sky.

Broady shakes his head, after what Allison and he have seen, Broady thinks it's foolish to hide out at a church. However, it doesn't stop what looks like hundreds of desperate people from flooding in. People cross the roads, oblivious to cars driving by.

"They've lost it," Broady cries out, making a left turn out toward Tudors Road.

As he drives away from the church, passers-by look into Broady's vehicle giving him strange looks, as if he's heading in the wrong direction. He begins to feel uneasy as he heads farther and farther out, with fewer people the farther he travels.

By the time he reaches Tudors Road, the uneasy feeling grows deep within him. On the open mountain road, there is no one in sight. He has to stay on this road for eighty kilometres before his next turn off. He begins to feel isolated, questioning his decisions. His heartbeat quickens. His thoughts begin to catch up with him and the tightness in his chest makes breathing difficult. He winds down his window. The musty air in the ute is making him claustrophobic. After only travelling a few kilometres it becomes overwhelming, he pulls the car over to the gravel on the side of the road. Pressing hard on the brake, the tires skid on the dirt. The car door flies open as he kicks it hard. He leaps from the car. A wave of emotion washes over him as the intense events from the past twenty-four hours come raging through his head. He paces back and forth, replaying the events over and over in his head. The women in the shopping mall, the car exploding on their way home, unknown creatures tearing up his place, Ray and Jen's blood-soaked apartment and the whole city turning on its head. Now having left Allison, he struggles to keep his mind together on his own.

Grabbing a stone from the dirt he throws it in anger out into the bush, slipping on the gravel dirt and falling to his knees. His eyes begin to swell; he shuts them tight and takes deep breaths.

The trees sway as a large gust of wind blows through them. Broady is reminded of a cloudy September afternoon when he took that picture of Charlotte on the swing. The wind was howling so much it was able to push Charlotte back and forth on the swing, much to her delight as she laughed and giggled. Dandelions blew in the wind capturing the perfect photo of her. He pulls out his phone and stares at it. Rubbing his eyes, his mind slowly quietens as he begins to focus again. Picking himself back up and dusting the dirt from his pants, he jumps back into the ute. He shakes his body and feels more like himself again.

He grabs the booklet from the passenger seat, double-checking that he's going in the right direction.

A long and winding stretch of roads some three hundred kilometres long. He jumps back out and bangs on the jerry cans making sure they are full. At least the man was honest enough with that, he thinks.

Driving off he looks at his watch. 10:00 am. Making some calculations with his fingers, he thinks he may be able to reach Abby's parents' property by midafternoon.

He turns the radio on, hearing only static and flicks through a number of stations without being able to get a clear signal. With the mountain ranges blocking a clear station he flicks the CD player on. Instantly, loud ethnic music blasts out of the speakers frightening Broady as he jumps in the seat. He frantically looks for the eject button, but it's broken. The loud chants of the music drive him crazy before fumbling at the volume button, turning it down before it clicks off.

Broady breaths out a sigh of relief.

With the radio off he realises just how quiet it is. He hasn't passed any other people in almost an hour. It begins to feel rather peaceful as he winds his window down, sticking his head out. He enjoys the cool breeze as it rushes over his head. The temperature starts to drop the farther out he ventures. Winding the window up, he shuffles around in his seat getting himself comfy for the long drive.

Chapter 4

Time rolls around, with the sun beginning to settle behind the trees in the mountain rainforest. Streams of sunlight break through and onto open paddocks as cows feed in the meadow as if nothing has happened and they have not a care in the world. The fading sunlight stretches over the tall grass, illuminating the plains in a golden yellow. The moments before the sun goes down are his favourite. Thoughts begin to flood his idle mind with memories of his very first date with Abby. Taking her on an afternoon picnic up on Mount Tamborine—at the top of the mountain stretch acres of paddocks. Despite his rugged appearance, Broady is a romantic and a true gentleman. He had surprised her, driving her all the way up blindfolded having earlier set up a little picnic table on a large rug with a bottle of wine. He remembers the surprised look on her face when he took the blindfold off. That afternoon was the first time the young couple kissed as the two collapsed on the soft bed of grass.

Broady smiles as old feelings begin to surface, reminiscing on more innocent times. As the sun begins to fade over the mountain, he notices a sign ahead. Winding the window down partially to un-fog the windscreen, a frosty breeze blows in, making him shiver. He is surprised how much cooler it is here. Thirty kilometres before the last turnoff Broady is shocked at how quickly the time escaped him. 4:35 pm, he sees, reading his watch. Making his final turn onto the road leading to Abby's parents' suburb, he takes one last look at the booklet. Having got his bearings, he discards the booklet onto the passenger floor to join the other trash. An old café sits nestled between the rainforest, having been there once before he notices that it's closed. The old timber building is dark, and no lights are on. Finding this strange he begins to worry if things have turned bad here, too.

Abby's parents live in a secluded property surrounded by sub-tropical rainforest at the edge of the town. Driving through the town he passes the small country state school that Abby went to as a child, the same school Charlotte will attend. The playground is surrounded by trees and luscious green grass. A nice little school, he's happy Charlotte will be going there. Broady tries to imagine Charlotte playing in the playground, hoping this will all be over soon.

The fuel light illuminates on the dash as he drives up the hill toward their street, but he's hopeful the spare fuel onboard is enough for the journey back.

All the driveways on the street are well concealed from the road, covered from the leaves blowing in the wind. Abby's parents' house is different. It has a perfectly bright white wooden house letterbox that sticks out like a sore thumb from the road. They could always tell the house by the letterbox, especially at night. Abby's father always kept his letterbox clean, keeping a rag in the back of his car when he checked the mail. Funny guy, really, Broady always thought.

Spotting the letterbox bright as ever he turns into the driveway; trees line the driveway providing a lot of cover. The dirt road is loud and bumpy, the ute's crappy suspension has Broady bouncing all over the seat. To Broady's dismay, there are no cars parked in the driveway and all the lights seem to be off. The large timber log house seems deserted. He flicks the car engine off and sits for a moment. No sound, and no lights on in the windows.

The car door creaks as he opens the door. He hops out looking around as the wind howls through the trees above. A white cloth shade curtain sways, catching Broady's attention. Not sure if it is the wind, he takes a closer look. No window open. A small shadowy figure moves quickly from behind the curtain. On edge, he slowly reaches behind his back pulling the pistol from the back of his pants, as he does, he hears a click; the front door unlocks and opens. Charlotte bursts through the fly screen door and it slams loudly against the wall.

"DADDY! DADDY! DADDY!" Charlotte screams out in excitement. Her long blond hair curls at the bottom and little blond ringlets bounce as she sprints toward him. An overwhelming sense of relief washes over Broady, grateful she is ok.

"Squirt!" he calls back, her nickname, given to her by Broady for her incessant love of squirting bath toys. Quickly he tosses the pistol in the side door of the car, bringing himself down onto one knee, she jumps into his arms.

"Charlotte!" Her name is called from inside the house.

Abby appears running out after her with a concerned look on her face.

"What did I say!" she continues in a bossy tone. "We have to stay inside."

"I know Mum, but look, it's Daddy!" she says innocently looking up, patting Broady on the shoulder.

"I know honey, but it's not safe outside . . . We have already spoken about this twice now," she says, still not acknowledging Broady at all.

"Hey Abby," Broady awkwardly says.

"Hi," Abby replies, making eye contact for only a brief moment. Her long curly black hair blows around in her face; she brushes it off to one side holding her hand up behind her ear.

"You've dyed your hair," he says, trying to make conversation.

"Uh-huh." She forces a smirk, crossing her arms and looking aimlessly toward the ground.

Charlotte giggles, moving her head back and forth between the two looking at them, it's been a while since she has seen them together.

"Daddy come and see my room!" she yells excitedly, tugging at his arm.

"Grandpa made me a fairy princess bed with fairy lights, wait till you see it!" She pulls on his arm and points toward the house. She grunts and groans scrunching up her little face as she tries to pull him along, eager to show her dad.

Stepping up the few steps onto the veranda, Abby calls out to him.

"Hey, Broady!" she says.

He stops and turns around.

"I'm glad you're here." Her face softens.

"Come on, Dad!" Charlotte yells. Becoming impatient, she

runs behind him and pushes him with all her might on the back of his pants.

"You're too slow, geez," she says, continuing to groan.

Broady smiles back at Abby before breaking into laughter at Charlotte's cute persistence. He plays along with her holding up his arms against the door as she shoves him inside.

The familiar smells of fresh timber re-ignite memories. With Charlotte still grunting as she pushes him along, he slows as he passes the wooden entry table. Old photos of Abby and her parents still line the top of the table with a few new additions of Charlotte up on the wall. It seems as though everything is still in the same place, the stone-tiled floor and timber-clad walls. The long hallway that opens into the kitchen and dining room. Broady can see that some of the furniture is still in the same place. With the surrounds, he feels somewhat nostalgic.

Turning his head around to see his daughter frantically pushing him along, she turns him into her room down the hallway. Standing at the open door he looks into Abby's old room, having now been transformed into Charlotte's. It feels somewhat surreal to him.

"Wait, Dad, STOP!" she says, crawling through his legs and standing with her arms out in front of him, stopping from coming in any farther.

"What are you doing?" he asks. "First it's 'go', now it's 'stop'?" Broady says sarcastically. "Geez." He rolls his eyes playfully.

She quickly runs off, jumping onto her bed and falling off the other side.

He cringes at her fall. "Are you ok?"

A few seconds later dim fairy lights come on. Shining over

the top of her white four-post bed, draped on top of the white mosquito netting and wrapped delicately down the poles.

"Ta-dah!" she says, springing up from behind the bed, her arms way up in the air with her mouth open in excitement.

"See? Told ya it's awesome," she says. She runs around the room explaining her set-up and showing him her belongings. While she moseys on around, Broady spots a picture frame on the side table. He walks over to it, picking it up. The photo inside the old wooden frame is of Broady and Abby when they were together at Abby's parents' wedding vow renewal ceremony. Broady was wearing a black button-up shirt, it's probably one of the few times he has dressed up. Abby's in a stunning green full-length dress, looking gorgeous with her makeup and hair done. Broady laughs at his scruffy dyed hair, looking like an idiot. The pair look so young. Broady recalls how stunningly beautiful Abby was that day, he remembers thinking at the time, not knowing how he managed to woo a girl who looked like that.

'Uh-hum,' Abby clears her throat; Broady turns to see her standing in the doorway leaning against the door.

"What's this doing here?" Broady says placing it back beside Charlotte's bed.

"Charlotte loves that photo; she says goodnight to you every night and looks at it when she speaks to you on the phone."

Charlotte runs over and hugs Abby. "You were so beautiful, Mummy," she says, looking up at her sweetly.

"Aww thanks, princess." Abby blushes.

"When you were young, I mean," Charlotte adds, blissfully unaware of her somewhat insulting statement.

"Wow!" Broady laughs, Abby too.

"Mummy, Mummy, can Daddy stay the night?" she begs, pulling on her shirt. "He can sleep with me in my room."

"Umm," Abby says, searching for an answer.

"We'll sort something out, princess," Broady quickly interjects, rubbing her head.

"YAYYY!" she squeals with excitement, running off down the hallway with her hands in the air.

The two parents stand close to one another, briefly making eye contact. Broady can sense she feels awkward again and is curious as to why. Moments pass as Broady tries to smooth things over.

"Yeah, so about that," Broady says. Feeling awkward now himself, it's the only thing he could muster out of his mouth.

"What's going on here? I haven't seen or heard anything all day," he adds changing the subject.

Abby walks off toward the lounge room. "It's worse than we first thought, it's now affected nearly every major city across the country, and populated cities are the worst areas," she informs Broady, flicking on the TV. "The whole country is in a panic, and to make matters worse there are so many conflicting stories. Every news station and state police say something different and there's been no official federal government statement," she adds, anxiously biting a nail.

The television is on showing graphic videos of the drama unfolding across the country. The main banner on SBS says *Terrorist Attack.*

Broady looks down, seeing Charlotte quietly playing with her dolls' house and teddies in the lounge room, totally oblivious. "Pumpkin, I'd like to speak with your mum quickly, could you go take your toys to your room for a moment please, precious?" he says, worried of what she might overhear.

"Ok, Daddy," she says sweetly. "But only if you have a tea party with me and Teddy."

Broady smirks and agrees. "I can't wait."

Charlotte excitedly grabs her teddy and runs off into her room.

"Dad coming over is the best thing ever, Teddy," she says, talking to her stuffed friend.

They both chuckle at their daughter's conversation.

Broady's face then drops. "Look, Abby, this isn't any terrorist attack, I can assure you." he says. Abby can tell he's being serious.

"What do you mean?" Abby queries.

"There is so much that's happened I don't know where to start," he says, holding his arms out, palms up. He starts slightly shaking his head as he stares up toward the ceiling, his thoughts race as he tries to recall and consolidate what's happened.

"It's ok, just try starting from the beginning," she says calmly, seeing he is visibly agitated.

"There are these things . . ." He stumbles trying to find the words to describe the beings he's encountered. "Creatures or something," he adds as he begins to pace back and forth.

"I saw on one of the news stations said that it could be a biological weapon, maybe it's turning people into these creatures or something?" Abby cuts in, trying to help come up with an explanation. Broady shakes his head

"They didn't look, sound or move anything like people do, ok?" he says rather abruptly, cutting her down.

"Explain it to me then, Broady!" Abby says, becoming defensive.

"Argh." Broady grunts, finding it difficult to explain what he has never seen before, he becomes irritated. He sits down on the couch placing his hands up over his face.

"Don't get shitty at me, Broady," she says abruptly. "See? This is your problem," Abby says.

Broady can sense an argument about to start. Overtired and exhausted he tries hard to gather his thoughts.

"I'm not taking it out on you, Abby," he says, trying to calm the situation. "I didn't get the best look, but they had dark-grey skin and bright yellow eyes. They moved like birds almost, hunched over with some sort of growth coming out of their back, like stumps above each shoulder blade. I've barely had any sleep; we saw the remnants of an old woman dismembered at the shopping mall."

Abby cups her hand over her face, horrified by Broady's explanation of what he's witnessed.

"We hid in my roof cavity and came close to being killed ourselves," he says, shaking his head. "Allison's parents . . . I'm pretty sure they're dead."

"Wait, Allison was with you?" Abby asks, surprised.

"Shit!" he cusses, standing up, pacing back and forth again. "We were at the mall, that's when everything turned upside down," he says anxiously.

Abby sits listening intently.

"That's when all these weird things started happening to me." He rubs his head, running his hand down over his face.

"What do you mean?" Abby says, looking intrigued.

"I have no idea, I almost see things . . . things that I didn't think were possible, things as they happen, or just before," he says, confused.

"Like a premonition?"

"I don't know how to explain it. It's like I'm there, but in some cases from a different perspective, watching something happen . . . And I've been having these crazy dreams." He plonks himself back down, tired and exhausted, unable to properly comprehend his experience.

Abby sees he's distressed and rubs his leg, trying to comfort him. "Broady, you're scaring me. I've never seen you like this before, showing so much emotion and energy. You're normally so calm and jaded."

Seeing Broady like this hits home to Abby, sensing that something unbelievable is happening—more than what she's seen on television.

Hearing what Abby says he sits straight up on the couch, immediately switching, reining in his emotions, becoming the logical thinker again. Not wanting to reveal too much more, he pulls away, grabbing the remote control and switches stations randomly.

Abby notices his change in persona and moves her hand away, curling up on the couch beside him. Abby, disinterested in watching what's on, stares at Broady curiously; he's glued to the set.

Broady stops, finally settling on a channel with the government emblem. It's a live press conference; a man in a military officer's uniform approaches a bench, covered in microphones. The banner on the television identifies the man as General Chief Admiral Robert Walker.

He begins addressing the nation.

"At approximately 13:45 hours Eastern Standard Time, reports began coming in from various locations across the country involved in

possible terrorist attacks. Information has now surfaced that there was an incident at the Biotech Research and Development Laboratory in Logan Central the day before. At this stage, we are treating these incidents as a biological hazard and have enacted strict national military quarantine measures. We cannot confirm whether the incidents have resulted from an attack, but strongly suggest that they are all related. No one as of yet has taken responsibility. We do know that a number of deaths have resulted. Further reports of what has been described as mutated beings of some description, with yellow eyes.

"Now, we do not have any conclusive evidence nor video or photographs but the descriptions at this early stage are widespread and linked to every incident thus far. We do not know at this stage whether these beings or creatures are of animal, human or otherwise origin. We do know, however, that these incidents all correlate after the sun has set. We have used this time to isolate and quarantine these areas across the country. Safe zones and military checkpoints have been erected across affected areas; anyone who is sick, injured or in need of shelter should attend one of these sites. They will be broadcast over the emergency radiofrequency. We request that during the quarantine proceedings, people remain indoors unless evacuated to a designated area.

"We will update you as further information comes to light."

Crowds of reporters yell out as the stern-faced General walks off without answering a single question, followed by fellow military staff.

Broady presses the mute button, turning to Abby. "I think it's a good idea we sleep in the attic tonight," he says with a concerned look on his face.

"Really?" Abby looks at him strangely, frowning and pulling her head back bewildered.

"If it's not as isolated as we thought it may spread farther out. I think it would be a good idea," he says calmly

"No way!" Abby's says. "It's gross up there, Broady; God knows the last time anyone was up there. Besides, the guy just said we'll be fine indoors," she says, pointing at the television.

Becoming annoyed again Broady adds, "Abby these things bashed my door nearly off the hinges, from what I hear they don't know much of anything. Besides, they only appear to come out at night. They don't know anything, they're just winging it." He stands firmly. "I'm not going to risk it."

"Fine . . ." Abby rolls her eyes and walks out of the room. "I'll go get the single mattress from the spare room and we can use the inflatable that is already up there as well."

He stares blankly at the wall in thought for a moment before looking at the clock in front of him.

4:45 pm.

"I'll go sell the idea to Charlotte," he says.

"Yeah, whatever."

He walks down the hallway, hearing Charlotte's sweet little voice playing in her room, tiptoeing up to her bedroom door. Pausing for a moment he rests his head against the hard door jamb and closes his eyes.

"Why yes, Miss Piggy, Daddy will be joining us shortly," Charlotte says in a posh voice. "I am very much looking forward to it," she continues.

Broady smiles for a moment at the innocence of it all as he gently knocks on the door.

"That must be him now," she says.

"Can I come in?" Broady says gently.

"You may," she says, still playing the part.

He closes the door quietly behind him. There looks to be a large guest list for the tea party. Charlotte has all her teddies spread around a little wooden table and chairs in her room.

Broady begins to think of how he's going to persuade his daughter to willingly sleep in the attic, and what a perfect way than through an imaginary tea party he thinks.

He sits down at a seat Charlotte's reserved for him. Playing the part for a few moments, buttering plastic scones as his daughter pours imaginary tea.

Such a beautiful and innocent thing, he thinks to himself. With all the drama of the past twenty-four hours, he is still able to keep himself cool in front of her.

"So, princess, I had the best idea!" He begins selling the idea.

"Why yes, Daddy?" she says, sipping her tea.

"Mummy and I were thinking about how we all can have a big slumber party."

"That's a great idea!" Charlotte jumps up.

"But you know," he says, looking around. "It might be a bit cramped in here, how about we have it up in the attic, like a campout?" he says enthusiastically.

"Really?" Charlotte turns her nose up. "It smells funny up there."

"True," he says. "I was going to make a tent; we can set up our beds and make a fort! Have torches . . . And you know what else?" he says, trying to lure her in.

"What?" she asks.

"There are two big skylights up there, so we can look up to the stars as we fall asleep."

"But I already have fairy lights," she says, pointing to her bed.

"How about I set the lights up and make it nice and cosy up there, then we can all play games together? Come on what do you say?"

"UHHHH, ok, Daddy," she says, running over and hugging him. "I love you," she says adoringly. Such a loving and affectionate child, Broady feels truly blessed.

"Love you too, princess." He kisses her on the top of her head as he holds her tight.

Hearing a scraping sound from the hallway, Broady turns around to see Abby dragging the single mattress down the hallway.

Turning around he says, "Hey, honey, I'm gonna go help your mum set up camp, ok? So we can play some more later, ok?"

"Ok, Daddy," she says, sitting back down to her tea party.

Walking out of Charlotte's room into the hallway he can see Abby pulling the drawstring down to the attic, the folding staircase creaks and crashes to the ground.

"Is this really necessary, Broady?" she says, looking at him rather unimpressed.

"Yes," he says. "Let me give you a hand." He walks over to help her with the mattress.

Abby just rolls her eyes as they lift the mattress into the attic.

It's quite dim, only a small amount of light peers through the skylights and the small windows at either end of the attic are dirty. The air in the room is stuffy and stale. The old wooden floorboards creak as Abby walks to the centre of the large open attic. She lifts her arm pulling on a cord attached to a single hanging light globe in the centre, only partially illuminating the room.

"Home sweet home!" she says rather sarcastically, clearly not a fan of the idea.

The attic has four timber beams from floor to ceiling positioned in a square around the centre of the room. The attic is a big open rectangle with a cathedral ceiling. Timber shelves screwed to the walls hold old boxes, suitcases and milk crates filled with junk; there are metal standing shelves pushed up against the walls, too. It's filled with old unused furniture and children's toys.

"Wow." Broady looks around amazed. "Do your parents ever throw anything out?"

"Not a thing . . . EVER!" she replies, embarrassed. "The inflatable mattress is up here somewhere." She begins pulling boxes out looking for it.

"Oh, wow, look," Abby says as she opens one of the boxes. He walks over to her and kneels. "Mum and Dad's wedding album," she says, pulling out an old photo album from the box. The box is filled with them, all marked with different names and dates.

"And look our high school yearbook!" Abby says.

Broady picks one out, blowing the dust off, right into Abby's face making her sneeze. Broady laughs.

"Sorry."

She glares at him, sniffing and wiping her face. She begins to flip through the album.

"You don't happen to have your Christmas decorations up here, do you?" Broady asks, standing up and looking around.

"Oh my god!" Abby bursts out laughing. "Look at your

hairdo, Broady," she says, turning the album over for him to see.

Broady squints in the low light and bends down.

"HA!" he says. "Nice socks!" he quickly flips it back on her.

She immediately stops laughing, wiping the smile straight off her face and pulling the book away, left feeling a little insecure.

"The Christmas stuff is always closest to the stairs. Over there." She points.

He rummages around finding a box marked *Christmas stuff*, opening it to find another small box filled with fairy lights.

"Perfect," he says.

"What are you doing with those?" she asks.

Pulling the lights out of the box and untwining them, Broady doesn't hear what she's said.

"Is there a power point up here?" he asks.

"Over there, it's the only one," she says, pointing to one of the beams. She inquisitively watches as he walks over bending down and plugging them into the point near the floor.

As he does the lights immediately begin to strobe, partially stunning Broady. Startled he steps back catching the heel of his shoe on a partially lifted beam and falls onto his backside. Abby begins to laugh as he quickly recovers himself into a lying pose. "So, I guess I'll just settle here then," he says, pretending to yawn.

"You're an idiot," she says, smiling. Broady smiles back as their gaze lingers.

"MUM!" a voice cries out, breaking the moment. "I'm hungry, what's for dinner!" Charlotte yells from the bottom of the stairs.

"Well . . ." Abby shrugs her shoulders. "Duty calls."

"I'll finish up here," he says as she heads back down.

Carefully standing on boxes, he wraps the lights high up around the wood beams, managing to get them to stay, twisting them around and across all four posts.

He moves all the junk out from the centre of the attic, pushing it out to the side. Noticing that the attic doesn't look very much like a camp now, he gets a great idea and runs down the stairs.

He opens the linen closet and pulls out some old sheets.

Hearing Broady rummaging around, Abby sticks her head out of the kitchen and frowns, wondering what he is doing.

"I'm just going to heat a frozen pizza, yeah?" she calls down the hallway.

"Yeah whatever," Broady replies, focused on his set-up. "Just make sure you're up here before the sun goes down." He carries an armful of sheets up the stairs

"Yeah whatever," she yells back at him sarcastically. Broady stops midway up the stairs, crouches down and peers at her through the gap in the stairs, raising his eyebrows at her. Abby grins, popping her head back into the kitchen.

Back up in the attic, Broady throws the sheets over the string of lights and up over the top to make a little blanket house, using some tape he found on a shelf to loosely secure it. Some rusty old nails he finds scattered around provide the perfect hook, banging them into the beam with a bit of old metal pipe.

Down in the kitchen, hearing all the commotion from up in the attic, Abby shakes her head.

"What the heck, Broady!?" she yells out, hearing him trample down the stairs.

"Almost done!" he calls.

"Well good, because I'm just about done," she replies, peeking down the hallway. Broady is carrying a bunch of blankets and cushions from Charlotte's room.

"I don't even want to know!" she says.

With the pizza ready and the sun beginning to set, Broady moves around the house securing the doors and windows. By 6 pm it's starting to get dark. As Broady begins to close and lock the back-glass screen door he peers outside. Surrounded by bush, the trees sway back and forth in the wind. He stares out into the backyard, listening to the wind blow through the trees. With the movement from the wind, his eyes begin to play tricks on him as he looks around for any sign of the creatures lurking in the bush. No longer focused on making an indoor camp, that sinking feeling begins to arise in his stomach again, worried about the night ahead.

"Hey, you ready?" Abby calls out to him, as he stares out into the wilderness. Quickly shaking himself off he refocuses his thoughts, turning around noticing Abby holding two wooden boards with freshly sliced pizza.

"Yeah let's go!" Charlotte yells, standing down the end of the hallway at the base of the stairs, holding her teddy.

"Hang on," Broady calls out, running over to the stairs.

"Give me a second before you head up," he adds enthusiastically. He runs up into the attic turning all the lights off. "Ok!" he calls out.

Abby and Charlotte slowly step up the staircase, it's almost pitch back.

"Broady!" Abby calls out, a few moments pass, she starts to become a little unsettled.

"Quit playing around!" she yells.

With the sound of a light switch, the attic lights up, revealing the makeshift tent with their bedding lying in the centre of the attic.

"Ta-da!" he yells, throwing his hands up in the air.

The fairy lights spread warm ambient light around, revealing a cosy little white tent; the beds are made neatly, covered in cushions, pillows and throw blankets. The dim light leaves the outer attic in darkness leaving only the centre visible.

Charlotte squeals with excitement, "Mum, Mum, Mum! Look!" she yells, running over and jumping on the bouncy mattress. Broady grabs her in a wrestle, tickling her as she giggles.

Abby stands there frozen in awe.

"Are you just going to stand there and let the pizza get cold?" Broady says.

She walks over placing the pizza down on the bed, her mouth wide open in amazement.

"See, not such a bad idea, hey?" Broady laughs.

Charlotte and Broady begin to dig into the pizza.

"Wow, Broady . . ." Abby's says. "You did a really great job . . . I'm impressed!"

He just smirks while chowing down a slice of pizza, winking at Charlotte.

Noticing the two enjoying each other's company Charlotte can't wipe the grin off her face, having not heard her mum compliment her dad in a very long time.

"Ooooo," she exclaims, making kissing noises with her lips.

Abby's cheeks go bright red as she tries to shy away.

"I'll give you kisses, little miss." Broady plays, mimicking her as he leans over.

"Eww, gross!" Charlotte responds, lifting a blanket over her head.

Broady dives over the top of her, playfully wrestling and poking her. She squeals and giggles, pulling the blanket off her head. "I love you, Daddy," she says, instantly warming his heart. He is grateful for having made it to her.

"I love you too, princess," he says, gazing at her, lost in the moment. Her puffy cheeks still remind him of her as a baby, he's amazed at how much she's grown.

"DAD . . ." She pokes his cheek. "You're staring again!"

He laughs. "You're just too damn gorgeous," he says, kissing her on the cheek.

Abby sits back, watching how Broady interacts with her. She can see that he's a great father, however, she would never reveal that to him.

"Ok you two, bedtime, miss," she interrupts, plonking herself on the bed.

"But Mum," Charlotte begins to plea. "I need a story and all my books are in my room."

"Well lucky," Abby says. "Look at what I found." She pulls on old children's storybook from behind her.

Charlotte screws up her nose. "How old is *that*?"

"I found it in one of the boxes," Abby says. "Grandpa would read it to me when I was little, about your age."

"So . . . Really old then." She giggles, Broady nudges her.

"Pull up, kiddo," he says.

"I'm only joking, Mummy, can you read it pleasssse?"

The three settle in with Charlotte cozied between them.

As Abby reads along, Broady rubs his hand over her forehead

and through her hair. He looks over at Abby while she enthusiastically reads her favourite childhood story; he can't help but feel a certain fondness for her, despite their roller-coaster past. Looking down, Charlotte is already sound asleep. Not wanting to interrupt Abby, he continues listening to her read, taking a moment of rest.

Broady wakens to the sound of a kiss. Having finished the book, Abby kisses Charlotte on her forehead and lies down. The two ex-lovers lay facing each other as Abby caresses Charlotte's hair.

"So much sweeter when she's asleep," Abby whispers.

"Nah," Broady says tiredly with one eye open. "She's cute even with her little sassy attitude; I wonder where she gets it from?" Broady says raising his eyebrows at Abby again.

"So . . . What's the plan, Broady?" she asks, ignoring his smart-arse remark. "You've always got something going on in that head of yours . . . Even though you don't communicate it with anyone else."

He grunts at her passive-aggressive tone and rolls onto his back.

"It's safe here, there is still power. I say we stay put for a while and see how it plays out," he says.

"What about your little girlfriend?" Abby asks in a sarcastic tone.

"Allison is like my little sister, Abby," Broady says. "She's at the military safe zone. She'll be safe there," he says, trying to sound hopeful.

Guilt starts to surface, having not considered Allison until Abby mentioned her. He attempts to block it out by changing the subject.

"So where are your parents?" he asks.

"They're in Europe. I spoke to them yesterday and they're 'living the dream'." Abby throws her hands up and rolls her eyes.

Broady's phone buzzes from inside his pocket, a moment later sitting beside the bed, Abby's does too.

Both look at each other with a puzzled look on their faces as they both turn to read the text.

STATE EMERGENCY SERVICE their phones read.

STATE EMERGENCY UPDATE: ALL SOUTHERN STATES ARE ON HIGH ALERT AS SUSPECTED CONTAGION SPREADING. ALL LOCAL RESIDENTS ARE TO REMAIN INDOORS. KEEP LIGHTS OFF. MORE INFORMATION TO FOLLOW.

"Contagion?" Abby says, looking to Broady for confirmation. "Does this mean it's some sort of virus or something?" she asks, looking confused.

Broady reads the message over a few times in his head, then whispers it out loud, hoping the spoken words will help unlock more clues and somehow make more sense of it.

He thinks back to Allison's parents' apartment; remembering their bodies were gone, he wonders if it could be true, although he's still sceptical of the idea.

"The things I saw, they didn't move, look or sound like people. I can't see how that is possible," he says.

"Maybe it's some sort of mutating virus that's infecting people. Changing their genetics or something. The government are always doing fucked-up experiments on people." Abby begins to work herself up, hopping up out of the bed and pacing back and forth, spinning the conspiracies off in her head.

"The message wasn't incredibly informative, Abby; let's not jump to conclusions just yet."

"What would you know, anyway? You said yourself that it was dark, and you didn't get a good look," she snaps.

Broady chuffs to himself. "Well, I'm glad you listened to me enough for us to sleep up here, at least you still have some sense," he fires back.

Abby ignores him completely. She lies down on the bed and faces the wall.

By this time Broady can't be bothered arguing with her and just lets it go.

He lays down, his overtired and exhausted body aches all over. His mind, however, keeps ticking; his senses are still on high alert now that the sun has gone down. As the wind outside becomes more intense, the surrounding trees howl. Sticks and twigs bang on the tin roof, making him hyper-vigilant.

He turns on his side and looks at Charlotte as she sleeps. After only a few moments watching her sleep peacefully, he pulls the blanket up to the bottom of her chin and tucks her in. Abby lets out a tired yawn and rolls over on her side, and while still giving him the silent treatment she watches as he pulls the blanket up over her as well. Cuddling up to Charlotte holding her tight, he drifts off into some well-deserved rest.

His sleep, however, is anything but; vivid dreams plague his restless mind. Seeing clear as day, Allison boarding a minibus in the car park of the military safe zone where he left her. As he is standing just outside the bus, she turns around looking out into the crowd of people lining up to board the bus. Her hair blows lightly in the breeze and she wipes it from her face. He feels a chill run over his body as he watches on.

His dream then shifts and he finds himself walking outside an old run-down service station. Lucidly, he looks around the completely unfamiliar surroundings in the middle of nowhere.

Hearing a faint clicking sound from behind him, he turns around as a creature launches itself at him. Locking eyes with its brightly illuminated yellow eyes—completely paralysing him with fear, he chokes, unable breathe.

Broady gasps for air as he jerks himself awake, propelling himself upright. The room is almost pitch black. His heart pounding out of his chest, he can hear it in his ears as sweat runs down over his face, soaking his shirt. It takes a moment for him to get his bearings as his eyes adjust to the dark. Only a dim stream of moonlight shines through the small dirty window up behind him. He lays back down breathing heavily, reaching his arm out to feel Charlotte's warm body still asleep beside him. He continues breathing deeply, managing to get his senses back in order. He mulls over the emotional intensity of the dreams, still unable to understand why now, for the first time in his life, he is struggling to maintain his calm and composed state.

As he settles back in taking a big stretch, a dull ringing starts in his ear. Not noticing at first, he begins to get comfy, as things begin to settle the ring becomes louder. He swiftly reopens his eyes, noticing the familiarity of the sound he's heard before. He becomes weary, as the sound of a toilet flushing emanates up the stairs.

He sits up immediately, looking beside him; he didn't even realise that Abby wasn't in the bed. The retractable staircase is down and dim light from downstairs shines up into the attic.

Broady quietly slips out of bed. Standing on top of the staircase, he peers down as shadows are cast from a moving light. The old wooden stairs creak as he bears his weight down on them. The hallway is dark and eerie, the light having moved into the kitchen tracing light onto the adjacent wall. He slips down the hallway, hearing the sound of the tap pouring water, he peers around the corner.

Abby is standing in front of the sink drinking a glass of water she's just filled. The room is lit by the torch on Abby's phone.

"What are you doing?" Broady whispers with angst.

Abby jolts. "Shit, Broady," she says loudly as she turns around.

"You scared the shit out of me," she says.

"Shhh," Broady whispers trying to hush her, lowering both hands down toward the floor.

"I needed to use the bathroom or is that not ok with you?" she replies, ignoring his subtle suggestions.

"It's not safe down here," he says, desperately trying to get his point across. "Turn your light off," he continues whispering, frustrated.

"Sorry," she whispers, tilting her head sarcastically. "I'll check with you next time I have to go to the bathroom." She huffs, tipping the remainder of her water out into the sink and peering out through the kitchen window.

The high-pitched frequency ringing in his ears becomes deafly loud and screwing up his face in dismay he wiggles his finger inside his ears, clicking his jaw and elongating his face, attempting to rid himself of the irritating sound.

"What is that?" Abby says curiously,

Too focused on his hearing he doesn't quite make out what she's said.

"Seriously, Broady, come over here," she says, waving him over as she stares out the window.

Just as sudden as it came on, the ringing stops and it's deadly quiet again. As Broady begins to regain some awareness he looks up as a dark figure leaps toward the house, smashing through the glass window above the sink. He brings his arm up over his face as the sudden impact sends shattered glass flying through the kitchen. Broady stumbles back out of the doorway until he hits his back on the hallway wall. Abby screams as she falls, knocking her phone out of her hands onto the floor. With the light still on it slides across the other side of the kitchen, casting shadows around the room. The dark figure begins squealing a high-pitched noise and Broady instantly recognises the sound. It's the same as the creatures from the mall and the ones from inside his apartment. On the other side of the island bench, all Broady can see is Abby's legs and arms kicking and waving as a dark figure bears down on her.

Broady shakes off the shock of the surprise as the adrenaline begins racing through his body.

He rushes back into the kitchen in an attempt to help Abby. The creature has managed to get on top of her, and she fights profusely, trying to hold the creature back. The noise it's making is deafening—screeching and clicking. Without a thought, Broady grabs onto its skinny leg attempting to pull the creature off. It loses its balance and falls heavily on top of Abby; she cries out but manages to push it off to one side. It turns its head around, and in the dim-lit kitchen, its eyes glow bright yellow.

Irritated, it squints, slightly opening its mouth. Pulling back its lips revealing sharp razor-like teeth it hisses and clicks loudly toward Broady. As Abby struggles to get up the creature pulls her back down, slamming her back into the ground. Broady wrestles to pull it off her again. Irritated, the creature kicks Broady. Its strength is incredible, sending him flying across the kitchen, slamming into the overhead glass door cabinets. He hits his head as he falls hard onto the ground, along with the broken glass and crockery which shatter on the tiles making a tremendous noise. Dazed and suffering a possible concussion, he is well aware that Abby is still in grave danger. He looks around on the floor, while his vision is fuzzy, he still manages to see a kitchen knife block that's been knocked from the bench onto the floor. Knives are strewn across the kitchen. He scurries along the floor on his hands and knees, slipping on pieces of broken glass. Shards slice into the skin on his hands as he desperately tries to grab the closest knife. Grabbing one tightly he jumps back onto his feet. The creature mounts Abby's back as she attempts to get up. Now with no way of defending herself she screams for help, in agony as the creature tears at her back, biting her on the shoulder. Broady rushes over, plunging the knife deeply into the creature's back between the two growths protruding out from either shoulder blade. It jolts up with a deafening screech.

The painful sound causes Broady to block his ears, lifting his hands over them and closing his eyes tightly. The creature knocks him down onto his backside, ferociously waving its arms around, desperate to pull the object out. Placing his arms out to break his fall they land on shards of broken glass. This time Broady can feel the sting; he lifts his hands seeing them blood-soaked with shiny glass pieces over them. He brushes them off quickly onto his jeans, feeling the glass scrape and dig deeper into his skin. He shuffles backward and against the kitchen bench as the creature frantically circles around and around with its arms out. Sharp claws protrude out from its hands, and waving them around it bangs into the benches, knocking everything off onto the floor. Broady continues to back up out of the way and into the hallway. The creature falls to the ground, viciously scratching and clawing on the floor. Unable to reach Abby, Broady's forced to go the other way around, down the end of the hallway. He picks himself back up, smearing bloody handprints on the wall as he levers himself to his feet. As he limps down the hallway there is a booming sound as the glass doors at the end of the house explode in. More clicking and screeching. Broady realises there is another.

He limps down the hallway leaving bloody handprints on the furniture as he stumbles into the lounge room.

"Broady!" Abby screams, though her voice no longer sounds like it's coming from the kitchen. As Broady turns the corner into the dining room, he sees Abby's feet slide outside through the shattered glass door and out onto the deck.

Broady gives chase seeing another creature holding Abby by her arm; she is limp and weak, covered in her own blood. She desperately holds up her free arm, unable to put up any fight. By the time Broady has made it to the deck, the creature has already managed to drag Abby some twenty metres and they've begun to disappear into the dark bush. He steps out in an attempt to rush to her aid when he's suddenly stopped by a faint, familiar sound. He turns his head to listen closer.

"Daddy!" Charlotte's faint cries reach her father's ears. He turns back, unable to see, nor hearing Abby's pleas through the howling wind. The shrubbery wrestles in the wind and through the darkness, there is no way Broady can see where she is.

His heart breaks momentarily as he feels torn. Quickly shutting down any emotion he turns away, focusing instead on Charlotte. He steps onto the broken glass as he re-enters the property; he pauses for a second, noticing how eerily quiet it is inside. He looks up and into the kitchen. Standing hunched over, its arms close to its body like a t-rex dinosaur, the creature and Broady lock eyes. Its bright luminescent eyes are captivating. Both the creature and Broady remain frozen as they stare at one another. Inside, Broady is frantically trying to analyse and make sense of what he is seeing.

"Daddy!" Charlotte's crying voice yells again out from up in the attic.

Breaking eye contact for only a split second he looks up in the direction of the hallway.

The creature screeches loudly jerking its head side to side.

Broady's stomach drops, realising the creature is trying to locate the origin of her cry. It begins to dart quickly into the hallway. Broady races through the lounge room and down the hallway after it.

"DADDY!" Charlotte screams, her voice crackles as if in tears, sending chills down Broady's spine. His heart races as the threat draws closer to her.

The creature's feet skid along the tiled floor as it attempts to turn around and climb up the stairs. As it begins to ascend, Broady grabs the supporting pole with his arm, swinging his body around and throwing himself up, reaching out as far as he can, manages to grab the creature's ankle before reaching the top, both of them collapsing on the hardwood stairs.

Charlotte stands at the top of the stairs holding her teddy, her hand in her mouth, tears pouring down her little cheeks as her bottom jaw quivers.

Now off balance, Broady pulls harder, the creature falls on its face, smashing its jaw on the staircase. Using this to his advantage, Broady grabs tightly onto the creature's ankle with both hands. Placing his leg up on the staircase he pulls the creature with all his might, pushing his foot against the staircase simultaneously. His powerful heave manages to propel the creature up and over himself as he too falls backward down the staircase. The creature slides along the tiled floor, skidding into the front door, driving the knife still embedded in its back even farther in. The creature screeches and squeals as it kicks and scratches around frantically. Broady takes a hard fall as he lands on his back, flipping over his head and tumbling down to the floor.

Broady wastes no time as the creature violently kicks and screeches around on the floor. Lunging all the way up in just a few strides, he scoops Charlotte up under one arm and places her down out of the way. He lays flat on his belly reaching down and grabbing the fold-down staircase. Not designed to be pulled up from the inside, Broady grabs at it wherever he can. He looks up, seeing the creature scurrying to its feet. Broady clenches his jaw and, using all his power, heaves the wooden staircase. The creature jumps up to grab the stairs as they leave the ground, missing by only a fraction. It continues to screech and click loudly.

He hops up, the dark moonlit attic still light enough to see the confused and petrified look on Charlotte's face. He picks her up, ducking his head as he moves to the far corner of the attic, banging his shin on an old compressor.

"Shit!" he yells as he limps on.

"Daddy, what's going on?" Charlottes cries.

"Shhh," he says calmly. "We have to be quiet, ok, baby?" he whispers.

Once in the corner, Broady drags the portable shelving from either side around him, making a tiny cramped little hiding spot. He squats down with not even enough room to fully extend his legs, the boxes and things stored on the shelf provide a small amount of concealment. Charlotte clings to her father tightly as he peers through the gaps in the shelving. The creature wildly bangs against the walls, the attic floor shaking and vibrating, Broady can hear things being thrown or knocked over from all around underneath them.

"Daddy," Charlotte whispers, "what is that?" Still confused and scared she looks up to her father for comfort.

"Shhh," Broady hushes. "We have to be quiet, ok, honey?" he says, moving the hair from in front of her face, careful not to rub his bloody hands on her.

"Where's Mummy?" she whispers tearfully.

"Mummy will be back; she went to find help," Broady fibs, unable to come to terms with the high probability she's dead.

"We're ok . . . We're ok." He speaks into the top of her head, more attempting to convince himself than just her as he gently rocks her back and forth. Her hair smells like baby's lavender shampoo, and amidst the commotion beneath them, the smell is somewhat comforting. The time between each screech and banging of walls becomes greater and less intense as the time goes on. For hours Broady doesn't blink, just peering up at the moonlight as it streams in from the window up high in front of him. He looks toward the sky, waiting desperately for first light. Charlotte, on the other hand, manages to drift off to sleep on her father's chest. He continues to stare blankly at the small bit of sky he can see from the partially open window. 4:30 am, his watch reads. With only another hour till sunup, he begins to feel hopeful. The house is now eerily quiet, and Broady wonders if the creature has fled. Peeking up to the tiny gap outside, the sky is turning dark blue as the sun rises. His tense body begins to soften as he relaxes, an overwhelming warm tingling feeling washes over his body as it does. The heart-pumping adrenaline flows out of his extremities and they become heavier by the second. His eyelids too, hard to keep open, close gently, and resting his head against the hard timber wall he no longer notices the uncomfortable position he finds himself in. Physically and mentally exhausted, he falls asleep.

Chapter 5

Soon after he dozes off, visions begin to disturb his rest. Flashes of an old white minibus sitting parked in the stadium car park, smoke encasing the surrounding area, Allison stepping up and onto the bus, peering back as she looks for something or someone. Broady becomes aware of his lucid dreaming, recalling this reoccurring dream and he tries to make sense of all of it, before another flash.

An old abandoned service station. He tries to wake himself up, feeling constrained his anxiety heightens, and he feels suffocated. Turning around, capturing the moment a creature lunges toward him. Captivated by the bright yellow eyes, he's again overwhelmed and paralysed with fear.

Gasping for air, Broady jolts himself awake. As he comes to, he's thankful it's only a dream. He looks down at Charlotte's innocent face tucked into his arm, her mouth dropped open as she drools down onto his shirt. The emotionally-charged dream has his heart still racing. Pondering for a moment, confused to the origins of these bizarre dreams, he wonders if they are real. To Broady, they feel very much so.

The sun streams light straight in through the window, the light illuminating the dust particles in the air as the beams shine into the dull attic. Birds chirp loudly outside, seemingly unaware of the horror executed only hours earlier. He rubs his eyes with his forefinger and thumb as he cradles Charlotte with his other arm. Thinking of their next move, he feels his hands rough and course. Pulling them away from his face there is dried clotted blood, more smudged over his jeans, some even on Charlotte's hair. Now aware, his hands begin to throb. He looks closer to see a shiny shard poking out. He pulls it out with his fingers.

"Tsssk." He jumps from the sharp pain.

Charlotte groans as she begins to wake. Pushing against Broady's chest she sits herself up with a cranky tired look on her face she gazes around, puzzled.

"What are we doing here, Daddy?" she asks, collapsing back on her father's chest.

"I had the worst dreams," she says. Broady looks down at her, concerned. The possibility of her having suffered some sort of traumatic amnesia worries him, with no idea of how to work through it.

Broady looks up toward the roof, taking a deep breath. He's unsure if she's referring to last night, thinking that it was just a dream. Not wanting to further query her and unable to think of the right thing to say, he softens it over.

"You're ok, sweetness," he sighs.

Unable to get the visions out of his head, they are accompanied by a strong gut feeling. He now feels compelled to find Allison.

He's not completely sold yet on the idea of premonitions as Abby mentioned, still sceptical, yet he cannot seem to shake this feeling. A good opportunity to prove them wrong, he thinks.

"Charlotte, how do you feel about a little road trip?" he asks quietly.

"Where are we going? Are we going to your house?" she asks.

"Well . . ." he says, putting it more excitedly. "It's more of a holiday, but we are going to get Allison to come with us!"

"Oh yay," she exclaims. "I like Allison, but where are we going?" she asks.

Broady rattles his brain thinking of the safest place he can think of quickly.

"To Nanna and Poppy's farm, out west," he says.

"Yeahhhhhh!" She jumps up, excited. "Can I ride their horses, Dad? Pleasssse?"

"Sure, honey, I'm sure Poppy will teach you."

Concerned yet relieved he's managed to keep her little mind occupied, he still has no idea of what to say about her mum or what's happening. His mind is still in disarray as to what's happened.

"Ok, let's go downstairs and get your things," he says.

"Ok, Daddy." She smiles.

A sinking feeling rolls over his mind, unsure of what downstairs looks like. The roof cracks and tings as the heat from the sun warms the tin roof. Pushing the metal racks out of the way, Charlotte stares at him strangely but says nothing as he drags them across the floor before moving toward the staircase.

"Just wait there a moment, honey," Broady says, holding up his hand as he lays down on his stomach again, lowering the stairs ever so slowly. Broady pops his head down through the staircase; looking upside down, the place is a wreck. Tables knocked over, pot plants and dirt skewed down the hallway, Broady's bloody handprints smear down to the lounge room walls where the couches and coffee tables are up-ended.

"Oh my god," Broady whispers to himself.

It's quiet, however, he believes it's safe.

"What are you doing, Daddy?" Charlotte says, beginning to look more concerned.

"Nothing, sweetness, it's all good, just lowering the staircase," he replies, looking back and giving her a big grin of reassurance.

She walks over to the top of the stairs.

"Just a sec, honey," he stops her. "Let Daddy go first."

Broady quickly jumps in front of her and heads down cautiously, while trying to maintain a sense of normality.

Charlotte's room is directly adjacent the stairs. He thinks of a way to distract her.

"Well, come on then!" He smiles. "Hurry up would ya!" he jokes.

Charlotte carries on walking down normally, as she steps onto the floor Broady quickly ushers her along, positioning himself to block her view of the hallway.

"Now straight to your room, little miss, we have a big trip to pack for," he says.

"Yeah, yeah," she replies, opening her bedroom door. Broady cringes as the door opens. Charlotte's room remains completely intact.

"Come on then," he says, making his way over to her wardrobe and grabbing her pink unicorn backpack from up the top of the cupboard. "Could you come help me please?" he asks. He unhooks some of her clothes from her wardrobe, stuffing them in her bag.

"Aren't you even going to fold them, Dad?" Charlotte says, frowning at her father. Looking down she notices his bloody hands.

"DADDY! You're bleeding!" she says.

Broady quickly hides his hands behind his back. "Oops." He laughs it off, jumping up and heading toward the door.

"You keep packing, honey, I'm going to pack us some food and get cleaned up, ok?"

"Ok, Daddy," she says. Quietly sitting down, she begins to neatly fold her clothes.

Broady heads out into the hallway and getting a full view of the mayhem, he's shocked by what he sees.

"Don't leave your room till I come back, ok?" he yells back down the hallway.

Charlotte places her teddy on the seat with the table and chairs and begins innocently chattering away to herself. "Dad's very clumsy sometimes you know, Teddy, whatever will we do with him?"

Broady smiles to himself.

The kitchen is a total disaster, open kitchen cupboards, some hang off their hinges, shattered glass and kitchenware scattered over the benches and tiled floor. Broady's bloody handprints smeared along the floor. He turns to the fridge, grabbing shopping bags from on top of it. Opening the pantry, he fills the bags with non-perishable, tinned and packaged food. Grabbing a couple of empty water bottles that lay on the bottom of the pantry he walks past the island bench to the sink. His heart sinks at the sticky pool of drying blood where Abby had been laying, and the trail out the back door. He looks away, trying not to focus on it. Emotion begins to run high as he races over to the sink, quickly filling a bottle. He chugs down water in an attempt to suppress his turmoil. A single tear escapes his eyes, running down along his cheek; he feels the tear pool on his earlobe and fall as he throws the bottle into the sink. Shaking his head, he concentrates on filling up the water bottles. He snuffles, wiping his nose and face on his shirt, snatching the bag off the bench and quickly heads out of the kitchen and into the bathroom.

Turning both taps on full, he washes the dried blood off his hands. Splashing some water on his face, he peers at himself in the mirror, his eyes are heavy and red, dark circles appear as bags under his eyes. He looks hard at his image, drawing strength to keep himself together for Charlotte. Looking back down into the sink he notices fresh blood mixing with water flowing down the drain. He snaps out of it, checking under the sink for a first-aid kit. He pulls it out from underneath the cabinet. Squirting disinfectant over both his hands he clenches his body as the sting of the antibacterial washes clean his wounds. He grabs a bandage, ripping it open with his teeth and roughly wraps them up as quickly as he can. He jumps up grabbing one of Abby's dad's jackets from the laundry basket and puts it on. He briefly checks himself in the mirror before heading back toward Charlotte's room.

Hurrying in he is suddenly stopped by Charlotte standing just inside the door, he's moving so hastily he nearly runs her down.

"Whoa!" he exclaims, stepping back.

"Ready to go, Daddy!" she says, standing innocently at the door, her pink backpack sitting tightly over her shoulders. She stands poised, ready, holding her teddy up under her arm.

Broady is amazed at how well she's managed on her own, having done her hair into two slightly messy ponytails that puff out the top sides of her head.

"Great job, princess," he says. "Nice job with the hair! Looking good!" he compliments her, holding up his thumbs.

"Mummy showed me . . ." She pauses for a moment, and Broady's eyes widen. "Is Mummy coming with us?" she asks, putting her hand up to her chin, thinking.

Broady promptly swoops her up as his eyes begin to well. Still himself unable to process what's unfolded, he has no way of explaining it to Charlotte, instead, he chooses to ignore the question entirely. He remains as composed as possible as he marches out the front door, inside, however, his heart is breaking.

Unbeknown to him, Charlotte peers over her father's shoulders, seeing her house in a mess. Frightened, she quickly ducks her head back into Broady's neck.

He places the kitchen bags in the back seat, settling Charlotte down in the front passenger seat he carefully pulls her bag around her arms, pulling her teddy from her grasp.

"Teddy!" she cries, pulling it back into her chest tightly.

Placing the pink unicorn bag in the back, in between the all of the past owner's junk, Broady looks at the jerry cans for a moment, deciding it safer to fuel up the truck now to avoid stopping if possible. The containers are jammed in tight as Broady tugs on them. Having had little sleep for the last two nights he becomes easily irritated jumping up on the back of the tray and throwing some of the man's junk on the side of the driveway. Charlotte tenses up, having not seen her father angry before she sinks in her seat. Looking through the back window he sees Charlotte, ducked down in her seat, and realising his error, he takes a deep breath to calm down. The sound of the wind and the cool breeze on his face help ground him. Managing to free the jerry cans, he jumps off and cheers, trying to lighten the mood.

"I did it!" he says, throwing up his arms. "That junk didn't stand a chance against me!" he roars.

Charlotte giggles at her dad's silly act.

Having fuelled the truck up, he opens the driver's door, forgetting about the pistol still tucked in the side door. He lets out a breath of disappointment, angry at himself for not remembering. Wondering if it could have helped save Abby, he begins to feel horrendously guilty. He picks it up tucking it into the back of his pants again as quick as he can; out of Charlotte's view.

He jumps in, flicking on the ignition. Three-quarters full, it reads.

Not quite sure it's enough, he plays confident.

"Yeeha, we're ready to go, captain," he says in a cheerful voice.

He starts up the old ute, grinds it into gear and turns the car around. Looking back in the rear-view mirror at Abby's parents' house he drives slowly down the driveway.

Strangely enough at that moment, he recalls the first time meeting Abby's father on the front porch. Remembering as if it were yesterday, holding her hand as he approached the front screen door, residual nervousness still in his belly at the sight of him. What he wouldn't give to go back to that awkward moment. Hard memories of a distant time long gone. Charlotte, too, looks back, turning around in her seat.

"Something bad happened to Mum, didn't it, Daddy?" she says, slumping back into her seat.

Choked up Broady manages to get out, "What makes you say that, honey?" he says as calmly as he can.

"I had bad dreams, but I think they came true," she says, propping her legs up onto the seat, wrapping her arms around them, her teddy squashed in between. A salty tear rolls down her cheeks, soaked up by her teddy's fur.

"Hey," he says, rubbing the back of her neck. "We don't know for sure; she could be going to get some help." He realises he's pretty much confirmed her suspicion. She doesn't respond, choosing instead to turn away and look out the window. Broady begins to speak before stopping himself and unable to find the words he leaves her alone.

As the car tyres hit the bitumen road, Broady steps hard on the gas pedal, upset and a little angry with himself for not being able to comfort his daughter. They veer off, back onto the windy mountain road.

The roads are deserted. Having not passed a single car in over an hour, Broady's mind begins to wander.

What are we going to do?

What is happening?

What are these creatures? And where do they come from?

Where is Allison? And why do I keep having these dreams about her?

What am I going to do about telling Charlotte about her mother?

These questions run over and over in his head, with no real answer. Anxiety starts to boil to the surface and his palms become sweaty tied up in the bandages. He grips the steering wheel tighter.

Attempting to shift his focus, he nudges Charlotte.

"Hey, kiddo, want to play a game?" he asks.

She stirs and turns over, exhausted from her broken sleep and emotionally drained from missing her mother, her eyes are shut and she's fast asleep. Taking his eyes off the road for a few seconds he stares down at her peacefully resting. Broady finds a small piece of happiness in her peaceful state, enough motivation to enable him to better consolidate his thoughts. He mulls over the rather peculiar things that he's been experiencing, wondering what they are. The ring in his ears, making the connection that it only seems to happen when the creatures are close . . . but why?

What happened back at the mall, and his dream from inside his apartment. Was he dreaming at all? How could he possibly know these things? They seem completely foreign to his previously logical reasoning self. He cannot deny, however, that they all seem connected somehow from the very beginning.

He sits with those thoughts, not one to usually believe the hype of silly psychics and voodoo he feels very much at odds with them. He concludes that the dissonance is the cause of the sudden emotional upheaval he's experiencing.

Looking down at Charlotte he remembers hearing her scream out to him at the stadium, and still, the reminder of the voice sends chills down his spine. What if he hadn't come? The thoughts become sickening, swaying his opinion slightly.

Remembering the visions of Allison getting on the bus, he wonders where she is going. Still unsure, he decides it best to go and confirm her whereabouts at the military zone at the stadium. Then he'll head to his parent's farm, north-west of Bundaberg.

It's far, at least five hundred kilometres from his home town. The farm is, however, very isolated. He would have to drive through hectares upon hectares of cane fields and into the cattle farming region.

His parents' farm has cattle, pigs, chickens, as well as a huge range of fresh produce they sell at the farmers' market. Broady's parents moved there when he was eighteen, taking over the farm from his grandfather. Broady's father, Phil, was an accountant before they moved, and his mother Margret was a homemaker. Broady's uncle and father didn't care much for farm life in their early years, moving away to make a life of their own, only to someday return to their roots. The irony of the thought brings a smirk to Broady's face. Seems he's set for a similar fate.

"Arrgghh." Charlotte begins to wake, opening her mouth wide in what appears to be an extremely satisfying yawn.

"Are we there yet?" she groans, unable to get comfy again.

"About halfway, honey," Broady replies, rubbing her head.

"I'm hungry," she says, opening and closing her mouth chewing the air.

He reaches his arm into the back seat stretching as far as he can. Charlotte 'eeps' as the car veers slightly off the road.

"Dad!" she yells.

"Got it!" Broady exclaims, pulling the two wheels back onto

the road, presenting Charlotte with some chips, chocolate and a water bottle.

"This is all we have for now; we will stop later," he says.

Charlotte doesn't complain, not often is she allowed to eat snack food.

She tears the packets open, gobbling them down almost without a breath. Broady laughs at her keenness.

"I need to go to the toilet!" she begs, wiping the smile straight off Broady's face.

The windy bush road doesn't have many great spots to pull over; he's forced to drive another kilometre before finding a large gravel patch on the opposite side of the road. Broady veers over the lanes and the tyres skid on the loose surface as they come to a halt. He switches off the car's engine off, instantly noticing just how noisy the old diesel engine was. He opens the squeaky door, stepping out onto the gravel. The wind has died off and a bitter stillness embraces the air. Charlotte jumps down from her seat heading around to the driver's side. Broady opens the back door, attempting to give her some privacy. Charlotte looks at him with displeasure on her face.

"Not here, Dad, what if someone sees?" she says, looking embarrassed.

Broady rolls his eyes. "Geez, girls are difficult," he says sarcastically.

"Girls are the best!" she rebuts, merrily grabbing her father's hand.

He leads her through the scrub finding a flat spot in between the trees and stops, seeing a large lake through the bush. He stands and looks away.

"You too, Daddy!" Charlotte says, opening her eyes wide and glaring at her father.

"Oh, righto." Broady acts offended. "Two years ago I was wiping your bum I'll have you know," he says. She doesn't reply.

Moving away, he wanders farther into the bush toward the water. The sky opens up as the tree line stops at the water's edge. A huge wide-open lake, part of the city's dam, water as far as his eyes can see. Dense forest and hills line the outskirts of the dam. The waters are dead calm, not a ripple on the surface, the water reflecting the blue sky and refracts the shapes of the hills and trees. Broady looks around in awe at the picturesque surroundings. The trees are a deep, vibrant green after the last big wet season. He bends down at the water's edge, placing his fingertips in; the cold water feels chilly but refreshing. He mesmerised momentarily as he draws circles in the water with his fingers.

"Rahhh!" Charlotte yells as she jumps onto his back.

Broady jumps, taken off guard by the tranquil surroundings and completely surprised.

"Argg," Broady groans in a deep voice. "You got me, you little terror, now it's your turn."

She squeals and giggles as she runs off. Broady gives chase, making eating sounds with his mouth.

"I eat little monsters," he shouts, Charlotte continues to giggle and scream, looking back behind her as she scurries through the bush back toward the car. As she reaches the edge of the bush, Broady hears the faint sound of a car.

"Charlotte!" he calls out to her with a fretful tone, she continues completely unaware; he quickly runs after her. The gap between the bush and the car is seven metres or so, and by the time Broady catches up, she's already standing wide out in the open.

The sound of the tyres on the road echoes down from the hills. Too late for concealment Broady hastily opens the car door telling Charlotte to buckle up as she climbs through the driver's-side door.

Broady can see the car is an old red Toyota hatchback; the rear end suspension is sitting lower than the front. The paint on the bonnet and roof is oxidising, faded and peeling off. The car slows down as it gets closer. Putting his hand up to his forehead he tries to peer in the windshield, but the reflection from the sky makes it difficult to see who is in the car, seeing only faint outlines of people heads as they bobble in the back seat. Broady's senses go on high alert as he reaches in flicking on the car's ignition. With his other hand, he casually reaches behind his back, gripping Ray's pistol that's tucked down the back of his pants.

"Who's that, Daddy?" Charlotte calls out.

The car comes to a complete stop beside them. Broady's heart begins to race staring at the car's tinted windows.

A few moments go by that feel like an eternity before the passenger-side window winds down, revealing a middle-aged Aboriginal man in the driver's seat, his beard patchy and grey. A heavy-set woman sits back in the passenger seat as the man leans over her. Children from the back seat unbuckled, lean over the front seats peering out the window.

"Hey, brother," he calls out.

Feeling less threatened, Broady releases his grip on the firearm. He stands on the ute's sidebar and looks over the roof to the man in the car.

"You going toward the city, yeh?" the man yells out with a strong Australian accent. "No good mate, the whole place is gone!"

"What do you mean gone?" Broady finds it hard to understand the man's meaning with his accent. "What about the military safe zone?"

"Ahh, I dunno brother, we further south than that, but north no good. Left when the sun came up, slept on top of the roof we did."

Broady can't help but smirk at the man's idea, sleeping on the roof seemed to have saved his entire family.

"Have you heard any more information on what's happening?" Broady asks, not sure if he'll get any useful information from the man.

"Last I heard it was a virus," the man says.

"BULLSHIT!" the woman next to him says, slapping him on the chest. "It's those scientists experimenting and plundering mother nature. This is what they get for decimating the land," she says, also with a thick accent.

Puzzled, Broady tries to find out more.

"So, they're people or animals?" he asks.

"I dunno, brother. Be careful though, mate, it's not just those creatures. People gone loopy, mate, better look after that little girl, yeh," he says concerned, pointing at Charlotte.

"Thanks for the heads up."

"Alright," the man says. A plume of smoke trails the car as the man accelerates off.

"Who was that, Daddy?" Charlotte asks as Broady steps back down into the ute.

"Just someone telling Dad to be careful. It's all good though, sweetheart."

"Was he warning you about the monsters?" she quietly asks, sinking her face into her teddy.

Broady turns the key, starting the engine. He takes a breath as he goes to speak but Charlotte butts in.

"I saw one you know . . . Last night in my dream. I think they took Mummy away," she says, sobbing into her teddy.

Broady looks over to her, his heart breaks at the sadness on his daughter's face. His eyes begin to well up, blurring his vision. He places his hand on her, massaging the back of her neck trying to comfort her. He doesn't speak, instead holding his breath for a moment swallowing his pain.

"Everything is going to work out ok," he says, trying to hold a straight face.

Charlotte looks toward him as he nods his head. She sobs and agrees.

Broady grinds the ute into gear. *Emotions won't help us survive*, he thinks, shaking them off; he wipes his eyes before gripping the steering wheel tight beneath his palms.

Chapter 6

Looking down at the watch on his wrist it reads 12:30 pm as they begin descending down through the mountain range. A large clearing of trees opens up on the horizon as they veer around a bend; thick smog covers the city. Patches of dark plumes of smoke billow up into the sky meeting the dense white clouds above. Nearing his town, abandoned vehicles litter the side of the road. They drive past the same church he saw heading out. He notices the large arched wooden doors are swinging wide open; a bloody handprint smeared down to the ground. There is no one in sight. Broady shakes his head at the needless lives lost.

As they head closer to the stadium, Broady is surprised to see no one in sight. He heads over the overpass, and Charlotte gasps in awe of the cars piled up on the motorway.

"There must have been a big smash," she says.

Over the curve of the bridge, the long straight road toward the stadium comes into view. The road in is blocked entirely. Broady stops before the roundabout. Car doors are left open, many with their headlights still on. Broady fears they may have become stranded before nightfall. *They wouldn't have stood a chance*, he thinks.

Broady rolls the car up the curb of the roundabout. Stepping down on the accelerator they jump up over the curb and onto the grassy island.

Startled, Charlotte bounces around in her seat. "Daddy!" she pipes up. "You can't do that!"

She begins to tell him off.

"Relax, honey," he tells her. "The road is blocked, and we need to find Allison, there's no police around."

She props herself up by sitting on her feet gripping the door handle tight, as she looks around curiously at the surroundings taking everything in. She doesn't say a word.

"Hold on!" Broady says cheerfully as he drives off the curb, the car bouncing along the road.

"Yeeha!" he cheers. Charlotte giggles at her father.

He's forced to drive on the opposite side of the road as the mountain of cars are blocking the road in toward the stadium, it seems somewhat surreal to him. As he slows down, peering over he notices some of the car windows and some panels are smeared with blood.

He gazes in farther, looking for the sign of any bodies in or around the area with no luck. Puzzled, he continues on. Zigzagging the ute through gaps in traffic on his left, up and onto the path, he stops the ute a few metres from the car-park entrance. The fences that were surrounding the outer perimeter of the car park have been pushed over in some areas, lying flat on the ground, while the other pieces of temporary fence lean and bend over. Large portable diesel power light generators have been knocked over as well, smashed and shattered on the concrete surface.

He switches the engine off, and all is deafly quiet.

"What are we doing here, Daddy?" Charlotte asks.

"Looking for Allison, honey, I told you already," he replies.

Charlotte screws up her nose looking at the grisly surroundings. "It's not very nice here, I don't like it."

Broady's smirks. "Come on, kiddo, let's have a look around." He unbuckles himself.

The two hop out from the car, Charlotte grabs her teddy that's fallen onto the floor. She stretches up high, feeling cramped after the long drive.

"What's happened here?" she asks as she looks around.

Large armoured vehicles that line the entrance are left seemingly abandoned, their doors wide open. As they walk past, Broady notices spent shell cartridges littering the ground.

"I have no idea, honey," he says, becoming more concerned.

It seems as though the man they passed in the hills was right, this place is no good at all.

"Stay close to me," Broady says, pulling Charlotte into line behind him. She grabs the back of his shirt, frightened as she follows along. Broady leads himself and Charlotte through the front gates, his gut churns as he navigates around the blood-splattered concrete, stepping around large dark red pools that sit every few metres. Assault rifles lay scattered randomly along the ground, along with other pieces of equipment. *What happened here?* Broady wonders, becoming more suspicious that again there are no bodies to be found.

Looking far and wide, he walks into a rifle on the ground;

kicking it as he steps. He stares down, wondering if it's worthwhile taking it, it didn't seem to help these guys out. Not taking a risk he picks it up, trying to remember how to use one, having only fired one at a shooting range on a trip to Las Vegas when he was twenty-two, right before Charlotte was born. He pulls the butt tight into his shoulder regaining some muscle memory, bringing the sights into line as he scans the surrounding area. His sights meet a large khaki tent positioned right outside the stadium. Hoping the tent is a command set-up, he decides it best to see if he can find out any information about other safe zones and whether there were any people evacuated by bus.

Midway across the long hot car park the sound of a car door slamming echoes in the distance behind him. Swiftly he turns, placing the crosshair in the direction of the noise. His heart quickens as they stand exposed out in the middle of the car park. For a moment there is no movement, he moves his sights side to side before noticing objects beginning to fly from the passenger side of a distant military vehicle. Shortly after, a person comes into view, pulling something from the vehicle. Too far for Broady to see clearly, he believes it's a survivor, scavenging for supplies perhaps? Still wary but not threatening, he drops the rifle down, deciding it's best they find what they need and move on.

Broady notices bright pink paint sprayed on the ground in front of him. Large circles sit at the end of long lines parallel to each other. Inside each circle sits large orange traffic cones, one of the cones appears to have been knocked over. As they walk by Broady can see the knocked over cone has a large thin pole with a metal sign protruding out the top. The sign is facing down

Curious, Broady bends down reaching with one hand to flip the sign over.

"BROADY!" a voice screams as the sign flips, banging back onto the concrete. He jumps up in a fright and circles around, his heart pumping blood into his ears as he looks around in all directions. There is no one in sight. The sound was so profound, almost as if someone was yelling right in his ears. It's an almost deja-vu moment having heard voices in the car park previously. After his panic settles and he begins to think rationally he realises the voice was of a woman. His thoughts move to Allison as he focuses on recalling the voice. It's too difficult to determine for sure.

"Daddy!" Charlotte yells, bringing his attention back. "What's wrong?"

Still startled yet convinced there is no danger he lowers the weapon and runs his hand over Charlotte's head.

"Nothing, princess, I thought I heard something," he says, softly still scanning the surroundings.

"Trr . . . aans . . . port . . ." Charlotte begins to stutter a word from her mouth.

Broady looks down, seeing she is attempting to read the sign he flipped over on the floor.

Transportation Point 1 it reads.

Delving into his mind, he recalls his dream of Allison boarding a bus. He rubs his eyes and presses his fingertips firmly against his forehead. "I'm losing my mind," he whispers to himself. His head pounds as he tries to piece together his fragmented thoughts, on top of the trauma that's already transpired around him. He closes his eyes. "Allison got on the bus here," he whispers, slowly beginning to trust his gut.

With his eyes shut he hears a faint sound of cloth flapping in the wind in front of him.

Opening his eyes, only a short distance from him, the entrance from the dark khaki tent flaps in the wind. A large transport truck is parked outside along with a military Land Cruiser.

As they approach, Broady's hairs stand up as all other background noise fades. He is focusing solely on the tent.

"Wait there, honey," he says holding out his hand in front of Charlotte. She stops as Broady continues lurking forward, his steps slow as he creeps over.

He stands just outside; the glare from the brightly shining sun makes it difficult to see inside the dark tent. Slowly, using the muzzle of the rifle, he pushes aside the flap of the tent. Still unable to see in clearly, he gulps, taking a quick step inside. He quickly scans the inside of the tent as his eyes adjust to the low light. There is no movement, no personnel appear to be anywhere in sight. The inside of the tent is a mess, portable tables appear up-ended and computer equipment, monitors and pieces of paper are scattered all over the floor. Towers of cardboard boxes are stacked along the walls of the tent. Fairly sure there is no immediate danger, he pokes his head back out of the tent, the sunlight blares in his eyes making it difficult to see; he calls out to Charlotte.

She runs over and wraps her arms around him. "I was scared all by myself," she sobs.

"Don't worry, kiddo, I got you," he says, squeezing her tight.

"Sit down there can you please, sweetness." He points to a

box to the left of the entrance. Still moving quietly, he walks through the room. A number of large whiteboards lay knocked over. Lying facedown, a bloody handprint smeared across the back of one. Broady bends down, lifting the board back up. A large map is pinned across the entire board, circles appear drawn on with red and blue markers. He bends over picking up the other boards and moves them together. It's a state-wide, detailed map. The names of towns and cities are marked in red on the board on the left, and above the names in bold reads *Confirmed outbreak*. On the right board, written in blue are the names of roads that Broady is familiar with, highways and main roads. There are straight lines drawn in blue on the map in the centre board that appear to encase many of the roads in and out of major cities. Broady only assumes that these could be roadblocks for quarantine. However, he's unsure.

He steps back, getting a better perspective of the entire map. His eyes widen as his hands tremble at the sheer size of the outbreak. He stares in awe before noticing two small green circles drawn on the map. He steps closer, looking at either whiteboard for any indication of what they are. Finding none, he places his finger over one, *Port of Brisbane*, another far inland, west of the coastline in Roma. Seeing no connection, he looks around, noticing another rather small green circle positioned directly over his suburb.

"I wonder if these are other safe zones?" he says, thinking out loud.

"Is that where Allison is?" Charlotte says, having overheard him.

"Possibly, honey, they may have moved her and some of the others away from danger."

But where? he thinks, continuing to look over the map.

Moving his head back and forth between the two circles at opposite ends, hundreds of kilometres apart. He wonders if they took her to the port and moved off the mainland. Or out west, looking closer he sees an airport there. He becomes frustrated, unsure of which destination. He stands back closing his eyes and pinching his fingers on the bridge of his nose. Recalling the old service station from his dream, he wonders if these are clues. Trusting his gut, he focuses on the service station, trying to remember anything that would stand out. After a minute he realises that the service station from his dream seemed like an old independent, having not noticed any major labels, it's unlikely it would be positioned near the capital city or anywhere near the port. He takes a giant leap of faith and decides they'll make a break for Roma.

"They're at Roma!" he says as he traces his finger along the main roads.

"How do you know that, Daddy?" Charlotte asks.

"I just have a hunch," he says. "Trust me," he adds, becoming more confident in his decision.

After tracing his way, he takes the time to look to the town his parents live in. He becomes more confident seeing Mundubbera, the town where his parents' farm is north of there. Not the usual road he would travel, he quickly memorises the main roads he'll need to remember.

Just as his mood begins to lift, he hears the sound of a tin can being kicked across the ground. Broady swings around raising his rifle, pointing toward the flapping entrance. "Quick!" Broady whispers to Charlotte signalling her to move toward him. She scampers behind her father, ducking down and peering through his legs.

His blood pressure rises as he feels the pulsating blood rush up his neck, heating his upper body. Nearing the entrance, he reaches back detaching Charlotte's arm from his legs, placing his hand up for her to stop. "Shh," he whispers, his finger up against his lips.

He edges closer to the entrance peering through the gap in the flaps.

Beside the Land Cruiser, a figure in a brown jumper with the hood up is crouched on the ground, seemingly sorting and throwing belongings off to the side. Using the element of surprise Broady leaps out of the tent pointing his rifle at the figure.

"Hey, you!" he yells startling the assailant who turns around. It's a young female. Seeing Broady's rifle pointed straight toward her, she frets falling backward against the car. Her hair is all matted and dirty, she stares down the barrel of the rifle bug-eyed.

"Shit!" Broady says, exhaling his breath as he lowers the weapon.

"Hey," Broady says again, attempting to inspire a response. The girl's eyes dart back and forth, the bottom of her boot-cut jeans are splattered in blood. Broady begins to feel sorry for the traumatised girl.

"Are you ok?" he says, taking a step toward her.

As he does, the girl snatches a black backpack off the ground and sprints off, dropping some belongings out of her bag as she runs.

"Hey!" Broady calls out to her, shaking his head as he looks around. He doesn't go after her; he watches as she sprints over the other end of the car park toward the lake and park area before dropping down out of sight.

"Who was that, Dad?" Charlotte says, walking out of the tent.

"I thought I told you to stay inside?" he says as he walks over to see what she had dropped.

He bends down picking up a black vacuum-sealed packet. *Beef stroganoff* is written on one side.

Broady realises it's an MRE used for military personal, otherwise known as a Meal, ready to eat. The girl must have been scavenging for supplies. He turns back to the Land Cruiser deciding to investigate. Poking his head in he leans over the front passenger seat into the rear cabin. The air is hot and stale. Opening the glove box a large hunting knife with a black handle falls out onto the floor, having been stuffed on top of the overflowing glove box. Its blade is tucked into a black leather case, he pulls on the cold steel handle of the knife with one hand, holding the case with the other, revealing a twelve-centimetre black blade. Broady feels the sharpness of the blade by running his thumb across the edge, it's razor sharp. Thinking it might be useful he pushes the blade back in its case, placing it on the seat. He jumps out and searches the cabin in the back. Full of boxes, he pulls one of them down onto the concrete floor, opening it up. Filled with wires and cables, he tosses it aside. He pulls down the next, revealing cartons of bottled water stacked in the centre. He drops the box and rips open the plastic carton pulling two water bottles out. His thirst is insatiable and he cracks the lid, chugging down the whole bottle. Charlotte watches her father in amazement as she tries to copy him, holding the bottle firmly with both hands.

He bends down, opening another box full of brown and tan military shirts and cargo pants. He lifts some out before looking down at himself. His jeans have two large bloodstains on each pocket, blood from the cuts on his hands. He stands up, ripping off the stretched and tattered shirt and putting on a fresh brown shirt. He tosses Ray's pistol onto the back of the cabin, undoing his belt, he begins to pull down his pants.

"DAD! What are you doing?" Charlotte says, pulling her teddy up, covering her eyes.

"I forgot a change of clothes and mine are dirty," he says, changing his pants.

"Geez," she says, still covering her eyes, feeling a little embarrassed. "Could have told me that," she adds, turning around. "How come you tell me to pack clothes and you don't even pack yourself?"

Charlotte removes the teddy from covering her face and stares out into the vast car park, noticing figures appearing at the far end.

"Hey, Dad, look!" she says, pointing over in their direction.

Broady looks over still doing up his pants when he sees what Charlotte is pointing at.

"Quick," he says, running over to her lifting her into the Land Cruiser. Grabbing his belt, he wrestles with it, putting it on as he swiftly makes way around to the driver's side, hoping he's able to start the engine.

He jumps in the driver's side, having forgotten to shut the passenger-side door, he reaches over Charlotte and slams it shut. He begins frantically looking around, inside the glove box and on top of the sun visor. Looking over, the figures in the distance coming closer. He counts five people walking toward them, too far for him to make out if they're military or civilians. He's unsure if the girl he startled has gone for help or if it's just some other people looking for supplies. He thinks it best not to stick around and find out. The closer they get the more agitated Broady becomes. Frustrated he looks around for another exit strategy. If he is quick, he can lose them in the stadium, he thinks.

He kicks the car door open, jumping down, he peers over the bonnet to see how close the people are. Still a few hundred metres away. About to slam the car door, a shimmer of sunlight hits his eye. The keys are hanging in the ignition, swinging back and forth reflecting the sunlight. Broady shakes his head. "Idiot," he mumbles to himself.

"What?" Peering out the window, Charlotte turns her head.

"Nothing, honey, Dad's just silly," he says, turning over the engine.

"Yes!" he exclaims as the car starts. Jumping back in the Land Cruiser, and swiftly pulling the car into drive, they speed off through the car park. He glances through the rear-vision mirror as the people fade out of focus.

"Erh! What's this?" Charlotte grunts uncomfortably, screwing up her face as she pulls the knife still inside its case up from underneath her.

"Oh oops!" Broady says, quickly reacting, grabbing the knife out of her hands.

"Hey, I was looking at that!" Charlotte exclaims.

"Sorry, honey, that's Daddy's knife. Not a great idea for you to be playing with that!" he says, tucking the knife into a thin pocket down the side of his cargo pants leg.

"That sucks!" she sighs,

"Hey kiddo, watch the attitude, would you!" Broady says.

Driving hastily, they drive up over curbs and around the countless abandoned vehicles. Again, driving up over the roundabout, Broady plants his foot on the accelerator as the tyres lose traction on the grassy centre. The Land Cruiser's suspension is stiff and the car bounces and jolts like a roller coaster, becoming all too familiar Charlotte seems no longer concerned as she bounces around in her seat.

"This is fun!" She giggles, holding up her hands.

Broady smirks, happy to hear his little girl laugh after everything that's unfolded.

Like deja vu he stops again on the overpass, looking north at the freeway. The cars are stacked like a car park, he's annoyed that he didn't have time to grab the map, only briefly looking at the main roads, he's unsure of any other way to travel; the freeway is the most direct route. Checking the fuel tank, he sees less than half a tank, not nearly enough to go around. He checks the back of the Cruiser, hoping to be lucky enough.

"Bugger!" he says.

"What's wrong, Dad?" she asks.

"We don't have enough fuel to go around; besides, Dad's not so sure he knows any other way," he says, slumping his head sounding defeated.

"Why don't we drive through the middle like the roundabout?"

Broady lifts his head, turning around and looking down onto the freeway.

She's right, parts of the emergency lane are free, and the grassy centre strip is completely vacant. Feeling optimistic, he drives the vehicle across the road and down the side of the onramp onto the emergency lane, managing to squeeze through gaps in between vehicles and onto the centre freeway grass. He stops the car and engages the Cruiser's four-wheel-drive mode. The grassy centre strip is uneven, and Broady can't think of a worse time to become bogged down. Before taking off he glances over at the stretch of vehicles left desolate. Windows are smashed, car doors left wide open; smears of blood run down inside the doors. Noticing again the absence of people's bodies, he's still confused by this. Surely, it's not possible for the creatures to have taken everyone like they did Abby. He wonders if the news was correct and this was some kind of contagion. For now, he places his thoughts to the side, focusing on the road ahead. Driving along the grassy centre Broady turns to Charlotte.

"What would I do without you, kiddo?" he says, reaching over and scuffing her hair.

"Hey!' she says, pushing his hand away.

"I'm the smartest kid in kindergarten you know!" she states proudly.

"I'll bet you are!" He chuckles to himself.

She continues staring out the window, intrigued by what she sees.

"Where are all the people, Dad? Did they seriously just leave their cars here?" she asks.

His tone changes as his thoughts and worries begin to creep back in.

"I don't know, honey . . . I don't know . . ." he says.

Chapter 7

Hours pass by driving drearily along the centre strip. Broady is stunned the entire way up is almost identical, feeling almost surreal. Up ahead is a sign to Toowoomba.

"That's the exit we need," he states as Charlotte sits up in her seat.

"Too . . . woom . . . ba," she sounds out "That's not it, Dad?"

"Roma is west of Toowoomba, honey; we're on the right track." He grins.

Broady stops short of the exit, and with the engine still running he hops out and walks toward the road. There is no gap big enough for the Land Cruiser to fit, and Broady begins to stress as he paces down looking back as far as he can for an opening. He heads back to the car and jumps in behind the wheel; he stares looking north, wondering how far he would have to travel before being able to cross. He stares at the fuel gauge as it edges farther toward empty. A few moments go by before Charlotte becomes restless.

"Uhh, earth to Dad?" she says, trying to wave her arms in

front of him, reaching as far as she can. She unbuckles herself. Broady is lost deep in thought.

"Umm, HELLO!" she says, waving her hand inches from his face.

Broady jumps back in fright as he is jolted out of his head.

"Haha," Charlotte giggles. "Scared ya!"

"AHH, you got me that time," Broady says, playing along. He switches off the engine giving him a moment to think. He stares at the blockade of vehicles. The poor individuals caught out in the open like that wouldn't have stood a chance.

Watching her father, Charlotte turns to try to see what he is looking at, before coming up with an idea.

"Why don't we just ram them out of the way?" she says.

"Ram," Broady mutters, mulling the idea over in his head. "Or push," he continues. "Yes! We'll push them," he says, becoming excited.

"What a great idea." He rubs Charlotte's hair again.

"Hey," she says, unimpressed, and fixing up her hair.

Using Charlotte's idea as inspiration, he runs over to one of the cars. Reaching through the wound-down window he takes off the handbrake and puts the car into neutral. He turns and with a big shove, using all his body weight, the car's tyres slowly begin to turn. The car rolls back about a metre before it crashes into the car behind, smashing the tow bar into the other's front bumper. Charlotte watches from the car as her father runs between the cars pushing some back, and the others forward across all four lanes. The setback cost them some precious daylight hours, but Broady finally manages to push the last car, having made a path just wide enough for the Land Cruiser to squeeze through. The hot mid-afternoon sun beams down on him, and wiping his forehead on his sleeve does him little good; his shirt is soaked with sweat. Finding only a small patch of dryness on the bottom of his shirt, he makes good use of it. He walks back over to the car, puffed and exhausted and pulls a water bottle from the back. As he undoes the lid, Charlotte pipes up.

"Wow I'm thirsty, Dad . . ." she says, looking at the bottle. "It sure is hot out here."

Broady frowns, perplexed, and looks down at himself and laughs, having just pushed eight cars by force.

"Here you go," he says, passing her the bottle he's just opened.

Opening another, he's quick to gulp the bottle down. His tongue swells as the water washes over it, soothing his dry mouth and easing his irritated throat.

"You must love water, hey Dad?" she asks.

"Why do you ask?" he says, taking off his shirt and grabbing another from the box in the back of the cabin.

"DAD!" Charlotte begins to freak again.

"Don't stress, I'm only changing my shirt," he tells her.

"Hey, is there anything to eat in there?" she asks, rubbing her belly.

"Let's have a look, shall we?" He shuffles around items and boxes in the back cabin, stumbling across a box with a sticker on the side, it reads *MRE*.

"Here we go." He pulls the box out using his fingernail to slice through the tape on the top of the box. Examining the contents, the box is packed tight with vacuum-sealed black packets, each one with a white label stuck on the front.

"Roast beef?" he calls out, picking one up.

Charlotte turns her nose up. "Nah," she says.

"Hmm, let's see. How about chicken and vegetable?" he adds, looking over to her.

Charlotte sticks her finger in her mouth and proceeds to make vomiting sounds.

Broady laughs, shaking his head. "You learnt that from Allison, didn't you!" he frowns.

"And since when did you become so fussy?" he says, digging farther into the box.

"Aha! Spaghetti Bolognese." He's sure he's found a winner.

"Ooo, yes please," she says, reaching her arms out for it.

He rips the top off and hands it to her. She looks at him peculiarly.

"We don't have any knives or forks honey, so just squeeze it out of the packet like Zooper Dooper ice block."

He rips the top off a roast beef for himself and rests his back against the rear tyre and begins to slurp out the contents of the packet. After a minute of uncertainty, Charlotte follows suit and begins to slurp the food out of the packet.

"It looks like dog food," she says as she squeezes the packet.

Broady can't help but agree with her, the salty giblets do somewhat resemble dog food. It's not exactly how he remembers his mother's Sunday roast beef tasting like. They both sit in silence for a moment, the ambient sound of noisy dragonflies buzzing around in the grass, like a twisted picnic amongst all the tragedy.

He squeezes the end of the packet like a tube of toothpaste, pushing out every last bit before wiping his mouth. He looks at his watch, having to clean the smudges of dried blood off the face with the sweaty shirt he left hanging off the side of the Cruiser. 2:37 pm it reads.

With only a few hours of sunlight left, Broady stands up and readies himself to move on. He wants to move out as far west as possible, away from the densely populated areas.

"Right, kiddo, let's get you buckled in," he says, twisting her legs around into the chair.

He checks all the engine lights and gauges as he starts the car, focusing heavily on the fuel gauge reading just over one quarter. Not knowing the size of the tank or how quickly they'll be able to get through, he silently prays they have enough to get to the safe zone in Roma. He turns the car facing the gap he's made. Charlotte squashes her face against the glass to see just how close they are. Charlotte squeals and awes as they narrowly drive through the gap, the Land Cruiser jolts subtlety as they nudge the front bumper on the last vehicle they pass.

"You crashed, Daddy!" Charlotte exclaims.

"Nah." Broady laughs. "Just gave it a little kiss," he says.

As he begins to make the way up the off-ramp, he gets a strange feeling, like they are being watched. As he drives slowly up the ramp, he peers out through the dirty windshield looking around. To his left about one hundred metres runs a road adjacent to the freeway, linking up to the off-ramp's intersection. On this road, three figures stand closely together, not moving. Broady stops the vehicle to get a better look, but with the afternoon sun behind them and the dirty window, it's difficult to see. He reaches over Charlotte's seat and winds the window down. He squints hard trying to focus on them. The figures begin to sprint north toward the intersection.

"Shit," Broady slips out as he quickly winds the window back up.

"What is it?" Charlotte says, becoming unsettled.

"Nothing, honey," he says, trying to calm her; locking her door. He accelerates off toward the intersection. The three figures are standing behind a row of concrete bollards on the side of the road.

Broady is confused as to why they have stopped. He drives by cautiously, the lower halves of their bodies are concealed behind the concrete barrier; only their upper torsos visible. There's a middle-aged man in his fifties with a thick moustache wearing a dark blue sweatshirt. He has a hard-looking face as he stares toward the Cruiser. His two companions, a boy and girl both appear to be around eighteen years of age with matching black-hooded jumpers. The two younger ones lean on the barrier panting heavily, their faces look tired and long. The older man leans over the barrier. Peering in through the dirty window, his facial expressions change as he spots Broady and Charlotte from a stern hard look to one of disappointment. His mouth moves as he talks to his two companions, and unable to hear through the glass Broady passes them by turning left and through the intersection, heading out into the industrial precinct toward the main road to Roma. He's hopeful they won't run into many people in such an area.

"What were those people doing?" Charlotte asks.

"I'm not sure, honey, they probably thought we were in the military and were here to help them."

"We could have stopped though and helped, couldn't we?" she quizzes him.

"They didn't seem overly friendly, I don't think they wanted our help," he says, rubbing her head. She turns in her seat, looking back at them, confused.

Heading through the industrial precinct the roads are wide and vacant, usually thriving with workmen and trucks bustling in and out. He's amazed at how wide the roads are when there are no trucks parked on either side, it seems surreal almost. Businesses are shut, their doors barred and locked, factories' large roller doors are closed and the gates are all padlocked. As they head toward the end of the road, he stops at the intersection with traffic lights flashing amber. He looks over and sees a mechanical workshop attached to a service station on the outskirts of the precinct.

"There's no red light, Dad," Charlotte says. "Why did we stop?" she asks.

"I'm just thinking, princess," he says.

Broady mulls over in his head whether or not he's going to try to find some fuel. With no power and no pump, he's unsure of his luck. He looks down again at his fuel gauge, not sure of how many litres the Cruiser has, he thinks it best to quickly duck in and out at least to check for any jerry cans in the workshop perhaps.

Broady turns the wheels about to take off when a loud bang on the passenger window catches his attention. Charlotte gasps as she is startled by a man at her window. With the hum of the diesel engine, Broady didn't hear anyone approach. He looks over to the man.

"Hey man, let us in," the heavy-set dark-skinned man says. Broady doesn't respond, instead just observing the man and staring blankly at him.

Seeing Charlotte visibly shaken, he looks over to her with both his hands on the glass.

"I'm sorry I scared you, little one. Please," he pleads, walking in front of the car and over to the driver's side.

"We need some help over here," he says, pointing down the street to where Broady came from. The man is sweating profusely and looks very anxious, his bandana over his head is wet and dirty. Movement catches Broady's eyes as he sees another man approach through the side mirror, a tall thin man with long dark hair wearing a tattered black singlet and dark ripped jeans. The man bangs on the back of the car forcefully, grunting loudly and aggressively, sending vibrations throughout the cabin, startling Charlotte as she jumps in her seat. The dark-skinned man takes a step back as the thin man approaches the window.

"Hey man, we need help, didn't you hear?" he says. "Open up the door," he says, his tone a lot less friendly than the other man's.

Broady notices the man seems to be scoping out the inside of the truck, his wide bug eyes darting around. Broady feels something is off. The thin man refuses to make eye contact and is pale and jittery.

"First you want my help, then you want me to let you in?" Broady says. He looks to the man with the bandana. "And you need my help over there?" He points. "For what? We just came from there, there's nothing."

"I can't hear you!" the man with the bandana yells. "Wind down your window!"

His eyes showing signs of guilt.

"HEY!" Broady yells, twisting his head toward the other man as he paces around the car. "What are you looking for?" he begins to interrogate him. "I'm over here!" Broady places two of his fingers up toward his eyes. The situation becomes increasingly tense, with Broady fearing their motives are sinister.

The long thin man briefly makes eye contact, his eyes are wide, his pupils dilated. The man has scratches on his cheeks and small scabs across his forehead, the stubble on his face is patchy and dirty. He steps toward the door, lifting the handle. Unfortunately for the man, the doors are locked. He becomes increasingly agitated as he repeatedly pulls on the handle, then explodes in fit of rage, bashing his fist against the glass. The toughened window doesn't break and Broady just stares at the man.

"Move!" Broady hears the other man yell. Seconds after the man moves, a metal pole of a street sign smashes through the driver's window. Charlotte screams as shattered glass flies throughout the cabin. As the pole penetrates through, Broady manages to push it forward, causing it to narrowly miss Charlotte. Both men attempt to pounce inside the car leaning in to grab the keys and the steering wheel, both men managing to wedge themselves in the window. Broady viciously fights the men, elbowing them. He panics, stepping on the accelerator. Both men trip over each other, the heavy dark-skinned man trips first ripping him out of the window and sending him plummeting down to the road. The car bounces as the man's head goes under the rear wheel. The thin man tries to gain control of the steering wheel, veering the car off the road. Broady manages to leverage the wheel straight and steps harder on the pedal. With the man's arms leaning over the pole, he grabs the street sign pole and pushes it up against the roof. The man loses grip on the steering wheel and falls too. Broady slides the sign from out of the car window and speeds away.

Looking through the rear-view mirror, the fallen man has made his way to his feet, he limps as he hopelessly gives chase. Frustrated, he picks up the sign, hurling it toward the car, which is now far, far away.

"The whole place has really turned to SHIT!" he yells, angry and upset. A few moments pass until his words sink in. That's the first time he's sworn in front of Charlotte, and he instantly feels guilty. Safe and far away from harm he pulls the car over. Charlotte is shaking and upset.

"Come here," he says, unbuckling her seatbelt. He opens his arms. She leaps across the seat and breaks out into tears.

"We're ok," he says softly, holding her tight.

"Why did those men want to hurt us?" she snuffles.

"People are scared and desperate. They don't really know what they're doing," he attempts to explain.

"But I'm scared, and I don't want to hurt anyone," she says, still sobbing.

"Fear can make a person do things they normally wouldn't do; it's just how it is now. We just need to be more careful, that's all."

Seemingly unhappy with his answer she crawls back to her seat, buckles up her belt and stares out the window.

Broady shakes his head, disappointed at himself for not comforting her better.

"I miss Mummy." She sighs before going quiet.

Like a knife to the heart, Broady knows no matter what he does or says, it won't replace the void in her heart from her mother's loss.

Broady takes off driving past a large brown sign, Regional Route 77, onto the Warrego Highway.

The farther they travel, the greater the distance away from civilisation. Kilometres of road stretch across before even passing a single dirt driveway. There are acres and acres of bushland, trees and big open grass fields, brown from the drought. Green hills litter the horizon. *Outback Australia really is a beautiful place*, Broady thinks as he surveys the surroundings. By late afternoon the sun is low in the sky and beams heavily through the front windscreen. Broady sits up straight, pulling the sun visor down, barely making a difference. The dirty windshield and reflection off the road do little to help. He smears the dust away from the dash. The fuel tank is sitting on empty; things go from bad to worse as the engine begins to chug and splatter as the car shakes and bounces back and forth.

"No, no, no," he pleads. "Come on!" His pleas go unanswered as the car comes to a halt in the middle of the road.

Charlotte awakes from her daydream. "What's wrong, Daddy? Why have we stopped?"

He pushes the car door open, stepping out onto the rocky asphalt, slamming the door shut.

Walking to the front of the car he leans his back against the warm bonnet. Broady slumps his head and shoulders, feeling hopeless. A breeze blows through the mounds of long grass in the fields beside him. He recalls the sound of Abby's laugh as they rolled in the long grass. This time, however, she's gone—and for good. Broady stands staring blankly ahead feeling somewhat detached, before finally accepting the overwhelming likelihood that she's dead. Feeling Charlotte's eyes stare at him through the glass he holds his body strong from trembling, his eyes, however, can't hide the pain as they well up with overpowering sadness. A few tears escape his eyelids, dropping down onto the road. He looks down as the droplets splat on the road and closing his eyes, he begins to lose hope in anything going right for them. Spending a few moments in self-loathing his head becomes light, and even with his eyes closed, he becomes tired and dizzy.

Only believing a few seconds have passed, Charlotte's voice echoes into his head.

"DAD!" she yells from inside the car.

As Broady opens his eyes a bright flash from in front blinds him.

Looking behind him the Land Cruiser is gone. His heart rate skyrockets in total confusion. He turns back around to a burnt-out minibus, sitting on the side of the highway down in a ditch; he examines the bus, looking eerily familiar to the bus he envisioned Allison getting on. He struggles to make sense of it. Up above the bus, he looks into the open fields taking note of the silhouette of a large tree perched up on the top of a hill. The tree is enormous standing well out in the open alone on a hill.

"DADDY!" Charlotte's voice echoes from behind him. Startled, he turns around stepping right into the Land Cruiser banging his knee.

"Ouch!" he cries out.

Charlotte giggles. "Geez, Dad, didn't you see the car there?" she mocks him. "You've been standing there for ages. I need to go to the toilet," she says.

He turns back looking at the sun, having dropped considerably since his last recollection. He feels disorientated, realising he must have slipped into some sort of trance again. He plays it cool in front of Charlotte, pretending everything is normal. He opens her side of the door. "Just go on the side of the road," he says.

"Are you serious?" she replies.

This time there's no time for mucking around.

"You're safe here with me, no one is coming, trust me. I'll even turn around and keep watch." He turns around and folds his arms. "SEE!" he calls out behind him.

As Charlotte does her business Broady 'keeps watch' looking out into the fields rehashing on his new vision. As he scans his surroundings, he sees an enormous tree, on the top of a grassy hill. Broady's eyes widen in disbelief. The outline of the tree matches almost perfectly with the vision in his head.

"Hey, Charlotte, I think we might have to camp out here tonight," he says.

"In the car? It doesn't look very comfortable," she says, pulling up her pants.

Broady agrees, turning around. The Cruiser's window is smashed and sitting wide out in the open. Broady looks around for a nearby property. With none in sight he looks back over at the tree.

"Nah, by that big tree over there." He points over toward the hill.

"Woah," she says. "We can be monkeys," she adds.

This gives Broady an idea. He opens the back of the Cruiser, grabbing a few water bottles and MRE packets, stuffing them into a big military rucksack.

"What are you doing?" Charlotte asks.

He lifts out some jackets from one of the boxes and throws it at her, covering her body and head completely. He laughs.

"Geez thanks," she says sarcastically, pulling the jacket from over her head.

"This is our camping gear," he says.

"Here, let me help you, Daddy," Charlotte says sweetly.

"It's all good, honey, Dad's got this," he says, smiling down at her.

"I'll carry Teddy then!" She says.

He lifts the pack over his back clipping in the chest straps for the short walk uphill to the tree. He grabs the rifle from the back, using the strap to hook it over his shoulder

"What about the rest of the stuff?" she asks.

"It's all good; we'll get the rest tomorrow." He stares at the horizon, keeping an eye on the sun. "Come on," he says, beginning to walk off.

Charlotte stands at the edge of the embankment and starts to grizzle.

Broady looks back to see her standing with her arms up to carry her.

He obliges and steps back, scooping her up and carrying her down the embankment. At the bottom of the shallow embankment, Broady steps on top of an old frail barbed wire fence. The wire draws down easily, with not much tension left in it. Walking up through the meadow the grass is up to Broady's stomach, well above Charlotte's head height. He looks at her as she reaches down grabbing reeds of grass.

"Good thing I'm carrying you," he says. "You'd get lost in here for sure."

Approximately halfway along, up the short slope, he pauses, turning around, wondering if he can see anything in the distance.

No movement at all for as far as his eyes can see. The eastern horizon is covered in a thick blanket of smoke. Neither passing cars nor trucks. In the distance a train lay stopped in its tracks, abandoned. The only sound comes from the whistle of the wind as it blows over his ears.

Although alone and somewhat in the middle of nowhere, there is a sense of peace Broady feels looking out into the vast planes, far away from any apparent danger, man or creature.

"Come on, Dad!" Charlotte says, tapping him on the shoulder. "Let's climb that tree and make a treehouse," she says, sounding excited.

Broady continues the ascent. *The wonders of a child's mind,* he thinks. Being able to disconnect so easily and focus solely on the moment.

Broady wonders when he will tell her the full extent of what's unfolded. He's concerned of her age and her ability to comprehend. The thoughts dawn on him as he looks at his daughter's sun-kissed face with glee in her eyes.

He decides to put it off for a better time. The first order must be their timely journey to Broady's parents' farm, picking Allison up along the way. He tries to shake off such woes, for the time being, deciding to play along with his daughter's delights. The longer grass dies off the farther uphill they trek. Placing her down he yells, "Race you there!" as he starts to sprint off.

"Hey, no fair," she pouts, chasing after him. "You got a head start."

Broady turns, running slowly backward for a time, enabling her to catch up.

"I'm going to beat you, Daddy!" she says, confident in her stride.

Reaching out for the tree at the same time Charlotte declares herself the winner.

"I won!" she gloats.

"Did not, did not," Broady reiterates.

"Did so, you're slow," she rhymes, poking out her tongue.

"Come here, you," he growls, holding both hands up like bear claws.

Charlotte squeals as Broady chases her around and around the tree and grabs her from behind growling as he does. She squeals again, only this time the sound she makes is not one of joy.

"Wait, stop," she says in a stern tone. Broady listens and drops down to one knee.

Charlotte turns around and hugs her dad tightly.

"It's ok, honey," he says, rubbing her back.

"I don't want to play monsters anymore," she cries into his shoulder.

It hits home that kids are much more perceptive than he first realised. He holds her for a few minutes staring at the sun as it begins its descent over the mountain ranges on the horizon. Fears begin to surge inside at the realisation of the very real threat that awaits after the sun goes down.

Broady swallows his fear, burying it deep down.

"You said you wanted to climb this tree," he says, shifting focus. "Come on, let's do this!" he adds encouragingly.

Knelt still, they both look up at the tree. The trunk stretches almost two metres in diameter. Its ancient trunk stretches high above Broady's head before fraying out large branches in every direction, up and up the tree stretches into the sky, each branch reaching far out, blocking the entire sky with its evergreen leaves, leaving only the horizon visible. The ground beneath the tree is dirt with only patches of grass, the tree blocking out the majority of the sunlight A little grove is made from the sprawling branches, creating a neat little area, big enough hopefully for them to nestle themselves in, like birds in a nest.

"It's huuuuge," Charlotte marvels.

"Right, Teddy goes first!" he says, quickly pulling Charlotte's teddy from her hand throwing her stuffed friend up and into the tree

"HEY!" she exclaims.

"You're next, I'll boost you up," Broady says, laying out his hands and interlinking his fingers tightly.

Charlotte steps in, holding herself firmly on the tree as Broady stretches his body lifting his heels off the ground. The branches are high, she reaches out managing to pull herself up, grabbing her teddy she turns around and sits on a large branch.

"Come on, Dad, your turn," she yells down.

Broady takes a step back, sizing up the daunting task of the leap.

"Alright, alright," he says, psyching himself up. He blows his warm breath into his hands, rubbing them together.

"Wait, hang on," he says, pulling off his backpack.

"Look out," he calls out before throwing the bag up into the tree, wedging itself in between branches.

"Come on, Dad, you can do it," Charlotte calls down.

He secures the rifle tightly behind himself before taking a run-up. He leaps up into the air kicking against the tree's trunk and grabbing the lowest branch. Using his legs, he leverages himself up, slightly slipping as he does.

"Be careful, Dad."

Regaining his grip, he pulls himself up and into the tree.

"Phew," he pants. "Tough gig," he adds, pretending to wipe sweat from his brow.

They sit like birds on a perch as Broady rustles around attempting to secure a more comfortable position. Grabbing out a jacket from the bag, folding it over itself to increase its cushion from the hard wooden branch, he sets it down in the groove in the middle of the tree. He sits on his backside and wriggles himself into a semi-comfortable position.

From high up they get a spectacular view down over the surroundings, seeing the shadow cast along the open planes from the distant mountain ranges as the last beams of sunlight run across the open fields. After the sun settles in for the night, the coastline looks dark and gloomy, Broady feels somewhat glad he decided against travelling there. As the afternoon moves swiftly into twilight, he prays that the decision was wise.

"Dad," Charlotte calls, breaking his thought. "I'm hungry, can we eat?" she asks.

"Sure, honey, sounds like a plan," he says, rustling through the rucksack.

"Is there any spaghetti left?"

"Yep," he says, lifting Charlotte's spirits.

"But it's chicken and vegetables for you tonight, miss," he insists, still trying to hold onto some sort of normality.

"Aww," she sighs crawling along the branch, resting herself opposite Broady.

Tearing off the packet's top, Charlotte says, "Pretty cool treehouse, hey Dad?"

"I agree," he says. "I think we should spend the night here, like monkeys, what you think?" he says, shrouded with fear he's reluctant to reveal his real motives behind it.

"Yeah that would be so cool," she says, squeezing the mushed goo out of its packet.

"YUCK!" she spits, displeased with her food.

"Eat your vegetables, miss; I don't want to hear any complaining out of you tonight."

"After your dinner, if you need to go, go now. There will be no bathroom breaks during the night, ok?"

Charlotte stops eating and sits silently for a moment. "Is that because the monsters come out at night?" she looks over at him, worried.

"There are no monsters, honey." Broady plays dumb.

"You remember my bad dream about Mummy," she says. "They're real, aren't they, Daddy," she says, staring right into his eyes.

Caught off guard, Broady remains composed.

"No, don't be silly," he assures her. "There are no monsters, but there may be wild dogs or animals out here, they may want to nibble at your leg." He says reaching out and tickling her leg.

She bursts out laughing, forgetting about the whole thing. Broady sighs in relief having dodged yet another bullet fired at him from Charlotte.

The two sit quietly as Broady lays back against a branch peering up through the twigs and leaves. The breeze drops off as nightfall approaches, the branches and leaves settle undisturbed. Through the tiny gaps in the tree, stars begin to appear in the sky spotting more and more as darkness takes over the sky. Charlotte begins fidgeting around.

"Uh, Dad, maybe this wasn't such a good idea," she says, unable to find a comfy position.

He grabs his rifle with one hand, holding out his hand to Charlotte with the other, switching places. He places the rifle down against the branch at his feet, pulling Charlotte along and resting her on his chest. She hangs her arms and legs out the side and rests her weight on him.

"Do you think we'll ever see Mummy again?" she asks as she sniffles.

Tired and out of excuses he answers softly. "I don't know, kiddo . . . I really don't know."

Hearing his daughter sob, he tries a softer approach. "What's something nice you could imagine happening?" he asks her.

She breaks from weeping and thinks. "I imagine that she got away, somewhere safe and that the monsters didn't get her."

"Perfect," he says, stroking her hair tenderly. "Then just focus on that." He begins to sing softly, the song he's sung to her ever since she was a baby on her first night back from the hospital, a segment from a Bruno Mars song, popular at the time.

By the end Charlotte dozes off, her mouth partially open.

"Works a treat, every time," Broady whispers to himself.

Glad Charlotte has managed to fall asleep so easily he wonders if he'll be so lucky, with Charlotte's added weight, his backside has already started to go numb. The jacket does not exactly provide the lumbar support of his orthopaedic mattress. He nestles in as comfortably as he can, attempting to rest his eyes at least. The sound of crickets chirping loudly flood his awareness, as his mind begins to slow, wondering briefly if they've been chirping the whole time. He opens one eye peering into the darkness briefly, his eyes overly heavy becoming difficult to keep open. Allowing his body to rest he nods off quicker than expected.

Chapter 8

Ding.

Broady stirs to the sound of something hitting metal, amid a light sleep, groggy and unsure if he's imagination, he takes no further notice.

Ding.

By the second time, however, awake and more aware he lifts his head briefly, staring into the blackness. The crescent moon provides little light to the landscape.

Ding.

Head up and fully aware now, Broady is convinced the sound is coming in the direction of the Land Cruiser. His eyes widen as his senses begin to heighten; he peers down still unable to see the car, his vision only extending a few metres into the long grass.

The dings turn to banging and crashing, Broady convinces himself that some survivors are ransacking the vehicle. Far away in the midst of the field, Broady reassures himself that they're safe, there's no way anyone would venture out into the fields, and he's grateful for the decision he made.

The bonnet of the car pops and buckles as it creases from weight bearing down. He finds it strange that people would jump up on a bonnet, however, with the strange things happening he writes their behaviour off.

He drops his head back against the tree, closing his eyes; he focuses his hearing listening carefully for voices.

The sounds stop, only a gentle breeze blows through the night caressing the long grass as it waves through. Believing they must have moved on, he becomes sleepy. A soft ring begins in his ear, subtle at first, he barely notices. The sound steadily amplifies right as Broady begins to drift off, ripping him once again back into reality.

"Oh my god." Broady can't help but slip the subtle words of terror out.

The all-too-familiar ring. Broady knows that the creatures are descending upon them.

He sits up peering down into the grass, turning his head around frantically. The rustling grass in his peripheral vision unsettles him, frightened the movements are something far more sinister.

A click reverberates from out in the field. Then another from a different location, then another. More and more clicking sounds vibrate from all around. They're surrounded!

He wraps his arms around Charlotte carefully, and quietly shuffles his body down into the centre, in the hopes of better concealing them.

As the clicking sounds grow, light footsteps begin to pitter-patter across the flat dirt below, twigs snap and leaves rustle. Paralysed with fear he lays there helpless; worried any movement will give away their position. He stares down at the rifle at his feet. He can hook the rifle's strap with his foot he surmises. He glances at Charlotte still peacefully asleep. He abandons the idea, too many possibilities for things to go wrong; if he failed to hook the strap and it plummeted to the ground, they'd be mincemeat.

The pitter-patter of footsteps below becomes more erratic as multiple creatures descend, frantically shuffling back and forth.

Broady prays they cannot jump nor climb, if not and they stay quiet, maybe they have a chance.

His prayers go unanswered as Charlotte stirs in her sleep, murmuring and tossing her head around, stopping then clapping her mouth together.

Inside he is beside himself with sheer terror; he gently caresses her head, hoping to settle her. Unsure if the creatures heard, the hairs on the back of his neck stand up, his ears prick back like a dog, sensitive to every movement below as if he were seeing with his own eyes.

Silence . . .

Not a sound emerges from below. His heart pounds, fearing the worst, he hugs Charlotte tight, shutting his eyes awaiting his fate. Light scratches on the tree's trunk trickle up from below, confirming his thoughts. He takes a deep breath, holding it in. Pins and needles radiate through his limbs in anticipation of their discovery.

From behind the blackness of his eyelids a distant shimmer of subtle light peaks through.

On the horizon, to the west, a few kilometres out a dim light moves slowly east along the freeway. Staring out through one eye, the light splits off into two as the light becomes closer . . . then three.

The light is followed shortly by the sound of vehicles speeding down the way.

A deafening screech bellows a few feet from Broady's ear. Remaining still, the creatures below click and screech fanatically as they scamper away, disappearing in the tall grass.

Broady lets out his breath the feeling returns to his hands and feet, he cannot believe his luck. He wriggles himself up pushing against a branch getting a better look.

The three vehicles are moving quickly and before long Broady gets a glimpse of them as their headlights beam light onto each other. It's a military convoy. The first appears to be an armoured vehicle, situated on top is a soldier mounting a turret with a large machine gun attached. The soldier calls out something looking down into the cabin, although it's too muffled to hear what is said.

The second vehicle is a large troop carrier the back covered by a large desert camouflage cover. He is unable to see if there are any troops onboard. The tailing vehicle is a Land Cruiser similar to the one Broady borrowed. The man on top of the turret shouts again and a bright spotlight beams up into the night sky before the soldier on top tapers it down in front. The spotlight is fixated on the abandoned Cruiser in the middle of the road.

The convoy slows down; the armoured vehicle halts about ten metres or so from the abandoned vehicle. Six heavily armed soldiers jump down onto the road from the back of the carrier. The six men fan out around the convoy as they chatter amongst themselves, each one of the men holds their rifle up. Two more spotlights light up from the driver and passenger side of the Land Cruiser, scanning around into the dark open plains.

The door of the armoured vehicle opens and a soldier wearing a black beret steps out onto the road, pistol drawn and aimed at the abandoned car, he slowly steps toward it.

As the spotlights from his vehicle shine through the cabin of the abandoned Land Cruiser, Broady can see the rustling of the grass as the creatures home in on them. So desperately wanting to warn them, he feels helpless, anything he does will no doubt lead the creatures back in his direction. If anything happened to Charlotte, he would not forgive himself.

All he can do is look on as the ambient light illuminates the tops of the tall grass. Only metres from the road one soldier steps out to the edge of the asphalt leaning out appearing to investigate. The spotlight from the Land Cruiser moves in front of the soldier illuminating the grass in front of him, subsequently exposing a creature that lurked in the dark. A loud screech bellows out from the tall grass from the creature as its discovery. In a mighty bound it leaps out toward him. A loud crack of gunfire echoes far out into the open fields. Bats and birds that hang asleep in nearby trees are startled by the noise, chirping and squawking as they fly off into the night sky.

"CONTACT!" he yells, before a deafening sound of dozens of creatures.

The soldier manning the machine gun begins lighting up the grass, firing his high-powered weapon aimlessly into the fields. Bullets wiz past the tree. Broady ducks down low as bullets thwap into the tree's trunk. The men huddle together moving close to their vehicles as they fire into the grass. Creatures appear leaping quickly out toward them; they are swiftly cut down by the barrage of fire slumping down onto the road.

"LET'S MOVE," the soldier in the black beret yells out,

running back into the armoured vehicle firing his pistol into the field. It's sheer chaos as the men scamper back into their vehicles. The Land Cruiser is first to move, kicking up dust as it spins the wheels taking off hastily in front. A roar emanates from the troop carrier as the big diesel engine puffs smoke into the air as it speeds to catch up. The armoured vehicle is last; spinning its turret around as it follows the other vehicles. Its spotlights shine brightly on thirty or more creatures giving chase. The sight is unbelievable,

"Holy shit," Broady calls out spontaneously, unable to keep his amazement in. The creatures run hunched over, screeching as they tumble over one another in pursuit of the convoy. The soldier fires back behind the convoy as more and more creatures funnel in from either side.

The headlights and muzzle flares from the machine gun fade out as they move farther and farther toward the coastline until the burst of machine gunfire become distant faint pops in the night.

Broady stares at the rifle at his feet, grateful he wasn't in a position to use it. With the insurmountable numbers of creatures, it would have most certainly sealed their fate.

Seeing the situation as some sort of god-like intervention, Broady silently prays for a moment, thanking the soldiers for their leading the horde away.

Broady is stunned that Charlotte did not flinch during the whole ordeal; she lay dead to the world, lost in her dreams.

He pushes the button on his watch, illuminating the time. 3:15 am.

Only a few hours till sunup.

He lies back, surveying the outskirts and listening intently. After only a short time his eyes become heavy as the adrenaline seeps out of his body, his legs ache and become heavy. He closes his eyes vowing to stay awake till sunup, but within a few minutes of believing they're safe, he falls back asleep.

Adrift once again, Broady finds himself walking down a deserted road, in the middle of the rural countryside. The sky is dark and overcast, another feeling of de javu as he looks over seeing a white minibus laying off the side of the embankment, its internals burnt and charred. Fear surges as he worries for Allison's safety. He turns his head, opposite the road, a service station is attached to a convenience store and diner. He lucidly looks back toward the bus, now gone, his head begins to spin with confusion. He tries to concentrate, taking in as much detail as he can. The service station looks old and run-down, paint peels off the weatherboards, and its dirty fuel pumps are old and bent.

A loud gunshot rings out encasing all his senses.

Charlotte's voice screams out from behind him, her voice so encapsulating it sends chills down to his core, taking his breath away as he fights to wake up.

Broady's eyes open, propelling his body upright he gasps vigorously for breath, frightened and slightly disorientated, his vision is cloudy as his eyes try to focus.

The sun is shining; he looks up into the canopy as sparkles of golden sunlight glitter through the tiny gaps in the leaves as they rustle about in the wind.

It takes Broady's eyes a few moments to adjust, he squints

making it easier to see. He realises he is still in the enormous tree. His dream was so realistic that he battles to reconnect with the real world, noticing the farther out they travel the more detailed his dreams become. Slowly he moves his head, pain surges down his neck and back as he stretches. Reality sets back in as blood flows back around his body. As his breath returns, he smacks his hands against his chest noticing it's no longer impeded by Charlotte's weight. Panic sets in momentarily as he looks down onto the dirt below.

"No, Teddy, we're monkeys, silly, that's why we're are in the tree," Charlotte says.

The sound of her sweet little voice settles him as he looks over, partially hidden behind a large branch, she sits perched, her teddy beside her.

"Charlotte!" he calls out, still partially panicked. "What are you doing over there without me?" he says annoyed, the branch is suspended a few metres above the ground; she's managed to crawl her way up and out onto the branch.

Broady calms himself down. "Come back here, sweetness, please," he says softly.

"Teddy wanted to get a better view," she says innocently. "You were still asleep; we didn't want to wake you."

"Never mind, careful now," he says, pushing against a branch and hoisting himself up. He reaches out his hand to bring her back toward the middle of the tree.

"You scare me sometimes, you know that?" he says lovingly as he pulls her in.

"I know, but I'm brave . . . remember?" she says.

Curious, Broady asks, "So how did you sleep?"

"Ok," she answers. "You're not very comfy you know . . . no offence."

"Righto." Broady laughs. He grabs the rucksack, counting the number of rations left. Only two, he looks down at the Land Cruiser still sitting in the middle of the road. He stuffs the jacket back inside, grabs Charlotte's teddy off the branch and goes to throw it in the bag.

"Eh . . . Eh . . . Eh," she mumbles, reaching out for her teddy. "Don't put Teddy in there, I'll carry her," she insists, grabbing her teddy back and hugging it tightly.

Broady throws the bag down from the tree, and securing the rifle over his back with the strap again, he bends down holding into the branch and swinging his body down. Steadying himself he falls a short distance before his boots hit the hard, dry dirt.

Turning around he looks up to Charlotte, she holds her teddy tight as she looks on nervously.

"Ahh, I don't know, Dad. It's too high." She shakes.

"You can do it . . . You're brave . . . Remember?" he says.

She crouches down, shuffling to the edge of the branch, extending both arms out she looks away scrunching up her face as she leans forward falling from the tree.

"Gotcha!" Broady roars tickling her stomach after he catches her.

"Wow you're so heavy, no more treats for you," he declares sarcastically.

"Pffft, yeah right," she says, rolling her eyes.

They head back down the hill toward the main road. Charlotte chuckles as she runs aimlessly through the tall brown grass. Broady grins at his daughter's innocence, seemingly entertained by the smallest of things, momentarily wishing he could view the world as she does.

Stepping up the embankment and onto the road, Broady looks west along the open freeway, the road extends into a mirage as far as he can see.

"Wait here," he says to Charlotte as she is about the climb up onto the road.

He begins walking back; a light breeze blows black soot up into the air. Down on the road lay dark patches of scorched road base on the surface. Small piles of soot and ash lay compiled at the centre, so light even a delicate breeze blows it away.

Perplexed, he bends down reaching out with his fingers. He stares up at the bright morning sun, before looking back down at the road, piecing together each little clue about the creatures. Believing that these could be the remains of the creatures having been killed from the soldiers, their bodies left only to be incinerated by the sun's rays. He pulls his hand back, wary, he's unsure if their remains carry some sort of contagion. The wind blows, kicking up more ash and soot into the air. Broady lifts his shirt up over his nose, remaining on the cautious side.

The contents of the Land Cruiser has been scattered across the road. He walks around the Land Cruiser picking some of the food and water, loading in as much as the pack can carry. It's heavy, but he heaves it up onto his back, tightening the shoulder straps and clipping in the chest and waist straps, jumping up as he secures them properly. The road will be long and difficult. He grips the side of the Land Cruiser's metal tray nodding his head as he rocks himself back and forth, psyching himself up for the journey. Grabbing two water bottles, one in each hand, he puts on his game face, knowing he has to remain composed, at least for Charlotte's sake.

Walking back toward her within a few feet, he throws her a water bottle.

"Hey, Charlotte . . . Catch!" The bottle hits the ground, skidding along and coming to rest at her feet.

"What was that?" he laughs, holding out both arms wide.

He twists open his bottle taking a sip. Charlotte picks the bottle up from her feet, taking a sip.

"Drink up," Broady says to her. "We have a long walk; we don't want to get dehydrated," he adds, casting his shadow on her. Noticing Charlotte looking to him he shuts his eyes, lifting his bottle high and chugging down the water, he slows peeking out the side with one eye. She follows suit, Broady sees by something so simple as this how impactful his behaviour is on her. As he lowers the bottle the sun shines into Charlotte's eyes and she squints, chugging down as much as she can. He finds within himself, despite their dreary situation, an upbeat energy in the hopes of motivating Charlotte along in their journey.

He hopes to come across a farm or residence soon, with the possibility of finding another vehicle. Having passed the town of Dalby an hour before they ran out of fuel, he knows there's still a few hundred kilometres to Roma—far too long to hike on foot.

"Righto, let's go," he rhymes, beginning their first steps.

The road is coarse and gritty, the outer bed of the road is chipped and broken. Unlike the smooth sealed road from town, tiny stones scrape along the ground under Charlotte's dragging feet. Broady begins kicking some of the larger stones along like a soccer ball, throwing his hands up in the air. "Score!" he chants, picking up Charlotte's mood, she plays along. He enjoys these moments as she runs along kicking stones and chanting. After a few kilometres, her pace begins to slow again. Having not seen a sign for some time he's unsure how far they've come.

"So, what's this 'I can't catch' business?" he asks, drumming up anything he can think of to keep her mind occupied.

"Last school holidays we had it down pat," he adds.

"I know, I know," she says, sounding rather glum. "But no one would play catch with me when I came back, so I couldn't practice. I forgot. Then . . ." she says, becoming dramatic. "When I went back to school, I was playing with Ben and he threw a ball and hit me in the eye, and hurt me, now I'm scared," she says, getting upset as she relives her experience.

Broady thinks for a moment, finding the right words that might help.

"Well, you know Uncle Ed," he says, looking down to her as she nods.

"When I was about your age, we were playing baseball and he hit the ball so hard and fast I missed catching and it hit me right in the eye, same as you!" he says, dramatising the experience. "I had a black eye for two weeks!" he says, covering his eye.

Charlotte giggles. "Really?" she asks. "What did you do?" she says, inquisitively leaning forward and picking up her pace.

"Well, for about two weeks until my eye got better, I didn't play with him again. But when all the kids in the street had a big game one afternoon, my fear of not wanting to was outweighed by my urge to have fun with my friends. I guess what I'm saying there is, if you really want to do something you have to keep doing it despite being scared, it doesn't mean you won't be.

Heck, I was hell scared when I went out, but you know what?"

"What?" she asks, intrigued.

"After a while with more practice, I got better, soon after that, I wasn't afraid anymore."

"Really?" she asks, looking hopeful.

"Yep, promise," he says as they continue walking. He bends down picking up a small rock.

"Let's give this a try," he says.

Broady walks backward a few feet in front of her, gently underarm throwing the rock into her hands, which she shuts quickly as it touches her.

"Yesssss!" she cheers "Like a Venus flytrap, hey Dad!" she states.

"Aha!" he cheers. "You do remember."

Happy his distraction is working the two throw small stones back and forth at one another, all the while Broady walks the journey backward.

"How come you always catch them?" she asks after a while.

"Coz I'm awesome!" he laughs.

"Yeah, well, try catch this." She grunts, cocking her arm back and throwing the small stone up as high and as far as she can, up and over Broady's head.

He turns running a few steps forward looking up above his head. Zigzagging down the road he catches the stone, falling down just in front of him.

"HA!" he yells in victory before something out in the distance catches his eye.

"Wow, Dad, that was awesome," Charlotte cheers.

"Hang on, honey." He steadies his pace, leaning forward as he squints.

From this distance, a black object lays off the side of the road. Out of place in such a remote environment, he is eager to see what it is.

"What are you looking at?" she asks.

"I'm not sure, honey, let's go take a look."

Focused on finding out what's up ahead as they edge closer. The object is off the embankment of the highway, a black truck or van perhaps.

Yet as they move farther up the highway Broady gets better view over the embankment. It's a short white minibus; its roof is charred and burnt. White paint is bubbled and flaked off the side. Perplexed, he stares at the burnt wreck.

"Allison," he whispers before sprinting off toward it.

"Is Allison there, Dad?" Charlotte calls to him.

Nearing the top of the embankment he flicks the clip off his chest and waist and settles the bag down at the top as he steps down. Moving alongside the bus he peers in the shattered and broken windows.

"DADDY!" Charlotte cries out from the embankment.

"It's ok, honey"—he looks back at her—"just stay there for me, ok?"

He moves up to the front, the door still open. Broady is hopeful Allison could have got out safely.

Cautiously he steps onto the bus. The floor groans and creaks as he bears his weight down. It's a bleak sight, most of the seat coverings have been burnt off, and bare metal mesh is left exposed. He grabs onto a railing pulling himself up into the passenger's section, noticing the rails are cool and no part of the bus is smouldering, leaning him to the presumption that the fire happened some time ago. Sunlight enters through two roof hatches that have been burnt through. The bus is pungent with the smell of charred plastic along with another foul, foreign sent. As he makes his way toward the back of the bus, checking every seat, the charred remains of a person lay slumped forward behind a seat midway through the bus. Broady gasps at the sight, covering his mouth and nose having found the origin of the foul smell. He looks away, and unable to stomach the sight he moves farther to the back the bus.

As he steps farther into the back, the floor creaks and buckles, his foot breaking through the thin wooden floorboard kicking up dust and ash into the air. He falls forward grabbing hold of a metal railing atop of a seat, zapping him. The shockwave penetrates through him. His vision is compromised by a picture of Allison sitting on the seat behind, her hand on the very same railing. Startled, he takes a deep breath breathing in dust and ash that's kicked up into the air. Coughing and spluttering he pulls his shirt up over his nose and mouth. Pulling out his leg he slumps into the seat he saw Allison sit. His backside squeaks on the mesh seat underlay as he sits down. Another zap radiates through his body, short recollections show the bus driving down the highway, and a billow of smoke pours up from the engine and driving off the embankment. Memories that are not his own.

"Are you ok, Dad?" Charlotte's voice yells out.

Shaking his head, he snaps himself back into reality and calls back out to her, "I'm fine, honey."

"It just overheated," he says to himself, rehashing his thoughts of the smoke billowing up from the bus's engine. As the ash gently begins to settle, he closes his eyes resting his head on the railing in front.

"Where are you?" he whispers, attempting to force another vision. He concentrates hard on Allison and the visions he just saw.

"Come on!" he begs, gritting his teeth. Nothing happens, he bangs his head on the metal seat becoming frustrated.

"Dad, come back out please," Charlotte pleads.

"Damn it!" he says angrily, bashing his palm against the rail, storming off the bus.

"What is it, Dad?" Charlotte asks, seeing her father angry.

"Nothing, honey, Dad's just annoyed. Just leave it, ok," he says slightly dismissively.

Broady picks up the bag, hoisting it back up onto his back, and continues to walk along the road. Charlotte doesn't make a sound and quickly follows suit.

For more than a kilometre Broady says nothing, Charlotte looks at her father seemingly chatting away to himself, agitated in his stride.

Broady mulls over in his mind the dreams and visions. Replaying them over and over again. The high-pitched sound in his head, the creatures. He believes they are all connected somehow. Angry, and feeling out of control, his inability to comprehend and understand, he feels like he is going crazy. He continues marching forward, the only thing he can control. Tears well up in his eyes, utter confusion as he struggles to maintain his sanity.

After more than a kilometre the panic begins to subside, his tunnel vision of the road ahead widens and he hears the sound of kookaburras, 'the laughing maniacs' his fourth-grade teacher used to call them. He chuckles at the thought, looking over his shoulder to where they are sitting, perched up in the gum trees beside the road.

Charlotte walks slowly a few feet behind; she hugs her teddy tight, quiet and reclusive.

"Hey," Broady says, bending down onto one knee. "Look, Daddy is sorry if you thought I was mad at you," he says, stroking her shoulders with his hands.

"You were angry," she says shyly. Never having seen her father behave in such a manner has frightened her.

"Yes, you're right, I was, but not at you . . ." he says, looking her in the eyes. "I was hoping to find Allison, Daddy is worried about her, and when I didn't, I was angry. It's nothing to do with you, ok sweetness?"

Charlotte's face lifts as she realises she's not in trouble.

"So, how about a game of I-spy?" he says, trying to cheer her up. "I know you love that game."

Her face lifts higher into a smile as her eyes light up. "I'm the best at that game!"

"Well, you are very clever," Broady boasts.

The game has reinvigorated the long march, the two play back and forth for a few kilometres. Much farther than he had hoped for.

Chapter 9

As the day drags on, and the sun beams down in the centre of the sky. Broady stops, unzipping his backpack and pulling out more water. They're running through their supplies of water quickly; he thinks as he rummages through what remains. On the plus side, there is now less for him to carry.

"How are you travelling, kiddo?" Broady asks.

"It's hot, Daddy," she says, slumping her shoulders forward.

The heat from the black bitumen road radiates up from the ground, making the relative temperature much higher, even more so for Charlotte being so much shorter. Broady sympathises with her.

"I know, honey. Here, drink up." He passes along a bottle of water, with Charlotte snatching it from his hands. There is no trouble this time as she chugs it down.

"When are we going to stop?" she asks, tired and very much over it.

"Just a little longer, I promise," he says, pulling the now lighter pack over his shoulders.

Charlotte walks toward him with both arms up. She wants to be carried.

He rearranges the rifle over the back of the backpack, tired and spent himself, he bends down, picking her up off the ground.

So much for lightening the load, he thinks. His journey just got a whole lot more taxing.

His shoulders ache from the heavy rucksack, having lost nearly all feeling in his feet some hours ago. He puts his woes aside focusing straight ahead, with the thoughts of finding Allison pushing him forward. After only a short distance Charlotte's arms go limp as she nods off, having a nap.

He looks to either side of him, for kilometres and kilometres there is nothing but bush and vacant land. Having not travelled this way before Broady is concerned that they again may not find shelter before sundown. The long straight road is glary as the hot sun scorches the road; the puddle of water made from a mirage on the horizon does little to help his cause. As he stares aimlessly at the illusion ahead, a small dot appears hovering out, he blinks wondering if it's just part of the illusion. A few moments later a bumper bar and the beige hood of a truck appear. Looking to be an armoured vehicle with a turret on top, the same type he saw the previous night. Broady sighs with relief. He prays that it is soldiers driving and not another stray having commandeered a vehicle as he did.

Moving toward them, more than one vehicle begins to appear. A string of vehicles drives along in a line heading straight toward them. Broady squints, placing his hand up over his brow counting the cars.

Six big troop carriers steam down toward them, followed by a green jeep a few hundred metres behind.

Broady stops walking forward, shaking Charlotte gently awake.

"Honey, I need you to wake up," he whispers in her ear.

Cranky and unhappy, she lifts her head.

He walks to the side of the road and places her down. She yawns loudly, wiping her face.

"Stand behind me," he says, reaching over his back and grabbing the rifle. He hooks it over one shoulder, ready yet not wanting to appear too threatening. Little good it would do him anyway, he concludes, he's just hoping they don't take it from him.

The two stand and stare as they approach; all the canopies from the carriers are pulled off. Troops sit lined up in the back of the truck. Not showing any signs of slowing the convoy kicks up large plumes of dust and dirt from the road as they roar past. Charlotte covers her face; Broady squints tightly holding his breath wanting to get a better look.

He peers at the soldiers sitting in the back of the troop carriers, some with helmets on, some without. Most of the soldiers have their heads down, slumped forward. Their uniforms are dirty, their faces smudged with dirt and ash. One leans out and spits out the truck on the opposite side. Another trooper points toward them, patting his comrade on the helmet, lifting his head to take a look. Most of the men's faces appear grim. Making eye contact with one man, he appears angry as he snarls at them before passing by. Broady twists with the trucks as they drive past.

A few seconds later, the jeep slows as it passes before suddenly hitting the brakes. The wheels lock up at it comes to a screeching halt.

A hard-faced looking man hops out of the passenger side, dressed in full desert camouflage. His uniform is neat and clean; three golden stripes are embroidered on his shoulder and he's also carrying a pistol on his hip. His tough stare puts Broady off foot.

"Where is your regiment?" he yells sternly. "Where are you from, soldier? Who is this child?!" he continues to barrage Broady with questions—there is no hope of answering them all.

The man's voice is deep and powerful; his interrogation makes Broady feel uneasy. Feelings of guilt immediately surface, seeing as how he very well stole this equipment from the Australian army.

The man glares at Broady, awaiting a response.

"WELL?" he yells.

"No sir, I'm not a soldier." Broady tries to act calmly

"You're not a soldier?" the man continues to barrage him.

Broady begins to sweat as Charlotte hides behind his legs, frightened by the man.

"You better start talking, son," he says, taking a step toward Broady. He pulls his pistol from his holster, tapping his finger on the slide.

Broady sweats, then decides to come clean.

"I'm from Robina, or at least that's where we came from, the military checkpoint anyway. This is my daughter Charlotte." Broady steps aside placing his hand on Charlotte's head as she cuddles her teddy. "My friend Allison, I left her at the stadium and drove through the mountains to a town west of Grafton to find my daughter, when we returned the whole place was completely decimated and deserted," he explains.

The man's face softens as he looks down at Charlotte.

"I borrowed some of the gear that was left behind," he says as he pinches at his clothes.

"Interesting story," the man replies sceptically. "So what brings you out here?"

"There was a map in the command centre, it had the locations of two other checkpoints, we figured we'd head there, see if we could find my friend," Broady says.

"How do you know your friend is there? Didn't you say she was at the safety point?"

"I saw civilian evacuation signs; I figured they were moving people out of the city. And to be honest, I chose Roma because I thought the port would be too densely populated an area, it was a fifty-fifty chance really."

"Hmmm," the man hums, pacing side to side.

"I suppose it is," he says, lowering his tone. "Well, I got some bad news for you, kid. The western front has been evacuated this morning, deemed no longer safe. We are the last of it. The rest of the company are moving to the ports and out to sea. These creatures don't seem to be good swimmers," the man explains, much to Broady's disappointment.

"I saw some of your troops last night," Broady interrupts.

"Delta company. They were dispatched yesterday afternoon to rescue a busload of civilians that were attacked—"

"Wait . . . I thought the creatures only came out at night?" Broady looks puzzled.

"They do, the creatures are not the only thing you need to worry about, kid."

"What happened to the people on the bus?" Broady asks, concerned.

The man steps right in front of Broady. "Delta team searched the nearby area until dusk, by then it was too late for them to head back, they made a run for the port. They didn't find anyone. They did everything they could." The man softens seeing the disappointment in Broady's eyes. "Sorry, kid," the man says, slapping him on the shoulder.

The slap from the man's hand zaps Broady again giving him a sharp pain in his ear.

The vision of Allison on the bus again, only this time not from her perspective. Now standing in the centre of the bus Broady looks forward, a bearded bald man in a red-and-black flannelette shirt fires a rifle at the bus, smoke billows from the engine before veering off into the ditch.

"You alright, son?" the man says, lightly shaking Broady's shoulder.

Broady opens his eyes wide, blinking them repeatedly. He rattles his finger in his ear, shaking off the sting. Broady comes to after a few seconds, as he realises what happened.

The man stares at Broady with a strange look.

"Yeah, yeah, I'm good," Broady says.

"We've been walking all day, I just have a migraine."

"Private!" the man yells over his shoulder.

A young thin man emerges from the back seat of the vehicle holding his rifle. "Yes, Sergeant!" He stands at attention

"Bring these two some water!" the sergeant instructs.

The man fumbles in the back seat before running out with two bottles of water, dragging his feet as he does.

"Here, Sarg," he says, handing the sergeant the bottles, before dragging his feet back into the jeep.

The sergeant grunts and shakes his head as the young soldier jumps back in.

Broady opens the fresh bottle, having finished a full bottle not long ago and feeling a little water-logged. He still proceeds to gulp it down not wanting to arise any more suspicion.

The sergeant bends down opening the bottle for Charlotte.

"Here you go, little miss," he says kindly. By the stature of the man's character, Broady can tell the sergeant is a good man.

"Jump in the back, kid," the sergeant says, walking back to the vehicle.

"We'll be fine," Broady calls out.

Stunned, the sergeant stops in his tracks.

"Come again?" the sergeant says placing his hand up to his ear in disbelief.

Broady repeats himself.

"Kid!" the sergeant begins to lecture him. "There is nothing out here, aren't you listening? Safe point Delta has been evacuated."

Broady doesn't budge, sticking true to finding Allison and heading to his parents' remote farm.

"Look, I'm sorry about your friend but you have to think about your little girl." The sergeant tries to sympathise with him.

"We have somewhere safe to go." Broady stays persistent.

"Suit yourself, kid." The sergeant stares a look of disappointment at Broady.

He moves his head to the side, tilting around. He stares down at the rifle, before looking up again at Broady then back down to the rifle.

Broady doesn't move a muscle silently praying the sergeant doesn't relieve him of the weapon. The sergeant stares for what feels like an eternity before he says, "Good luck, kid." He turns around, stepping into the jeep, he slaps his hand on the side twice before the car accelerates off, kicking up dirt and stones off the road, flinging them at Broady and Charlotte. They both turn away covering their faces.

"Yeah thanks," Broady says, spitting dirt from his mouth. "For nothing," he adds sarcastically, turning around and heading off.

Charlotte stands looking toward the vehicle as it speeds off. Innocently she copies her father. "Yeah! Thanks for nothing!" she yells.

Broady chuckles to himself as he walks on. Charlotte quickly falls in line.

Doubt begins to creep in as he worries if he has made a terrible decision turning down the sergeant's offer. His head hasn't been clear since this whole thing started, driven now largely by deep urges and emotions along with strange dreams and premonitions he can't fully understand, steering away from his normal logical thinking. He looks up toward the blue sky hoping he is right.

The two cool off briefly in the shade of a nearby tree, a quick rest and recoup as they both slurp down some food. As noon passes and the afternoon begins, they hit the road again. This time however Charlotte is exhausted after eating, taking slower and slower steps. Broady pauses looking west with nothing yet in sight. He holds in his frustration knowing at this pace they won't make it anywhere before sundown. Broady doesn't want to take that risk again.

"Want a piggyback?" he calls back to Charlotte.

Instantly reigniting Charlotte's mood, she races over to him. Rearranging his pack, facing it forward, holding onto the rifle he bends down. Charlotte jumps up onto his back.

"Here we go!" he yells as he groans and stumbles, using the rifle as a cane propelling him up.

"Now put your feet in here." He says grabbing her foot and placing them at the bottom of the strap giving her some leverage.

She giggles as she says, "Giddy up, horsey," she cries out in laughter.

Broady is thankful he's cheered her up. Her laughter has brought him a second wind as he marches on, occasionally making horse noises and trotting sounds, much to Charlotte's delight.

They trot on; Broady's relentless determination to find Allison safely gives him the resilience to push through the pain he feels shooting down his knees and into his burning feet. His shoulders aches from the weight of the rucksack now topped with Charlotte on his back. Unbeknown to him, in the depths of his subconscious, most of his resolve comes from his guilt for not having been able to save Abby.

Sandwiched between the two, the sweat pours out of him, feeling like the melted cheese in a hot toasted sandwich. Roughly three kilometres farther down the road, in the distance, Broady spots a building on the side of the road. Although from this distance, it appears only as a small smudge. Broady is convinced however it is a building; either that or the heatstroke he is suffering has progressed into full-blown hallucinations.

He picks up his pace, panting heavily as he tries to move his weighed-down body quickly. Sweat pouring down his head, the salty sweat runs into his eyes burning them, yet still he doesn't blink, fixated on the structure ahead.

"Uh, Dad, your all sweaty and gross," Charlotte says, screwing up her face as she wipes her hands on her shirt.

"I can walk now," she says.

"There looks like a building up ahead, we might be able to rest there," he struggles to say, gasping for air.

As Charlotte dismounts, a breeze blows by brushing across his sweat-soaked shirt. The feeling is utter bliss and Broady lets out a big sigh. He closes his eyes and revels in the sensation for a moment, before switching the rucksack onto his back once again.

As they near the building the hairs on the back of Broady's neck stand up, he grips the rifle more tightly as parts of the building comes into focus. A big white awning extends out from the building. Two concrete driveways metres apart. Trees encircle the building still partially obscuring his view. The closer they move, the more eerie it feels. Before they even pass, Broady knows what it is, having seen the front of the building before, like the bus from his dream.

A service station.

Chapter 10

Metres from the driveway, Broady can see the old white weatherboard building, paint peeling and flaking off its surface. Three cars are parked, each one is parked facing inward having been driven straight into the car parks at the front of the building just right of the entrance door; the vehicles are covered with dust and dirt. An old white Holden Commodore, next to a blue seventies Ford Fairlane and a newer model Hilux. A black sign out on the grass by the road says, *Café Open, Coffee, Cold Drinks, Hot Food.*

The cheap metal Venetian blinds are spun shut however they're broken and kinked in places. Through the broken blinds, it appears dark and desolate. The building extends far back from the shopfront, giving the possibility that the owners may live in a residence behind.

A sinking feeling arises from Broady's stomach and he wonders if he is meant to avoid the service station.

He walks slower past the first driveway. Charlotte stands still behind.

"Aren't we going in there, Dad?" she queries him.

Broady stops and turns. "No, honey, something doesn't feel right," he says, still at odds. His doubts fester in his gut making him feel nauseous, further perpetuating his distrust added with a realisation that these visions only accompany bad events.

Despite being low on supplies and no other forms of shelter in sight, Broady decides to keep moving.

"Come on, let's get out of here quickly," he says, ushering her over with one hand.

Charlotte stares at the building momentarily, as she lifts her foot moving toward her Dad a scream for help resonates from the building.

The sound seemingly confirms Broady's suspicions. "Quick," he says, bending down. "We have to hurry."

A loud bang, like the slamming of a door accompanied by a smashing sound, emanates from the building.

Charlotte stops moving and turns back to the building.

"What are you doing?" Broady growls, whispering.

"Daddy, someone needs our help." She pleads.

"I know, honey, it's ok. We're going, it's not our problem," he says, brushing off her request.

"NO!" she yells, stomping her foot angrily.

"Shhh," Broady whispers, crouching right down.

"That lady needs our help," she demands.

"It's not safe for you," he says, attempting to persuade her.

Charlotte, however, won't have a bar of it. She crosses her arms and stands tall.

Broady's mind races as thinks of ways around the situation. Wanting to avoid a full-blown tantrum as he doesn't want to draw any more attention to them. His heart pounds as he sees Charlotte glare at him, he knows he's not getting her away without a fight.

"FUCK!" he blurts out.

He stays low, making his way over to Charlotte. Taking her by the hand and pulling her down into a crouch position the two scurry up the driveway, making as little noise as possible.

Broady leads Charlotte between the Holden and the Ford, taking cover beside the vehicles. He gently opens the rear door of the Fairlane. Having been convinced by his daughter, he changes his mind, deciding to enter the building.

He turns to Charlotte and whispers to her. "Now listen, honey . . ." his words are interrupted by another loud bang from inside the house. Broady pops his head up, peeking through the break in the dirty window. The shop is dark, a shaft of sunlight illuminates through a doorway. It looks to be the kitchen. Broady sees no movement.

"Listen," he continues, "you have to stay here in the back ok, honey? Lock the door and stay low."

"But I want to stay with you," she says, scared.

"I know, but you want me to go in there, and it's not safe for you."

"But I'm scared," she cries.

Broady doesn't like this idea at all as he looks around.

"Ok, jump in the driver's seat, and you see those buttons on the steering wheel?" He points to the horn. She nods and agrees, climbing over the centre console and into the driver's seat.

"You push down on those hard if someone comes and I'll come running out, ok?"

Charlotte drops her bottom lip. "You promise?"

Broady pushes his worries aside, looking her dead in the eye. "Promise," he says confidently. "You look after Teddy." He closes the door slowly, gently nudging as it clicks shut.

He pauses for a moment, his hand trembles as he grabs hold of the rifle. He pushes it hard into his shoulder steadying his shakes as he makes his way toward the front doors, remaining crouched down.

He presses his face up against the door peeking in through the gaps in the blinds. Still clear. Grabbing hold of the handle he gently opens it.

A small bell attached to the door softly chimes as it opens. Although faint, to Broady it sounds like Big Ben. His heart thumping in his chest, he holds the door with his foot, poking his rifle in the door and scanning the shop. The shop is a mess, packets of food and produce lay scattered all over the floor on the three aisles to his left. There are no people, however, so Broady sticks his head back out, signalling the thumbs up back to Charlotte who is eagerly staring at him through the passenger-side window. She props her thumb up before he heads into the shop. With no lights and no power, the shop is dark from the blinds drawn, only scattered thin streams of light emanate through.

Adjacent to the front door behind the counter is a swinging door with a circular window. It's bright behind the door as sunlight streams through the window illuminating a cylinder of dust particles onto the floor.

He moves through the room tactically like the countless war movies he's seen, moving over behind the swinging door.

Quickly bobbing his head up, he gets a glimpse through into the kitchen. It's empty. The kitchen proceeds left in a straight line with benches on either side. On the right sits a sink with a closed window with no blinds above it. Directly across from the door is another doorway, separated by a beaded curtain hanging down from the arch.

He places his hand on the swinging door, pushing it forward gently as he steps through. He holds the door as he closes it, not wanting it to make noise if it swings.

The air is damp and musty, like the smell of a McDonald's kitchen and burnt oil. The floor is sticky and grimy as his shoes lose some traction. Pointing his muzzle through the beads, it appears to be the entrance to the back residence. Another loud bang and muffled screaming emanate from the wall to his left behind the kitchen, muffled sounds of a man yelling—Broady is unable to make out what's being said. The beads in the doorway sway with a light breeze blowing cool air into the musty kitchen. Through the beads is a short hallway. Seeing the hallway is clear he pokes his rifle through the hanging beads, they tinkle on the metal muzzle. He reaches out with his hand gently pushing them to one side, enough room for him to move through. As he goes to lower the beads the wall next to him vibrates with another loud boom, shaking the wall and startling Broady he drops the beads and they swing, noisily crashing into one another.

"Get off me!" a muffled scream of a woman radiates through the wall.

Broady clenches his jaw as the beads clash together, worried he's given himself away. He pauses for a moment and gripping the rifle tightly he feels his sweaty palms slip along the rail. He wipes them on his pants.

He moves into a small open room. Surprised, a heavy-set dark-skinned woman sits on a single recliner chair, she leans against her hand as her fingers partially cover her face, teardrops stream down her cheeks. A step farther into the room and he can see several people in the room. To the far right, below a large window with see-through drapes sits a large green three-seater fabric couch, an elderly gentleman sits on the couch gently rocking an elderly woman back and forth, gripping their hands together. The elderly man's face is badly bruised, his right eye is swollen and puffy, and a small cut in the man's forehead weeps blood down onto his face. The woman is openly crying. Another man, middle-aged wearing a white business shirt, his sleeves rolled up with a slick haircut sits in the corner of the room on the floor with his knees up, his head down, tapping a mobile phone against the top of his head. On the far side of the couch on the floor sits a young teenage couple, a boy and girl, the girl is sobbing into her hands, she's visibly shaking and seemingly terrified.

The vibe in the room is dreary; none of them even raise their head, despite Broady entering brandishing a rifle. Something awful has happened here, he thinks.

With the sound of a struggle still ensuing in the next room, Broady quietly steps through the room into a corridor to his left with doors at either end. Laughter erupts from the room to his left, along with a muffled sound of a woman screaming as if her mouth was gagged. Broady now assumes more than one male is in the room. He begins to panic as he realises the gravity of the situation. Holding the rifle tight he steps a foot closer toward the door, the floorboards creak as he approaches. He swallows hard as he creeps closer.

"You're making it worse, bitch!" a man yells through the crack in the door, slightly ajar followed by a loud slap.

Broady presses the tip of the rifle against the door, his adrenaline soars in anticipation. Sweat beads on his forehead as his heart pounds in his chest. He opens his mouth, breathing deep into his lungs as quietly as possible, and holding his breath he pushes the door open with the rifle. Much to his surprise the door doesn't creak or groan, instead gliding like a well-oiled machine. A thin man with short mousey brown hair stands in the corner opposite Broady. He's leaning on a dresser; a silver revolver rests on top. His face is gaunt and rough; he stands hunched over, with his hand down his pants, his eyes wide with glee as he strokes himself. Fixated, the man doesn't notice Broady enter the room.

To the right, an overweight bald man with a long beard sits upright on the bed, shirtless. Undoing his belt while another two men stand beside the bed holding the woman's hands out, the man on the opposite side of the bed next to the window is also shirtless, Broady noticing a sun tattooed around the man's navel. The woman's hair covers her face as she struggles and cries out as the men restraining her laugh at one another.

The overweight man pulls his pants down to his underwear, his hairy arse crack pokes out.

Broady snarls in disgust.

"Show us your pretty face," the man on the bed's croaky voice says brushing her hair away, revealing her face.

"ALLISON!" Broady yells in surprise.

The man and his accomplices turn around. Broady realises he's just blown his cover.

The thin gaunt man pulls his hand from his pants; they drop to the floor as he reaches for the revolver. Before he even has time to think, Broady pulls the trigger twice, hitting the man in the chest. The situation has just exploded. Stunned, Broady blankly stares at the gaunt man as he slumps to the ground, blood seeping through his shirt.

A split second later the man closest to him holding Allison down runs over charging Broady, pushing him up against the door pinning him, his rifle pressed up against his chest. Now fighting for his life, Broady knows he's in real trouble. While the man is busy trying to grab hold of the rifle, Broady places his foot up against the door. With all his strength he springs his torso forward, leveraging his weight behind his foot, pushing the man back. The man trips and stumbles over a cushion on the floor; falling onto his back. Broady quickly snatches the rifle back. The ground shakes as the man hits the floor hard. Swiftly taking advantage of the man's bad luck, Broady swings the rifle around, holding the sights up to his eye staring down the barrel at the man, now on the floor. Lifting his head, the man foolishly holds his hand up, attempting to deflect a bullet. Broady can see the shock in the man's face, almost in disbelief with his mouth widened; Broady can see the fear in the man's eyes. Broady fires a single round, hitting the man in his cheek. His head springs back almost in slow motion onto the floor with his mouth still open. Not at all what he expected to experience, feeling pity for the man, helpless as if he knew exactly what was about to happen.

Before Broady can think any more, the overweight man leaps

from the bed, his pants around his ankles. His grotesque hairy sweaty chest bears down hitting Broady in the face. The two hurtle toward the floor. Landing on top of him, the man's sweaty body slips and slides over Broady making him slippery to grab a hold of. Broady attempts to manoeuvre the rifle, now wedged between them. Broady struggles to breathe as the rifle agonisingly digs into his rib cage. The man uses his sheer size to his advantage. Face to face, Broady can smell the man's foul breath as he yells.

"I'm going to fucking kill you, you fucking CUNT!" he screams ferociously, spitting over Broady as his long coarse beard rubs against his face.

Broady gags as he inhales the putrid smell, tasting it on his tongue. He holds his breath as he frantically tries to free himself. The man leans all his weight onto Broady grabbing hold of the rifle, he laughs in Broady's face as he struggles to move. The man raises his body driving his elbow down hard onto Broady's cheek. Only partly connecting yet with still enough force to open a small cut underneath Broady's eye, his slippery arms slide off to the side; with a loud bang as the man's elbow drives down still farther into the timber floor. Broady doesn't feel the blow, too hyped on adrenaline. Not wanting to take a full blow Broady wraps his arms and legs around the man's sweaty back. He wriggles and squirms as he yells profanity into Broady's ear.

His head up beside the man's, Broady catches a glimpse of the knife he has nestled in his side pocket. He grabs the black handle, pulling it from its holder and drives it into the man's side as he cries out. The man tries to pull away, Broady holding him close pulls the knife from his skin plunging it farther around into the man's back.

The man coughs and splutters. Broady closes his eyes as blood sprays from the man's mouth onto his face. Delving the knife in deep he pushes the man to the side, pulling it out as the man rolls onto his back. The man desperately wrestles Broady grabbing hold of Broady's hands on the knife. Broady mounts on top of the man, both hands firmly on the knife. The man is strong; despite being wounded he pushes the knife back. Broady shifts his weight higher up on the man's torso. He draws one arm back up high, lifting himself off the man he drives down hard smacking the back of the knife like a hammer on a nail. Now inches from the man, he drives up again pushing down this time with all his weight like a sledgehammer, the knife plunges into the man's chest with a deep crackling sound. The man cries out as the knife penetrates his chest, just left of his sternum. With their eyes now level, Broady holds his weight down firmly. Gurgling sounds seep from the man's mouth as he gargles for breath shaking violently. The sounds soon become a faint crackle before a light whistle carries the last of the man's foul breath from his body. His arms go limp and he lets his grip on the knife go and the tension in his body leaves, his eyes however still open, glazing over as the life seeps away.

Broady continues to press his weight against the man, in an intense state of shock unable to move, staring at the tiny droplets of blood splattered through the man's beard.

"Broady!" Allison screams. Her scream pierces Broady's core, eerily familiar, remembering his name being called in the vast emptiness of the stadium's car park.

She jumps over the end of the bed, helping Broady up to his knees. She starts crying.

"I can't believe it's really you." She sobs, burying her head into his shoulder shocked by the sight of him. Aching and bleeding slightly from the cut under his eye, it immediately begins to swell up. He comforts her holding the back of her head and squeezing her in a tight embrace.

Pulling back and grabbing hold of her hands, tears stream down from her face, her hair messy and knotted. Looking down at her hands covered in dirt along with her clothes as if she's been dragged along the ground outside.

She delicately places her hands on Broady's face; clearly traumatised her hands tremble as the tears well in her puffy eyelids.

"You came back for me," she says, spluttering into a laugh. Only moments ago, fighting for her life as a group of thugs attempted to gang rape and likely kill her, she's in total disarray. Her eyes flicker back and forth as she stares into each one of Broady's eyes with a look of disbelief. She gently caresses his cheek, lightly running her thumb over the weeping cut below his eye.

"Tsssk." Broady flinches, looking back at her. Before he has a chance to think, Allison jumps forward locking her soft lips onto his in a passionate eruption of affection, the force of her adoring kiss, knocks Broady off balance and bumping him back.

"Argg!" he cries out, as the two unlock lips. A wild pain shoots up Broady's back. Allison frets seeing the agony on his face.

"Are you ok?" she asks, seeing him stumble on his feet. "Let me help you," she says.

He groans and grunts as Allison helps steady him. The adrenaline has now left his body and the fight and fall from the overweight man landing on top of him begins to take a toll. He looks down at the overweight man's lifeless body with a feeling of pure hatred; he pulls the knife embedded in the man's chest out, wiping the blood off onto the man's underwear and sliding it back into the side pocket of his cargo pants.

He limps over to the rifle left unattended on the floor. He leans his weight against the wall, his body stiff and aching as he leverages himself over. Allison supports him, her hands firmly gripping his hips as he picks the rifle up. Letting out another grunt, he straightens himself.

Allison scoops herself up under his arm, and the two hobble out through the doorway like wounded soldiers. As they turn the corridor into the main living area, the others just stare, not knowing who was going to appear. Broady cold stares back at each one of them. Anger begins to surge in the fire of his belly as his breath quickens. He unhinges himself from Allison, standing strong as he yells out.

"Are you guys fucking kidding me!" he erupts in a tirade, frightening the elderly couple on the couch, the woman flinching.

Broady passes back and forth, the rifle swinging down beside him. Everyone in the room has their head down sheepishly.

"You were all just going to sit there while and do nothing while those scum tried to . . .!" Broady chokes up, pointing toward Allison. Emotionally charged, he's unable to finish his sentence. Terrified of what might have happened to Allison, he walks off in a huff toward the back of the dwelling stopping at the end in front of a sliding glass door. Staring out through the glass, the rear of the property has no fence; a large partly built shed sits on a clearing on right side of the property, having no external or internal walls, just a bare slab, steel frame and a roof. The rest of the backyard is littered with junk; an old trampoline sits toward the back, its cover partly torn. Long grass grows up through the torn cover as is the case for most of the yard. An old rusted car, with no hood or door panels sits surrounded by grass as tall as the car. The rest of the yard is dirt. A portable toilet sits to the left. Broady wonders if the dwelling's toilet hasn't worked for some time.

"Wait . . ." he stops moving, frozen as if he has seen a ghost. "What happened to the other guy . . . ?" He turns to Allison and grabs her by the arm. "The guy who was holding your other wrist?" he demands an answer.

"Uhh . . . Uhh, he . . ." she begins to utter, before her words are cut short.

BEEP . . . BEEP . . . BEEP.

Before she can muster an explanation, Broady darts out of the room. Slapping the beads to the side as he runs through the store, gripping the rifle tight. He bursts through the door kicking it with his foot. The door swings open, shattering the glass.

"Charlotte!" he calls out, bringing the rifle up to his eye, frantically looking around for the other man.

Racing over to the car he notices the car closest to him is missing, tyre marks showing the vehicle sped off in a hurry. Sick in his stomach he races over to the car Charlotte was in. He doesn't see her from afar.

"NO, no, no!" he yells, running over to the passenger door.

Panic surges as he flings the door open. Sitting on the floor on the passenger seat is Charlotte, crouched down holding her teddy.

"Oh, thank god," he says, looking toward the sky with a massive sigh of relief. "Are you ok?" he asks, stepping down toward her. "Are you hurt?" he asks, checking her over in a frenzy.

"I was scared," she says. "I saw some man jump into the car and drive away," she explains. "I waited till he left; I didn't want him to see me," she adds.

"Smart thinking, kiddo," he says, rubbing her head and messing her hair. He thanks God for Charlotte having the wits to think.

"Hey!" she says annoyed, before noticing Broady's face. "Daddy!" she exclaims, holding up her hands to her mouth. "What happened to your face?" she asks, her fingers gently touching his cheek.

Thinking quickly, he answers, "I slipped over, honey; I hit my head on the bench."

"Silly Daddy," she says, shaking her head. "See what happens when I don't come with you?"

Broady laughs. "Yeah righto, kid," he says, helping her out of the car. Hearing the sound of footsteps on broken glass they both turn around to look.

"ALLISON!" Charlotte cries out, running over to her excited. Allison bends down as Charlotte races over, jumping up into her arms.

"We found you!" she shouts ecstatically.

"I know," Allison says tickling her on the stomach making her giggle. "You did such a good job," Allison praises her.

Broady stares down at the tyre marks left on the ground, wiping his hand down over his face feeling sick at the close call, had the man not been able to start the commodore and instead hopped into the car Charlotte was hiding in . . . He dares not think further. He grits his teeth at the danger he placed her in. Allison, seeing Broady slumped over appearing stressed she walk over to him, rubbing her hand on his back.

"Hey, are you ok?" she asks.

He straightens up, stretching his neck. He turns his head looking over at Allison as she holds Charlotte up on her hip both with a subtle look of joy on their faces; he manages to refocus his thoughts.

"Yeah I'm good," he says.

He walks out onto the centre of the road; he looks west as storm clouds begin to roll in, distant flashes of thunder in the mountains. There is no sign of a fleeing vehicle. Broady assumes the man is long gone by now, and good riddance, too.

A raindrop falls from the sky hitting Broady on the top of the head; he raises his head as another cool drop touches down on his eyelid, delighted in the sensation.

"Come on, let's get you inside," he hears Allison say as the rain rolls through.

"Broady, come on!" she calls out, heading back through the front entrance.

He takes another look west down the highway; the visibility of the road begins to diminish as a front of heavy rain heads toward them. In the very few moments spent on his own, his mind races over the incredibly traumatic event he's just experienced. He never believed he would take the life of anyone, let alone three, and in such a grisly way. Recalling the sheer closeness of the overweight man, still able to smell and taste the man's breath in his throat, he feels nauseous and he attempts to block it from his mind. He walks back over to the car, grabbing the backpack from the back seat of the car before heading back toward the entrance.

Chapter 11

Entering back through the main doors of the service station, he turns, locking the bolts on the floor and ceiling. A breeze still blows through the smashed glass at the bottom corner of the window. Broady looks around the room for anything to block it with. Seeing a sturdy wooden magazine rack next to the entrance, he begins to pull the heavy wooden cabinet positioning it over the door. It scrapes loudly on the pieces of broken glass on the floor like nails on a chalkboard. Broady doesn't seem to notice, positioning himself on the other side he shoves it with his shoulder. Standing back up, Allison and Charlotte stare at him, Charlotte has both hands covering her ears. They look at him discontented.

"What?" Broady says throwing up his hands.

Charlotte screws her face up. "My kindy teacher makes that sound on the blackboard when we're too loud," she says. "Blahhhh." She pretends to vomit and shivers.

Broady laughs. "Yeah, well you're blahh!" he replies childishly.

The three walk back through the kitchen into the dwelling

behind. As Broady walks back through the beads still swinging away, his body immediately begins to tense up.

The heavy-set dark-skinned woman sitting on the single recliner hops up from the chair and wraps her arms around Allison.

"Oh, honey," she sobs, "let me look at you." She pulls back looking Allison up and down, tears start to fall from her eyes before pulling her back in an embrace. Broady sees she seems to genuinely care.

"Are you ok?" she asks.

"I'm fine," Allison replies. "Broady came to save me, like my very own guardian angel," she says cheerfully, smiling back at him.

"Thank you, Broady," the woman says. "We're all very happy you're here."

Broady can barely wipe the frustration off his face; still very much upset, it's difficult for him to accept the woman's gratitude. Instead he stares with a stone-cold look at everyone sitting in the room.

Sensing the tension, Allison walks over to him.

"It's ok, Broady, they did everything they could, Geoff over there tried to stop them." Allison points to the elderly gentleman sitting on the couch holding his wife.

"See what they did to him?" Allison points to Geoff's eye. "They had us at gunpoint Broady, everyone was frightened and didn't expect something like this to happen on top of everything else," she says.

Looking around again at everyone, he can see she is right; he softens slightly looking at the dark-skinned woman.

"You're welcome," he manages to get out.

"Hey!" Charlotte pipes up, still mounted on Allison's hip.

"We wouldn't have even come in if it wasn't for me!" she voices, demanding some sort of recognition.

Allison turns to Broady with a surprised look on her face.

"Is that so?" she rhetorically asks.

Broady swipes his hand through his hair. "I'll tell you later," he says, brushing past them toward the back of the dwelling.

Allison turns to Charlotte. "Well thank you then, my little gem," she whispers, tickling her again.

Broady pushes the dirty, stained, tan-coloured drapes back, pulling on the sliding glass door making sure it is locked. He scans the room further looking at all the room's possible entry points.

"How about I introduce you to everyone," Allison says.

Broady, seemingly uninterested, continues poking around the room, pulling on windows and doors.

"This is Geoff, and his wife Elaine," she says as Broady leans over them checking the window behind them.

"Nice to meet you," he says.

Feeling uncomfortable, Broady goes to walk out to the kitchen. Allison grabs him by the arm; she glares at him, insinuating his abruptness. Broady stops and turns around, allowing Allison to continue.

"This is Jannette," she says, motioning to the dark-skinned woman. Jannette steps forward holding out her hand, she is dressed in a long-sleeved ankle-length African dress, and her hair wrapped up high in a bun.

"Nice to meet you, Broady," she says calmly. She turns her

head slightly as she holds her hand steady, gazing into his eyes as she tries to figure him out. Broady steps forward.

"Likewise, I'm sure," Broady says, shaking her hand.

They both spend a moment looking at each other, both still very sceptical of one another.

"The two over beside the couch are Sean and his girlfriend Miah," Allison interjects, continuing to introduce.

The two young teenagers lift their heads, simultaneously saying "Hey".

Broady nods his head up at the two sheepish-looking kids.

There's a pause for a moment before she introduces the last person, her face and tone drop as she points to the sharp snappy-looking chap in the corner of the room.

"Oh yeah, that's Rick," she says half-heartedly.

"Yeah yeah, save the best till last hey!" he arrogantly bellows.

Allison rolls her eyes as Rick springs himself up, now out of harm's way he struts around.

"Great," he says, throwing up his hands. "What do we do now, hero?" he says, mocking Broady. "We are in the middle of fucking nowhere." He begins ranting, Charlotte jumps in Allison's arms as Rick raises his voice. Broady begins to grit his teeth, Rick already gets on his nerves.

"These crazy fucking creatures come out at night that no one knows anything about; just about decimate everything and everyone we've ever known. Only to be commandeered by some fucking redneck hillbillies. And now we're stuck in this shithole, unable to make it to any sort of safety," he carries on aimlessly.

Wanting to further dampen his spirits Broady whispers, "Actually, the military checkpoint has been evacuated."

There's a large gasp as everyone in the room looks around in disbelief at each other.

"Great," Rick says sarcastically, holding up his arms he nods his head, before dropping them down hopelessly by his side.

"Just cool it, would ya!" Allison interrupts his ramblings.

Rick casually walks over to Allison getting right up close to her face. Broady begins to tense up, puffing out his chest, tilting his head back he clenches his fists as his face boils with rage from the remnants of the fight just moments ago.

"Or what?" Rick challenges her.

Allison stares back at him shaking her head. "You're such a dick." She taunts him, knowing deep down he's nothing but a spineless wimp with a big ego.

He moves his head to the side toward Charlotte. "So glad your dad has come to save us," he says quietly.

Infuriated, Broady storms over grabbing Rick by his tie, twisting it around tightening the knot around his neck.

"You don't speak to her," he growls deeply, inches from Rick's red face as his blood supply is obstructed from his tie.

"Broady," Allison yells, holding her hand on his shoulder. He looks over, seeing Charlotte frightened by the conflict and releases Rick, shoving him back out of the way.

"Yeah, yeah," Rick says sarcastically still attempting to uphold an alpha persona.

"Girl's pussy got you on a tight leash, eh boy," he says smugly.

Tipping Broady over the edge, he steps forward clenching his fist, cocks his arm back and punches Rick square in the nose. Everyone in the room gasps, Sean and Miah rise from the floor as Rick stumbles back, tripping on the coffee table in the middle of the room banging his elbow loudly, before falling onto the couch.

"Ooowww," Sean exclaims.

"Damn," Miah says.

Broady steps forward aggressively as Rick covers his face.

"I'm not here to play games with you. You keep your mouth shut until we're gone. As soon as morning comes, Allison, my daughter and I are out, you understand me!" he shouts.

Rick assumes defeat nodding his head, cupping his nose as blood runs down his face.

Broady turns around lowering his voice he walks over to Charlotte.

"I'm sorry, baby," he says holding out his arms as she climbs into him. Kissing her gently on the cheek. Seeing that he's startled everyone more than they were already, he begins to feel guilty adding, "Look, I'm sorry, everyone. We don't have time for this," he says, pointing toward Rick.

"Put the gun down then, we don't need any more people dead," Jannette says.

"Pfft, I don't think so," Broady says dismissively, infuriating Jannette.

"Just sit down, son, and calm yourself," Geoff says calmly, patting his hand down beside him.

Broady takes a moment realising these people are not his enemy and breathes deeply, taking Geoff up on his offer, he sits down next to him, propping Charlotte up on his lap.

The situation de-escalates and Jannette stands strong, taking over the room.

"Well," she announces, "since we'll all be spending some time together, we might as well get to know each other," she says with a hint of sarcasm. She raises her eyebrows at Broady. She looks down at Charlotte nestled in her father's arms as she looks back at her. Her sceptical look fades, turning into a warm smile,

"And who might you be, gorgeous girl?" she says lovingly.

"Charlotte," she replies, still a little withdrawn.

"Well that's a pretty name," Jannette says, attempting to soothe her. "Well my name's Jannette," she says. "And how did you manage to get aaaallll the way out here?" she asks her.

"I live with my mummy and poppy in New South Wales, right before . . ." she hesitates, fumbling with her bottom lip. She begins to sway gently back and forth as she rolls her tongue around the finger now in her mouth.

"Right before Daddy came and scooped you up before the holidays," he says, quickly stepping in and changing the subject, poking her in her ticklish spot. She jumps and squirms and begins to laugh.

Jannette looks on as Broady tries to hide away his pain; she doesn't press any further.

Broady coughs, clearing his choked-up throat. "Then when we headed to pick Allison up from the safe zone. But she got away from us, didn't she," he says, wresting with Charlotte.

"Safe zone, huh!" Rick pipes up, shaking the blood off his hand. "The military can't even keep us safe from people let alone whatever the fuck is out there."

"Hey!" Broady growls.

Rick holds up his hands backing down. "Right, right, I'm sorry," he says and sits back down.

"Hey, go over with Allison, would you, kiddo?" Broady

whispers into Charlotte's ear, tapping her on the bum as she scoots over to her. Allison looks over to Broady for guidance; he nods to the side, gesturing for her to take Charlotte out of the room. Allison bends down taking Charlotte's hand. "Let's see if we can find you something sweet to drink." The two head out back through into the kitchen.

"What about you?" Broady asks, turning to Janette, secretly deflecting the attention away from himself.

"Me?" She places her hand on her chest. "Well, damn, we were at home watching the television," she says before Broady interrupts.

"Wait we?" he says with an intrigued frown.

"My husband Earl and I, we were watching the late-night news in bed when we heard a loud bang from downstairs. My husband Earl went down to take a look." She pauses and begins to choke up. "And that was the last time I saw him. All I can remember is him screaming for me to get out. I'll never forget how terrified he sounded," she says before the tears come bursting out. "I hid in the closet all night when I finally worked up the courage to come out, I went outside and there were Geoff and Elaine, who live across the road. I got a ride with them to the stadium, that's when we met Allison on the minibus."

"Damn, I'm sorry," Broady says bowing his head sympathetically. He turns to Sean and Miah. "What about you two?"

"Like Jannette we were just at home, well . . . Miah's parents' house, they were out for the night. Except we weren't watching the news, so we had no idea of what was happening. We heard all this commotion outside; I opened the window and leaned out to have a look, that's when I saw one of those creatures. It looked right at me. It was dark, but its eyes glowed bright yellow. I froze . . . Miah pulled me back in and we hid under the bed," Sean says, getting worked up.

"We were both terrified," Miah says. "I didn't see anything though; I had my eyes closed. All I heard was this clicking sound." She shivers, reliving the moment.

A collective agreement hums throughout the room, as Broady looks to see everyone nodding their heads.

Their stories converge, trying to piece together their description in the hopes they will better understand what's going on.

"Dark, grey-looking skin," Geoff adds.

"They move quickly . . . hunched over, from underneath the bed it looked as if they were on tiptoes," Sean says, adding to the description.

"We heard on the news it was a viral outbreak," Elaine says.

The energy level rises in the room as the survivors begin to work together.

"Like a virus," Elaine adds.

"Uh uh . . . No, sorry." Jannette waves her hand in disagreement. "Those things aren't humans, ok?" she says, becoming more passionate with every word. "They're demons, I saw one up close. Those growths you see out their back, that's their burnt wings. Fallen angels cast down from heaven. They're here to bring about the end of days. That's our punishment for straying too far away from our Lord Jesus Christ," she says, closing her eyes and looking toward the ceiling.

Broady didn't notice at first, but now sees that Janette holds a string of rosary beads; she rubs her thumb in circles around a cross on the end.

Fed up, Rick laughs as he stands up.

"Look, I'll tell you what's really going on and it's not the fucking end of days or any bullshit bible nonsense. It's the fucking government and the military right…" He paces passionately and pissed off. "They've been experimenting on humans mixing our DNA with animals, birds I'm guessing, hence the growths from their back; probably trying to create some sort of super soldier and it backfired now they're out, and now we are supposed to rely upon them to save us from their own shit," Rick says. He slumps back on the couch, puffed, having expended immense energy relaying his thoughts. As the group begin to bicker at one another, the sounds begin to drain out as a dull ringing takes over Broady's hearing, drowning out the outside noise.

Hearing only his heart beating in his ears, he becomes light-headed as his vision narrows.

Recognising the now all-too-familiar signs right before he has a vision, he quickly stands up and attempts to walk out of the room for some privacy. As he steps forward he stumbles, tripping over Geoff's feet and partially collapses, banging his left arm loudly on the coffee table in an attempt to hold himself up.

The sound of Charlotte's laughter echoes in his ears. Broady looks around as he finds himself walking through a grassy field next to a dirt driveway, holding out his hand feeling long reeds slip through his fingers. A blurred vision of a house in the background sitting up on a slight hill at the end of the driveway. Visions of Charlotte ahead of him are blurred against the backdrop as she runs ahead toward it. A silhouette of a man appears, separating from the house.

"Papa!" she sings out, her arms up and out as she begins to sprint ahead her golden locks bouncing with each stride. The dull ring in his ear becomes louder with every second. Closing his eyes, he shakes his head, in an attempt to dampen the noise.

Startled, Jannette looks over seeing the colour drained from Broady's face.

"Hey, hey, hey, honey, take it easy," she says, hopping up from her seat.

Broady opens his eyes slightly disorientated, having to refocus on his surroundings he begins to slowly sit back down, with Geoff guiding him from behind. Feeling the blood begin to circulate back into his head the ring slowly dissipates, and his heartbeat begins to slow.

"What's going on with you?" Jannette asks curiously. Allison runs back into the room. Having heard the commotion.

Reluctant to answer, he looks toward Allison. She looks at him with worry.

"At the beginning of this whole thing, Allison and I were at the shopping mall and heard a massive explosion. Ever since then I've been getting this ringing in my ears, mostly when those creatures are near, and crazy dreams, blacking out sometimes when I'm wide awake. Seeing things that just aren't possible, things that . . ." Broady says before stopping, seeing everyone's eyes glued to him. Feeling uncomfortable he's relucent to continue sharing.

Jannette looks deep into Broady's eyes as if she knows he's not telling the full story. "That's a gift from God," Jannette says softly. "He's given those things to you to warn you." She nods confidently.

"PFFFT," Rick exclaims. "Ringing in your ears after an explosion . . . that's called tinnitus my friend, and crazy dreams, yeah . . . I think we all had those since this started, probably blacking out from severe PTSD. Haha, gift from God." Rick walks off. "What is wrong with you people," he says, walking out, laughing and shaking his head.

Feeling vulnerable, Broady hops up, moving over toward Allison. By the strange looks everyone is giving him he is glad he didn't share the full extent of the visions he's been experiencing.

Allison places her hand on Broady's chest as he walks up to her and gazes into his eyes. "Hey, are you alright?"

Broady only keeps her gaze for a short moment before he looks away, burying his emotions back deep down inside.

He stands straight, changing the subject.

"So, it's going to be dark soon, we need to think about sleeping arrangements."

"I call dibs on the main bedroom," Rick announces as he walks back through the corridor.

"Oh, and by the way, the toilet won't flush, so yeah hold your breath," he says, patting Allison on the shoulder as he walks back to sit on the couch.

"Ugh." Allison rolls her eyes in disgust. Everyone in the room shakes their heads at Rick's arrogance.

"What?" he looks around as everyone stares disapprovingly. "How was I supposed to know?" He shrugs.

"The main bedroom." Sean sits up off the floor. "Where Broady blew those guys away . . . It's all yours."

Rick pauses for a moment with a dumbfounded look on his face realising the error in his choice. "I'll take the other room then," he says, changing his mind.

"We're all going to stay in the same room tonight, alright?" Broady says firmly, much to Rick's disliking. "We should shut every door, and barricade the glass doors and windows, push that dining-room table up against the sliding door and move that bookcase in behind the couch, securing the window. That way we'll all be safe."

"Yeah well who made you the boss?" Rick says, standing back up in a huff.

"You can either fall in or fall out, no one cares," Broady says. "Or do I need to put you out?" Broady threatens him.

The two lock eyes, Broady doesn't back down, not when the safety of Charlotte and Allison are involved. Seeing the determination on his face and not wanting to cop another punch, Rick subsides. He moves over to the side of the room and sits on the ground crossing his legs like a sulking child.

"Right, let's do this, it's not long before sundown." Broady claps his hands, rubbing them together. The main living and dining area are small, a five-by-eight metre room. The short corridor to the left has a bedroom door at either end and a bathroom and toilet door in the centre. Broady and the group clear a large space in the centre of the room pushing back the tables and recliner.

"Geoff, can you give me a hand?" Broady asks.

"You think you two can manage to drag that bookcase in front of that window?" he says, looking at Sean and Miah, who nod.

"Hey, let me help you," Allison says, following Broady as he heads toward the bedroom.

"Nah, you mind Charlotte, keep her in here."

Rick just sits his back against the wall with his eyes closed.

"Get your ass up, boy!" Jannette growls throwing a cushion, hitting him in the face.

"Nah, I'm good, looks like you all got it handled." He grabs the cushion and placing it behind his head, lies down on the floor. "Thanks," he replies smugly.

Broady leads Geoff through the corridor to the door of the main bedroom.

"Hey, prepare yourself, ok?" Broady warns him as they enter the bedroom.

"Oh my . . ." Geoff stops at the doorway; he goes white at the sight of all the blood on the floor and covers his mouth.

Broady sucks it up; going somewhere else in his head, he grabs the overweight man's legs.

"Come on, Geoff, we need to move these guys out of the way."

Reluctant, Geoff puts on a brave face, holding his breath as he enters into the room. They both drag all three bodies, placing them on top of one another to the side of the room.

It's a grim sight; Geoff stands upright shaking his head. "Jesus," he says, looking down at the three dead men. "I'm really sorry, Broady," he says shamefully.

Broady looks at Geoff, sporting a black eye and cut to his forehead. "No, Geoff," Broady says, "I'm sorry for going off at you all, especially you, I know you tried to help Allison and I appreciate it." He places his hand on Geoff's shoulder, squeezing it gently, making amends with Geoff. Geoff's eyes begin to well up as he stares down at the men. A proud man he holds himself strong, swallowing his emotion.

With the bodies out of the way, Broady moves beside the queen mattress lifting it up.

"Hang on," Geoff says, pulling the sheets off. Broady looks closer seeing tiny flickers of blood splatter on them.

"Good thinking!" he compliments him.

They carry the mattress out of the room, Broady shutting the door behind them.

The living room is dim, with all the drapes drawn and windows and doors partially barricaded, Broady looks around.

"I guess this will have to do." He sighs, hoping it will be safe enough.

"Here we go." Jannette walks back into the room from the kitchen, holding a lit candle in one hand and a packet of candles in the other.

"These should do just fine," she says proudly.

"Right, Geoff, Elaine, you guys take the queen," Broady says as Geoff helps her down to the floor. Sean and Miah drag two single mattresses from the other bedroom and push one to Broady as they settle theirs back beside the couch where they were sitting.

"I'll take the recliner," Jannette announces.

"You sure?" Broady asks.

"Yeah I'll be fine; you got your girl and baby to worry about," she says with a wink.

Allison and Broady look at each other awkwardly.

"Oh no, we're just friends," Broady reassures her.

"Mmmhmm," Jannette says, raising her eyebrows as she rolls out a blanket.

Broady is quick to turn away, pushing the single mattress up against the corner of the room shoving Rick out of the way.

"Hey man, watch it!" Rick says, scurrying to his feet. "So where am I supposed to sleep then?" he says, looking around at everyone comfortably sitting down.

"Well, since you were such a *big* help," Broady says, "you get the couch."

Rick scoffs, he goes to contest, before he looks around as everyone in the room gives him a scathing look. He jumps onto his back on the couch.

"Fine, suits me anyway," he says.

Everyone sits silently on their beds for a moment. The light in the room is dim from the candles as they cast shaky shadows onto the walls and ceiling. Broady looks up to the corner window, seeing the thunderstorm having passed rather quickly the last sliver of the light outside begins to fade.

"We best blow these candles out after dinner, just to be safe," Broady says.

"Pfft," Rick blurts out "What are a few measly candles going to do?" he says as he stares at the ceiling.

"What is wrong with you, man? I mean, what is your problem?" Broady fronts him again.

Rick ignores him, just lying quiet as he closes his eyes.

"So, what's for dinner?" Allison says, breaking the tension. "There's a whole convenience store next door, why don't we just, I dunno, take some of the food?" she adds.

Sean laughs. "Nothing like a good old ransacking to top the

evening off, hey!" he says, rubbing his hands together.

Broady laughs at Sean and nods.

"Let's go take a look then, shall we?" Allison says, picking up one of the candles, lighting it off another. She cups her hand in front protecting the flame from the draft as she walks off; everyone follows except Rick, who just lays there silently with his eyes shut.

Like kids in a candy store the group run through the aisles grabbing items from the shelves, tearing open packets of chips eating them as they rummage through the store. Broady paces up the aisle, with Charlotte in tow. He grabs a can of vegetable soup up off the shelf and begins to read the nutritional panel, like he would when the two went shopping. Charlotte looks up, screwing up her nose at what Broady picked out.

"Ew, Dad, I'm not eating that, it's cold," she says, displeased.

Jannette looks up, lifter her head from a bag of chips, farther down the aisle. "Come on, Dad," she says. "Let the little one have some fun, after all, it could be the end of the world," she says, throwing Charlotte a chocolate bar.

"Yeah!" they all cheer. Charlotte looks up at Broady with puppy-dog eyes. Broady caves to the peer pressure, nodding to her. Charlotte's eyes light up as she tears the top off the chocolate bar. Broady walks around the aisle toward the fridge, running into Allison as she stands behind the aisle stuffing her face with a box of chocolate chip cookies. She stops, stares at Broady with a guilty look on her face, with a mouth full of biscuits she smiles awkwardly.

"Carb loading, are we?" Broady chuckles to himself as he walks by.

Broady stands in front of a fridge full of soft drinks. "Oh yeah!" he exclaims, opening the door and pulling out his favourite can of soda.

"Grab me one," Sean calls out, walking over to him.

"So where are you guys headed?" Sean asks.

Broady pauses, looking at him for a moment.

"I mean before when you said the three of you are leaving in the morning? Where will you guys go?"

"My parents live on a farm a couple of hours' drive north-west of here. It's pretty remote and self-sustaining. Mum grows just about everything there, you name it. And my old man, he looks after all the livestock, mainly cattle, but they have chickens and pigs as well. I'm thinking it's a good place to start," Broady says. "They put in a ridiculous number of solar panels when the government were offering the big rebate, so I'm hoping there is power on out there as well." He continues rambling about the place aimlessly staring at the can of soda in his hand. Getting a strange feeling he looks up to see them all staring at him. Jannette and Geoff peep over the shelves on their tiptoes, with only their eyes, nose and the tops of their heads visible.

"Can we come with you?" Miah quietly asks, walking up behind Sean, wrapping her arms around him.

Broady looks around the room as they all stare in both hope and desperation.

"Like you said earlier, all the safe zones are abandoned or overrun, making a run to the port seems too dangerous, especially that we don't even know if anyone will still be there … We would essentially be trapped … Sitting ducks waiting to be plucked,"

Geoff says, making a number of good points.

Broady feels the pressure as they all watch, listening on the cusp of his every word.

"Ok, but on one condition," he says, as they sigh in relief, Sean and Miah cheering.

"What's that?" Jannette asks.

"We leave Rick's ass behind," he says coldly, wiping the smiles of everyone's faces.

Keeping his head straight he looks out the corner of his eye at Sean, who is looking around the room at everyone's reaction before he makes contact with Broady again. Broady lets out a sly smirk and laughs, breaking the ice.

"Funny man!" Sean says, tapping him on the shoulder.

They all chuckle at Broady's gag, as they walk back through the kitchen into the room.

"What's so funny?" Rick says as the group enter the room, seeing them all still laughing and smiling.

"Oh, just how we're gonna leave you out here to fend for yourself," Jannette says, sporting a hint of attitude, as she throws him a packet of corn chips.

"Wait, what?" Rick sits up quickly with a concerned look. "You're joking, right?" Rick says, a real look of worry taking over his face. Suddenly the big ego seems to fade away showing a glimpse of his true nature.

"Relax, Rick, no one is leaving you," Allison says, seeing his genuine concern, handing him a chocolate bar.

"Mmmhmm," Jannette hums, raising one eyebrow.

Rick immediately looks relieved, quickly unwrapping the chocolate bar shoving it in his mouth, gorging himself, barely giving himself time to chew before the whole thing is stuffed in his mouth.

"Gross," Allison steps back disgusted.

"Yeah, gross," Charlotte mimics her.

"Watch it, kiddo," Broady tells her off.

"We're going to head out to a farm, north-west of here. It's remote, but hopefully it will be a safe place to lay low for a while," Broady informs him.

"Great, like a bunch of hillbillies," Rick says, swallowing his last mouthful of chocolate.

Everyone sighs, rolling their eyes and turning away from him as he lies back down on the couch. The group sit quietly as they chow down on their looted goods. Broady looks up, peeking out through the small gap beside the bookcase in front of the window. Only just able to see the sky as twilight rolls around quickly.

As Charlotte finishes off the rest of her snack, Broady turns to her and says, "Right, kiddo, toilet and bed for you," he stands up, turning to the rest of them,

"I suggest you all do the same, I don't want anyone opening any doors or windows throughout the night."

"Thanks, Dad," Rick says.

Broady leads her out toward the toilet, waiting just outside the door.

"It stinks in here!" Charlotte says through the door, grossed out.

Opening the door adjacent into the bathroom, he walks over to the flyscreen window beside the bathtub. Before closing it, he peers out, noticing how strangely quiet it's become, no crickets nor birds chirping. No wind blowing through the trees. Just an eerie stillness.

"Hey!" Allison says, creeping up on him.

"Shit." Broady jumps, surprised.

"You all good in here?" she asks.

"Yeah . . ." He pauses. "This is going to be a long night," he says, before closing the window.

They all settle in for the night, Sean blows out his candle.

"Goodnight all," Sean and Miah both say.

"Goodnight," the rest reply.

Geoff and Elaine too blow out the candle beside their bed and lay down for the night.

Broady doesn't lay down, instead propping himself up against the wall with a pillow behind him. Charlotte lies down in the corner using Broady's lap as a pillow, and he gently strokes his hand through her hair, looking down at her as she peacefully drifts off to sleep, the dim flicker of their candlelight shines on her cheek. As all goes quiet, the noise in Broady's head begins. Still rubbing his hand through Charlotte's golden locks, he prays they make it through the night safely. Allison crawls forward resting her head on Broady's other thigh. She looks up at him and whispers.

"You never told me that you were having these crazy dreams?" she says before Jannette interrupts.

"Now you two kids don't stay up too late now?" she says, calling out across the room in a mischievous tone, pulling the handle back on her recliner and blowing out her candle on the side table.

"Thanks, Mum, we won't!" Allison calls back, giggling.

"Mmmhmm," they hear.

Broady breathes deep, racking his brain.

"I'm not just having dreams, Allison; some are while I'm fully awake. I feel like I'm losing my mind," he whispers down to her.

"What do you mean?" she says.

"Remember back at the mall, just after the explosion?" he says.

"Yeah." She nods.

"Well, it's hard to explain but when we were heading out into the loading dock, I saw the police officer and the checkout girl, I saw them get attacked," he explains.

"Yeah, but we heard gunfire so it's easy to assume that," she says trying to rationalise it.

"No, before the gunshots, it was as if I was there . . . Don't you remember? You asked if I was alright straight after."

Allison pauses for a moment pondering on what Broady has said. "Yeah, I do remember, you looked all spacey, holding your ear," she says.

"And another before they burst into my place. I'm telling you, these visions are intense. I've never felt anything like it, it's screwing with my head, I feel all over the place," he says becoming distressed; he rubs his hands hard over his forehead.

Seeing his emotional state Allison reaches out grabbing his hand.

"Hey, hey, hey," she says, calming him down.

"Broady, I've never seen you like this before," she says.

"What, crazy and losing it?" he replies.

"No . . ." She pauses. "Vulnerable," she says, gazing into his eyes. Caught off guard, Broady looks away, aimlessly looking around the room

"You always hold your cards close, I was beginning to think you were some kind of robot," she says, giving him a cheeky look and breaking the tension.

"Come on now, I'm never like that with Charlotte."

"No, true, but with everyone else, you're like shut off from your emotions . . . Who knows, maybe Jannette is right, maybe what's happening is some type of biblical apocalypse and maybe you've been given some type of gift to . . . I dunno, save the world or some shit."

"More like save your ass," Broady laughs quietly.

"Shut up," Allison says, whacking him on the chest playfully.

"See, there you go again. Broady. Sealing off emotions *again*," she says, mocking him.

"I think it's time we get some rest," he says, ending the conversation, shuffling back down the wall and closing his eyes.

"Mmmhmm," she hums, mimicking Jannette.

Allison rolls over, using his thigh as a pillow. With his eyes closed, Broady feels someone's eyes watching him. He opens them seeing Rick lying on the couch, his head propped up on the armrest, spinning his broken phone on his chest. Rick just stares at Broady without so much as blinking. Broady wonders what's going on inside his head. He grabs the rifle that's wedged between the wall and mattress, lifting it up under his arm staring back at Rick. A few moments go by before Rick turns over closing his eyes. Broady watches him suspiciously, not trusting the man one bit. Blowing out the last candle on the floor in front him, Broady keeps his eyes open as long as he can.

Chapter 12

A faint 'ting' wakes Broady, so subtle and quiet he wonders if he heard anything at all. He listens intently for a moment. With the absence of any ringing in his ears, he assumes that all is well, closing his eyes down again. Then again, the sound coming out through the kitchen. Broady sits up grabbing the rifle, his ears pricked back hearing a faint rummaging sound in the distance. He looks around the room, only a few slithers of moonlight shine through the tiny gaps from the bordered-up window. Broady wonders if someone is trying to break in and take some food. His mind moves to more sinister motives, wondering if the man who escaped from the room has come back. Holding Allison's head gently, Broady hops up onto his feet replacing his lap with a pillow. Charlotte has already rolled off and is nestled in the corner curled up with her teddy.

Not wanting to attract any attention he shies away from lighting a candle. He reaches down, silently grabbing the rifle and moves toward the kitchen. He quietly parts the beaded divider looking down into the kitchen. The room appears well lit, from his eyes having adjusted from the darkness in the living room. Moonlight shines brightly through the window to his left; next to the door. The kitchen appears empty, and he wonders if he's being too overly cautious. As he goes to lower the beads the rummaging sound ensues through the swinging door from inside the diner and convenience store.

Broady steps through the beads lightly as he approaches the door. Looking down at the tiled floor, dim moonlight shines through from the next room. He steps closer.

The circular window in the door is smudged and dirty and in the poor light, it's difficult to see through. Suddenly in his peripheral vision, a shadow is cast through the gap in the bottom of the door, moving across. The hairs on the back of Broady's neck stand up as he looks back down. He begins to sweat as he stands by the door, waiting for any more movement.

Moments go by and he begins to wonder if his mind is playing tricks on him.

Placing his hand on the swinging door, he gently pushes it open a few inches. Pushing his face up against the architrave he peeks through with one eye. The dining section just in front of him is well lit from the moonlight streaming in from multiple gaps in the broken blinds, it's empty. The three aisles to his right that extend to the back of the shop are not as easy to see. Broady is only able to see the first metre down each aisle before the shelves begin to cast shadows, blocking the light from the front door. Staring into the blackness, he begins to sweat as he fears what may be lurking there.

As Broady cautiously steps through the door, grabbing it firmly, assisting its closure, another rustle comes out from the centre aisle. Broady ducks down, his back against the wall of fridges as he creeps down the last aisle swinging his rifle between the end of the aisle and the middle. Stopping midway down, the sound on the other side of the shelf stops. Broady's heart races fearing he's been discovered. He holds the rifle up to his shoulder pointing it in the direction of the next aisle, gripping it tightly with his sweaty palms. With boxes of food in the way, he's unable to see across into the next aisle. Still, with the rifle up against his shoulder, he removes one hand and reaching forward pulls a large packet of toilet tissue off the shelf. As he does, bright yellow eyes stare back at him. Broady chokes, frozen for what feels like an eternity as he stares into them sending chills down his spine.

A loud hiss brings his attention back as the eyes turn away jumping from the shelf. A black cat meows loudly, running off down the aisle having been startled by Broady's ambush.

Broady lets out an enormous breath of air, having been terrified half to death.

"Just a cat." He whispers a pep talk to himself, shaking his head.

Broady looks through the shelf, the cat had been happily munching away of a half-eaten box of biscuits left behind from earlier. He wonders if he should go after the cat. *Probably will cause more noise*, he thinks.

He walks back through the diner over to the front door. Looking through the glass window out into a flawless evening. The moonlight shines brightly down on the open fields from across the road. He sees a large dark body of movement from across the field. Just a herd of cows moving along nearby.

Broady begins to calm down as he stares into the peaceful night.

After a few seconds, he settles himself, deciding to try a get some sleep. Turning around, his head a little slow to follow, still peering outside into the fields he bumps straight into something hard. Startled, Broady jumps back raising the rifle high.

"Hey, hey, hey, it's just me," Rick whispers, holding up his hands.

"What the fuck are you doing, Rick?" Broady whispers, rubbing his head after the two had clashed.

"I heard a sound, I woke up and saw you were gone. I figured I'd come see if you were alright?" he whispers.

"Yeah, I'm fine, thanks. It was just a cat," he says dismissively, suspicious of Rick's motives.

Still sensing the tension between the two and with no one else around Rick attempts to smooth it over. "Hey, man, look I'm sorry about earlier, I didn't mean to upset you, Allison or your daughter," Rick says.

Broady eyeballs him for a moment, wondering if he is genuine.

"So now that no one is around watching, you're sorry . . . Right." Broady looks at him coldly, pausing for a moment. "It's all good out here we should head back," Broady says, pushing past him.

Rick stays a moment looking out the front door.

"Are you coming or what?" Broady whispers out across the room from the swinging door.

Moving into the kitchen the room suddenly goes dark, as cloud cover moves over the brightly shining moon, blackening the kitchen.

"Shit," Rick whispers, pulling his phone out of his pocket and turning on the flashlight.

"Hey, I thought that thing didn't work?" Broady looks at him.

"I keep it off to save battery, I've been checking for a signal every so often," Rick replies.

"Hmmm." Broady nods his head, surprised at his forward-thinking realising he knows very little about the man.

Rick freaks as a loud crash echoes though the diner area followed by a loud shrill. He jumps toward Broady, grabbing on to his shirt. The phone in his hand shakes violently as he holds the light up to the door.

"Relax, man," Broady calmly says, placing his hand on his shoulder. "It's just the cat." He informs him, laughing at Rick's cowardice. As he turns back around a sharp pain stabs him in the ears with a deafening ring. Broady stumbles, falling against the wall, cupping his ears.

"Hey, man, are you alright?" Rick says.

A loud boom erupts, blasting through the glass front doors. As Broady stumbles back upright pushing against the wall, Rick stands there in a panic, frantically trying to turn the flashlight on his phone off—a pointless endeavour. Broady turns, grabbing a mop and broom hung up beside the swinging door and wedging them across the door between the sink and counter. He grabs Rick by the collar dragging him back through the beads and into the room. The commotion has woken Jannette who's already lit a candle.

"We have to get out of here!" Broady insists discreetly.

Geoff, Elaine, Sean and Miah sit up in their beds.

"What's going on?" Jannette enquires, looking over Broady's shoulder.

A loud all-too-familiar screech echoes through the corridor. Jannette's face drops in sheer terror, her jaw dropping and her eyes beaming like a deer in the headlights.

Allison rolls over as Broady leans over her, placing the rifle down he rips Charlotte from her bed, her body limp still in a deep slumber.

"What is it?" Allison mumbles in a daze.

"Get up, we have to go *now*!" Broady says. Seeing the urgency on his face she jolts, electrified.

A loud bang comes from the kitchen as the swinging door hits the wooden broom and mop handles. Multiple screeching clicking sounds reverberate through the tiled kitchen.

"They won't hold for long," Broady says urgently.

"What do we do?" Geoff asks.

"Out the back door, quickly," Broady says to them all.

The group scurry to their feet as Geoff and Sean push the dining table out from in front of the sliding door. The incessant thumping of the swinging door sends panic through the room.

Charlotte begins to stir, lifting her head up from Broady's shoulder.

"Daddy, what's happening?" she grumbles.

"Hang on, honey," he quickly silences her.

Geoff pulls on the sliding door, it doesn't budge. He yanks at the door again and again; the glass door shakes as anxiously rips at the handle.

"Fucking thing!" he cries out in frustration.

"Hang on!" Sean says bending down, his hand shakes as he grabs hold of the pin on the deadbolt on the bottom of the sliding door, pulling it up.

A loud crack from behind them and Broady's stomach drops knowing full well the origin of the cracking wood.

"They're coming!" Allison screams. Geoff pulls the sliding glass door, Sean and Miah are the first ones out they run frantically out into the yard.

The swinging kitchen door bangs on the wall as it bursts open. Looking back, Broady sees the glowing eyes of a creature as it bounds toward them.

"Quick, you go!" Broady says pushing Geoff along, Elaine by his side.

Broady grabs Allison's wrists pulling her out the door behind him.

As he steps out onto the concrete patio, a creature dives across tackling Geoff to the ground pushing Elaine into Broady, making them both fall to the ground. In the scuffle, Broady loses his grip on Allison's wrist. He holds Charlotte tight as he scrambles to his feet. Geoff's attempts to fight off the creature are short-lived as it grabs a hold of his neck in its mouth pinning him to the floor. Geoff screams out for a moment before his screams are silenced, muffled by the sound of blood gurgling into his lungs as he coughs.

Allison reaches out her arm, helping Broady up.

A loud screech erupts as Jannette moves hastily outside. She bursts through the door from the force of another creature jumping onto her, knocking Allison over. He loses sight of Allison again as the three tumble along the ground. Broady steps out from the patio onto the dirt yard, in the distance, he can see Miah's white dress illuminated by the moonlight running through the field.

"Close your eyes, baby," Broady says, pushing Charlotte's head into his chest as he goes after them. As he quickens his pace, in the corner of his eye he sees a dark figure race toward the two teenagers. He stops in his tracks; Miah's white dress disappears as she falls, letting out a ghastly scream.

Surrounded, Broady frantically looks for a place to hide. Seeing only the portable toilet and having little option, he desperately runs toward it flinging the door open, he plunks Charlotte down onto of the toilets seat and squeezes himself in.

"Where's Allison?" Charlotte cries.

"FUCK!" he yells, having lost her in the scuffle.

"Broady!" Allison's voice cries.

"Daddy, you have to help her!" Charlotte begs.

Broady pants heavily, not wanting to expose Charlotte believing they made it in without being spotted.

"Broady!" she yells again, her voice louder as she draws closer.

"Daddy!" Charlotte cries out insistently, breaking his procrastination.

Taking the chance, he quickly opens the door, stepping out into the yard. He grabs Allison by the arm as she runs by, she screams in fright. Broady cups her mouth muffling her cries.

"It's just me," he whispers in her ear, yanking her back toward the toilet. He quickly glances around, noticing three creatures preoccupied as they gnaw at the bodies of Geoff, Elaine and Jannette, who never made it off the terrace. They climb in and Broady shuts the door, sliding across the flimsy plastic locking mechanism. Allison climbs up onto the toilet seat, picking up Charlotte and placing her in her lap. The sound outside is ghastly as the creatures rip and tear at the flesh of Allison and Broady's newly made companions, like a pack of hyenas having made a fresh kill. Allison covers Charlotte's ears, sparing her the awful sound.

"Help!" a sickening scream calls out. The voice sounds like Sean. Allison looks to Broady for guidance the whites of her eyes amplified as her head quivers uncontrollably. The cramped toilet barely housing the three of them, Broady slightly shakes his head.

"Anyone?" Sean yells out again, his voice becomes louder as his hard footsteps sprint in their direction.

A creature screeches out, within only a few metres of the toilet.

Sean's deathly screams cry out as a loud thud hits the dirt below them. The toilet rebounds as something bumps it hard. The three wobble and bounce against the walls as the toilet recovers.

"Ehhhh," Charlotte lets out in a panic. Broady is quick to hold his hand up to her mouth, his face inches from hers.

"Shh, shh, shh, we're ok!" he lightly whispers, attempting to settle her.

The horrific sound of Sean's demise can be heard only inches from the door. Tears run like a river down Allison's face as she closes her eyes, shying away. A sickening gurgling sound is squashed by a thunderous thump, like the smashing of a watermelon. The noise penetrates Broady's whole body, as the teenager he got to know a few hours earlier is killed in the most sickening way. The shivers wriggle in the back of his throat, accompanied by the thick vulgar reek of urine and faeces inside a damp unventilated toilet; Broady's stomach churns. He tries desperately to hold it down, as the acid from his stomach climbs up his oesophagus.

Unable to vomit in fear of giving away their position, the sick climbs into his mouth. He swallows it back down, forcing it with a large gulp, some bile shooting out the side of his mouth onto his shirt.

He focuses his attention, placing his hand on the lock firmly pushing it across holding it there, he crouches down and holding his head up with his hand against his knee, his nausea slowly subsides as the noise outside the toilet recedes. He looks up seeing Charlotte cradled in Allison's arms as she lightly whispers into her ears. Although pale and afraid, her hands stay steady as she nurtures Charlotte.

The night drags on and the feeling of time passes by ever so slowly for the three. The sound of pitter-pattering feet across the dirt yard is constant; multiple creatures screech and click, their chatter and noises are somewhat lessened as Broady listens intently, his ear up against the door. Occasionally passing within close proximity to them, Broady tenses each time they do, bracing himself and wondering if this will be the time they are discovered.

Crashing and banging sounds emanate as the creatures tear up the dwelling. Believing they have moved from out in the yard Broady stands upright stretching up high on his tiptoes he tries to peer through the tiny dotted holes lining the top of the plastic-walled toilet. Unable to see much at all only noticing the sky on the eastern horizon as it begins to lighten. He fixates on the horizon watching intently. Minutes feel like hours before the sky beings to gradually lighten, increasing the intensity of the rummaging inside the dwelling, becoming wild before complete silence in almost an instant—as does the dull ring in his ear.

Broady frowns, perplexed, the ringing going largely unnoticed during the ordeal only becoming apparent after the crisp silence.

"I think they're gone," he whispers to Allison who drops her tense shoulders in relief. "Let's just sit tight for a while to be sure," he adds. Allison drops her gaze down to Charlotte as she lay cradled in her arms having fallen asleep.

Broady too breathes a sigh of relief as the two smile at one another.

Broady slides his back along the plastic wall until he hits the ground, leaning his head back to rest, his knees up to his chest tight and cramped, unable to extend them freely. Both physically and mentally exhausted Broady shuts his eyes for what feels like only a moment.

Chapter 13

Feeling his legs begin to ache severely, he opens his dreary eyelids. Like the feeling of a huge hangover his head pounds, his body heavy and stiff. He blinks numerous times, the whole interior of the portable toilet is lit brightly with morning sunlight. Disorientated by the swiftness of dawn he attempts to stand.

"Tsssk," he utters in agony as his legs shoot stabbing pains up into his spine, both numb and tingling, waking Allison as he does. He pulls himself up with his hands gripped on the small wash bowl, managing to get up onto his feet. He lets out a loud pent-up breath.

Allison yawns stretching her neck, her eyes heavy and red. Charlotte grizzles as she wakes, also displeased with her short, broken sleep. Allison rocks her, gently comforting her.

"Wait here," Broady says. "I'm going take a quick look around."

Pulling back the plastic lock he pushes the door, tensing his body pre-empting a nasty sight. Only opening the door slightly, he slips out into the yard stepping on a blood-covered patch of grass and dirt. Getting the jitters, he quickly jumps off to one side.

It's a grim sight as he shuts the plastic door behind him; a string of blood loops up from the ground and halfway up the door. As suspected, but not surprisingly, Broady notices once again the absence of any bodies. Droplets of blood lead a trail toward the patio from the stained grass where he suspects Sean to have laid. He wonders if his body was moved by the creatures after they attacked him.

Cautiously he moves toward the patio, the sight of which is no better. Hundreds of small bloody footprints paint the surface; Broady bends down taking a closer look. The prints share a similarity to those of a dog. With the absence of any heel print Broady begins to question whether these creatures are or were human.

He peers over to the large pools of blood; sadness takes hold remembering Geoff's last moments. There are two others just next to them outside the door. Broady shakes his head at the hopelessness of their escape. They didn't stand a chance, he thinks, having barely made it out himself. He stands back up taking another look around the yard, seeing a bloody and torn white piece of cloth partially suspended by the tall grass. He closes his eyes for a second as he recalls Miah's end. He shakes his head at such a young innocent life lost. He grits his teeth before stepping over the puddles of blood into the doorway. Holding both hands out in the doorway Broady is reluctant to enter. The bloody prints are scattered throughout the carpet floor, there's a large scrape mark along one of the walls. Their bedding lay in tatters, ripped and torn with the cotton filling of quilts spread throughout the living room. Sticking his neck in farther he looks down the corridor to the kitchen. The house appears quiet and empty. Broady turns to make his way back outside when the sound of plates crashing together echoes from the kitchen. Broady freezes in a moment of shock, his heartbeat skyrockets as he slowly turns around. He breathes quietly listening intensely. Again, the faint shutter of crockery coming from down the corridor. Needing to make sure the area is safe for Charlotte and Allison, Broady knows he has to go back in. He steps lightly inside the dwelling, walking carefully around the scattered bits of broken furniture hoping to find his rifle. Tiptoeing all the way to his single mattress, the rifle appears missing. Alarmed, he begins anxiously rummaging around through the torn bedding and pillows, finding the rifle wedged against the wall and mattress, he sighs in a split second of relief.

With his rifle held high he walks down the corridor, the beads hanging from the doorway lay broken on the tiled floor. He carefully steps over them to avoid slipping. He bends down scanning the bottom cupboard doors, noticing nothing; he stands back up and peeks up through the circular glass door. A faint vibration reverberates as a knife sitting on the counter vibrates against the metal bench top. Broady is quick to jump back looking closely at the cupboard below. The door moves ever so slightly. Tension rises as Broady fears a creature may be hiding. He points the muzzle directly at the door and stands anxiously waiting. His palms begin to sweat as he reaches out, his hand shakes, hovering over the handle. He holds his breath. Taking a big gulp, he grabs hold of the handle pulling it open and jumping back readying his rifle to fire.

"Fuck!" he gasps before letting out a pent-up breath.

Rick lay inside the cupboard, having stuffed himself in sometime during the night. Broady sighs in relief before noticing Rick is bleeding heavily.

"Holy shit!" he says, dropping the rifle, falling to his knees to aid him.

Rick's white business shirt is torn and bloody, he whimpers as he slides his legs up and down.

"Rick, I need to take a look," Broady says, placing his hands on top of Rick's as he nurses his abdomen.

As Broady pulls his hand up, Rick shrieks, pulling himself away. His face is drowned in a look of pure terror as he breathes short, shallow and panic-stricken breaths.

"No, no, no," he cries out, cowering farther into the back of the cabinet.

"Hey, man, it's ok. They're all gone," Broady says. "I need to take a look, to help you, ok?" Broady slowly places his hands back.

As he pulls one of Rick's arms away, he's shocked by what he sees. The gash across his stomach is long and deep. Ricks hand slides over his abdomen as he holds in part of his intestines. Broady gasps jumping back up.

"Shit, shit, shit, shit, shit," Broady says hopelessly, his hands on the back of his head.

"Don't bother," Rick gasps, blood spraying from his mouth as he coughs. "There's nothing you can do." Rick groans, accepting his fate as he gasps harder for air.

Rick raises his hand; his arms shakes as he points back down the corridor.

"Geoff . . ." he says struggling with every word, his eyes glaze over. Broady, confused, wonders if he's hallucinating.

"He was dead . . ." He coughs, choking as he speaks. "Then . . ." His arm drops.

"Then what?" Broady says, confused.

Rick exhales deeply; his arm covering his stomach relaxes as his intestines bulge out.

Broady quickly bends back down, pushing Rick's hand back up and applying pressure.

"THEN WHAT?" Broady yells impatiently, hanging on the answer.

Rick's body goes limp; his eyes remain open.

"SHIT!" Broady yells, pushing back up to his feet, annoyed and confused. Rick's final words have left him with more questions than answers. What did he mean by it? Saw Geoff dead? Then what? Frustrated, Broady wipes his hands on a cloth in the sink. Accepting he may never figure out what Rick was saying, he places it in the back of his mind. Broady walks through the dwelling and back outside, broken glass cracking under his heavy footsteps.

He walks up to the portable toilet. "It's clear," he says as he pulls on the plastic door.

Charlotte is crying, her entire face is wet with tears. Allison is still cradling her.

"Daddy!" she cries, throwing herself on him.

"Hey, hey, hey," Broady says calmly.

"She thought you weren't coming back," Allison adds, as Charlotte buries her head into his shoulder.

"Hey, here I am!" he says, pushing back her red and distraught face.

"I told you the monsters were real!" she says, tearfully looking at him.

"I know, I'm sorry for not believing you," Broady says, cuddling her tight. He looks over her shoulder to Allison, the two share a look, having known all along. Feelings of guilt surface as he wonders whether protecting her from what's happened was for her benefit or his.

"Come on, let's get out of here," Broady says, carrying Charlotte in his arms.

The trio walk toward the house. "Cover your eyes, baby," Broady whispers to Charlotte, the grim sight of the bloody mess is enough to give grown adults nightmares.

"Close them tight," he says, seeing her peeking through; he gently pushes her head back down as they walk through the dwelling.

Allison gasps at the sight of Rick's body lying in the kitchen, mortified she begins to hyperventilate, and she too closes her eyes placing her hand on Broady's shoulder as he leads them through. Having previously thought the convenient store was a mess, he's surprised as he looks around. The shop looks completely ransacked, the aisle shelves have been all knocked over and the entire shop contents lay scattered all over the floor. The glass fridge doors are either cracked or shattered, leaving shards of glass covering the floor, the floor is wet from split cartons of milk. Allison almost loses her footing on the slippery tiled floor, the combination of liquid and tiny glass shards is like walking on marbles, she pulls heavily on Broady as she regains her step.

The three move slowly toward the door, having been completely smashed they're able to walk straight through.

The bright morning sun beams into Broady's eyes, partially blinding him as he's unable to shield his eyes from the rays. They step from under the cover onto the gravel road.

He leads them to the old Ford Fairlane.

"Shotgun!" Allison calls, seemingly having totally supressed her awful experience, she runs out toward the car, hopping in the front passenger seat, her mood having shifted noticeably. Broady opens the back door, placing Charlotte down on the back seat, a deja-vu moment having placed her on the very same seat yesterday. He looks forward into the front seat with concern for Allison.

He walks over to the driver's-side door and hops in. First, he checks the ignition not wanting to feel foolish again—unfortunately, no such luck this time. He searches the glove box and sun visor, before reaching down with his hand, scraping it along the carpet floor. A jingle sounds as he bumps what feels like a chain of keys.

"Yes!" he cheers, picking them up. "Now come on, old girl," he says talking to the car as he singles out the ignition key from the chain, plugging it in and turning the car over.

The car starts beautifully.

"Woohoo!" Allison cheers.

Checking the fuel seeing it just over halfway Broady announces, "It's going to be a good day; I can feel it!" he says, attempting to remain positive. "I'll quickly grab some things before we head!" Broady says, jumping back out of the car.

The mood shifts as everyone is grateful, they'll soon be on their way.

"I'll have some chocolate please!" Charlotte yells through the back window.

Broady laughs at his daughter's cheek.

"Yeah get me some too, please," Allison agrees.

He walks back in, a confident stride in his step as things start to turn around for them.

He grasps miscellaneous items he can reach off the floor, not bothering to move the shelving; they'll be at his parent's farm before midday at this rate.

He joyfully strolls back to the car; Allison smiles at him as he passes by.

"Here you go kiddo, go nuts." He throws the plastic bag into the back.

"Road trip!" Allison cheers as Broady hops back in. He unhinges his rifle from his back placing the muzzle facing down on the floor with the butt propped up against the seat.

Charlotte rummages through the plastic bag. "Hey, Dad, can I have this?" she asks, holding out a Snickers bar.

"Yeah, sure, but when we get to Nanna and Pop's it's fruit and veggies for you," he says, looking into the back seat, much to her dismay.

Broady puts his hand out as if to place the car into gear, instead grabbing only air.

Confused he looks around,

"You change gears on the steering column, dummy!" Allison says cheekily. She and Charlotte both burst out laughing at Broady, who takes it in good faith happy to hear them both laughing.

He reverses the car back out onto the road, taking one look back toward the service station, the place that's harboured some of the most horrible experiences. A feeling of relief washes over him, as he turns back around ready to leave the place and memories behind. Looking over to Allison, the sun shines through the window onto her tanned skin sitting sideways in her seat, her legs laid out along the long three-seater cushion as she leans her arm over into the back playfully fighting with Charlotte over chocolate bars, the two laughing hysterically. Warm feelings of home and family take root, as do feelings of affection toward Allison, having almost lost her yesterday.

"What are you looking at?" she says teasingly, smiling back at him.

"Nothing," he quickly blurts out, facing forward.

He can still feel her gaze lingering a while longer, he shifts the car into drive attempting to ignore her.

"Hold on!" Broady announces as he steps his foot hard on the gas pedal, shunting Allison back into her seat as he laughs playfully.

"Haha! You're *so* funny," she says, poking out her tongue.

"Do you even know where we're going?" she says.

Broady pauses as he tries to recall the map.

"Yeah, yeah," he says, acting confidently and hoping to find some signs along the way.

Now reunited, the trio begin their journey farther west.

Chapter 14

The road is long and straight, it's not long before the hype of leaving the service station begins to diminish, the fields of empty crops and dirt give little inspiration leaving time for reflection.

Allison turns in her seat, leaning her arm over into the back seat; Broady looks over his shoulder as she gently strokes the hair from Charlotte's face. Only an hour in and Charlotte is already asleep, her mouth agape as her head rests awkwardly back, chocolate covering her mouth and still holding the empty wrapper.

Allison rests her head on the seat aimlessly staring out the back window as she gently strokes Charlotte's leg.

"What's up, mate?" Broady asks, seeing her declining demeanour.

She doesn't respond, her head swaying side to side as they drive over patched potholes in the road.

"Hey, you alright?" Broady asks again.

"Yeah I'm fine," she responds, sounding less than.

"Come on, talk to me we have plenty of time, I'm here for you, you know that, right?"

Allison raises her head off the seat.

"I was really terrified yesterday, you know," she begins.

"First it was the mall, and then you and I stuffed in your ceiling. But that was nothing compared to those men attacking me, and I was pinned down on that bed." She pauses as she begins to choke up, covering her nose and mouth.

"It wasn't that I was terrified of dying . . . I was. But that was the first time I felt completely helpless . . . and alone." She pulls her legs up onto the seat, wrapping her arms around them as she leans against the door.

Broady feels guilty having left her, believing it wouldn't have happened had he not.

"I'm sorry that happened, Allison," Broady says reaching his arm out to her.

"It's fine," she murmurs, before going quiet.

"I may have left to find Charlotte, but I would never abandon you, I promise."

Broady realises that now Allison having lost her parents, it's probably hitting home for her now, thinking that she's all alone. Broady can't imagine how she must feel. He backs off leaving her to process her own thoughts and feelings, concentrating back onto the road.

Another hour rolls by with the car silent, absent from anyone speaking. The exhaustion from the past seventy-two hours really starts to settle in, fatigue rises high as his body begins to ache, feeling every bump and bruise, his eyes heavy as he blinks longer and longer each time. He rubs them as they ache to close. He looks over to Allison; emotionally drained, she too has fallen asleep.

"Get some rest, kid," Broady whispers over to her. He repositions the rear-view mirror so he can check back on Charlotte. He looks around trying to find anything to help keep him alert. He winds down the window, sticking his head out letting the cool breeze blow over his face; looking up he sees eagles circling up high above them. He wonders if they are circling them waiting for some fresh roadkill. He leans back in following the birds as they circle off. With the birds now gone he places his arm up against the door leaning his head into his hand. With his head lightly rested against his hand he feels more and more relaxed. As the highway nears a junction, still in a daze Broady fails to see the road coming to an end. He rubs his eyes again as his focus becomes blurry. As he moves his hands away, he's startled by the large crop of sugar cane straight ahead of him.

He gasps as he slams the breaks, not realising just how long he was rubbing his eyes. Charlotte and Allison are both flung forward hard into their seatbelts. Allison, shocked, slams her hand against the dash as the car comes to a screeching halt only metres from the guard rail.

"What the hell, Broady?" Allison yells, slapping him with the back of her hand.

"My bad!" he says.

Allison just glares at him, seeing how tired he is, she asks, "Did you fall asleep, Broady?" she says angrily.

"Nah nah," he quickly covers. "Just a lapse of concentration, I'm all good."

Allison shakes her head not believing him one bit. Charlotte begins to burst out crying, startled from the abrupt stop. Broady reaches back to comfort her.

"It's ok, honey, we just stopped quickly, everything is ok," he says calmly.

"Yeah, it is now I'm driving," Allison proclaims, opening the passenger door and climbing out, she storms over to the driver door opening it.

"Right, out you hop," she orders him,

"Didn't you fail your Ps like three times already?" Broady jokes.

"For your information it was once and that's only because the driver instructor hit on me and I told him to go and get effed!" she rages before peering into the back seat seeing Charlotte sitting there cuddling her teddy. She adjusts her tone lowering it down.

"Besides after what we've both been through, I'd be pretty annoyed if we died in a car accident because you were too stubborn to ask for help," she adds.

"Alright, alright." Broady chuckles at her boisterous attitude, sliding over into the passenger seat.

Allison jumps in, shifting the car into reverse she pulls back to the stop sign at the T intersection.

"Which way?" she asks, looking side to side.

"North . . . We need to go north," Broady says.

"Ok, which way is that, smart arse?" Allison says abruptly, still sporting a ton of attitude.

"Right, go right," he says, continuing to laugh.

Still upset from being woken, Charlotte sulks from the back seat.

"Come here, honey," Broady says climbing over the front seat and into the back.

Nestling in beside her, she cuddles up under his arm resting her head on his chest.

Rubbing his hand through her hair, somehow still soft and silky he begins singing her bedtime song as he takes in the subtle smell of her children's shampoo still lingering in her hair, the smell reminding him of bathing her as a baby, bringing a calmness to his breath.

As he quietly sings away, he catches Allison gaze as she looks back through the rear-view mirror with a sparkle in her eye, Broady quickly looks down burying his feelings with it.

Like magic she's asleep before he even finishes.

"Aww," Allison gawks adoringly. "So cute, Broads!" she adds gleefully.

"Hey, you just keep your eyes on the road, ok missy?" It doesn't stop her smirking as she continues driving along the road.

The farther north they travel the drier it becomes, acres and acres of dry dead grasslands. The only greenery sits in a few square blocks, where large-scale irrigation hangs on long poles above the ground.

"I have no idea where the heck we even are," Allison states, as Broady unbuckles his seat belt, gently pushing Charlotte off him.

"What are you doing?" she asks, straightening herself up in her seat.

"Keeping you company is what I'm doing, you ok with that?" he says sarcastically, climbing back over the seat into the front.

Allison smiles as she bites her bottom lip.

"What are you smiling at?" he asks her.

"Nothing," she says cheekily, copying his answer earlier. "So, you're kind of like a hero of sorts now you saved me? Oh, save me, Sir Broady," she says, playfully giggling and making fun of him.

"Twice, actually!" he rebuts.

"Well, let me kiss you, frog, and I'll turn you into a prince," she continues mocking him, leaning over and making kissing gestures.

Broady sinks his neck down, pushing his face up against the glass. "Cut it out, would you!" he says.

"Come on, just one kiss." She leans over, poking him in the ribs, hitting his ticklish spot; he breaks out in a chuckle.

The car veers off to the side of the road; the car vibrates radically as the tires hit the rumble strips.

"Hey, hey, hey!" Broady yells leaning over and grabbing the wheel, as he pushes the wheel, steering the car back onto the road, Allison plants a sneaky kiss on his cheek.

"Mwah!" she chuckles, as his cheeks begin to blush. "Oh, are you blushing, prince?" she mocks him.

He turns around pretending to check on Charlotte, hiding his embarrassment with a smirk on his face.

As he waits for the flushing of his cheeks to dissipate, he notices a car through the back window as they pass by; the vehicle has its door left wide open. Finding it strange, the car seems somehow familiar. He quickly dismisses it as having not seen another vehicle for some time.

As he turns back facing forward his neck kinks. A sharp pain radiates down his neck.

"Argh!" He groans.

A sudden white flash blast, momentarily blinding him. He quickly shuts his eyes.

Opening them a few seconds later he finds himself standing at the letterbox of his parents' property, running his hands over the top of their blue rusted letterbox holding Charlotte's hand with the other. As he raises his head to look up the driveway another white flash blinds him.

"Are you alright?" he hears Allison ask.

Regaining his vision, he shakes his head, Allison stares at him with concern.

"Yeah I'm good," he says. "Just kinked my neck."

"You had one of those premonitions again, didn't you?"

Broady looks back at her, perplexed.

"Don't go hiding things from me, Broady Fitzgerald, not after everything we've been through, ok?"

"Nah it was nothing. I did have a flash, but just of my parents' driveway, I was running my hand over their letterbox," he explains.

"Well that's a positive thing!" Allison says optimistically. "Looks like we're gonna make it after all," she states.

"Yeah I guess," he says rubbing his fingers against his lips.

"You guess?" Allison asks, puzzled. "Why, what else did you see?"

"Nah that was it," he says, sounding less than convincing. He sits for a moment pondering silently as they drive.

"Previously when I've seen something, there's a strong urge or desire or whatever," he says, struggling to find the words.

"Like a gut feeling?" Allison interrupts,

"Yeah, like I come out of it with a knowing, so to speak, what to do, where to go."

"And this time?"

"Empty," he says.

"Well, so far as you have told me you've always come out better off. You're probably reading into it too much, I wouldn't worry," Allison says, trying to comfort him.

"Yeah . . . Maybe . . ." he says, pulling his left foot up onto the seat and resting his arm across his knee as he peers out the window. His mind is going in circles, replaying visions over and over.

"Hey, let's all play a game!" Allison says, hoping it will lift Broady's mood. He looks over out of the corner of his eye with an unimpressed look on his face.

"I-spy." She laughs, remembering how excited he became when he played with Charlotte the time when they all took a road trip down south to the beach.

"I'm not five years old, you know!" Broady says.

"Oh, come on, you love it!" Allison says, still giggling like a schoolgirl.

"We can't, Charlotte would be very annoyed if we played her favourite game without her."

"Ok, ok, ok. I have another one," she says, jumping up in her seat getting overly excited. "Truth or dare!" she says mischievously.

"Oh, here we go!" Broady says, rolling his eyes. "How is that going to work while were stuck in the car hey?"

Allison shuffles herself in her seat and sits up straight.

"Ok just truth it is then," she says laughing playfully.

"What kind of stupid sissy game is that?" Broady snarls, mocking her as he grabs a bottle of water.

Allison completely ignores his comment and begins, "I'll start you off easy. What age did you lose your virginity?" she asks.

"Pffft!" Broady spurts a mouthful of water all over the dashboard, coughing and spluttering he turns around to see if Charlotte is still asleep.

"This is a set-up; this isn't even a real game!" he says.

She bursts out laughing at his reaction. "Come on, answer or I win!" she says.

Embarrassed but not wanting to be bested by her, he goes along with it. "Eighteen. After my high-school formal."

"Ha! Boring!" she blurts out, laughing.

"Get out of it!" Broady fires back defensively. "Ok, smart arse, your turn," he says.

"Easy, seventeen, my friend had a bonfire in the woods on her property, me and my boyfriend at the time snuck off into the woods, up against a tree!" she says, raising her eyebrows.

"Classy!" Broady adds.

"See, you're doing great!" she says as she attempts to pry as much as she can. "Ok, I got a good one," she says. Taking a deep breath, she composes herself and in a soft voice she looks into his eyes and asks, "Have you ever thought or felt anything more toward me than just friends?" she says with a subtle wink.

"Oh snap!" Broady calls out, not exactly surprised by her question. He scoffs as he racks his brain for a suitable answer. Knowing full well ignoring her will only deepen her inquisitiveness.

It's true that up prior to this morning Broady didn't have any feelings for Allison, stuck in a slump of his previous situation, detached from his feelings. However, he recalls the fact that he's been slightly drawn to her since the beginning of this messy situation.

"Hmmm," he contemplates, seeing Allison anxiously awaiting

his answer, hanging on every word. He decides to play her at her own game.

"Feelings . . ." he says, smiling. He leans over, seeing her cheeks blush having laid it all out. Holding her gaze he softly says.

"I have this feeling like I really need to pee!" he says before bursting out in laughter. "Pull over, would ya!" he says, having bested her.

Feeling embarrassed, she pushes him away, pulling the car over to the side of the road.

"You dick!" she yells as he hops out.

Broady continues to laugh at himself as he crosses the road finding a large tree a small distance from the road. Allison rolls the window down.

"You're answering me when you come back, I hope you know," she yells to him across the road, holding both hands up beside her mouth projecting her voice.

Broady ducks behind a tree to relieve himself, buying him some time to come up with a clever answer. To his right Broady sees a creek bed running parallel to the highway, cane fields lining the opposite side. He recognises some of the terrain, the creek bed runs through his parents' property.

"Hey, we're pretty close," he calls out as he finishes his business. Allison doesn't reply.

The sun sitting directly up above, it seems like his estimations were correct.

He pulls his zipper back up, looking down as he climbs back up onto the highway adjusting his belt.

As he raises his head a voice calls out, "That's far enough!"

A rough-looking man, his shoulders and arms red with sunburn stands behind Allison, his shirt wrapped up over his head, his large hands covering her entire jaw, Allison struggles, her voice muffled from the man's hand. Pushing it down momentarily she cries out.

"BROADY!" She screams in pain as the man holds a short-bladed pocket knife up to her throat.

"Hey, let her go!" Broady yells at the man taking a step closer.

In response the man presses the knife harder against her throat, the tip of the sharp knife piercing her skin and a tiny trickle of blood runs down her neck, Allison wails in distress.

"Ok! Ok! Ok!" Broady freezes, holding up both hands as he desperately thinks of a way out of the precarious situation. The look on the man's face is one of utter desperation, looking agitated and exhausted he twitches, moving erratically behind Allison.

"Be cool, mate, it's all good" Broady calmly calls out, edging closer,

"I'm taking your car!" the man growls.

"No dramas, it's all yours," Broady says remaining calm.

"DADDY!" Charlotte yells in a fright, having awoken to the commotion.

The man, seemingly taken by surprise, turns around with a crazed look in his eye.

"Shut up!" he yells toward Charlotte in the backseat. Shocked, she jumps in her seat and begins to cry loudly.

With Charlotte bellowing from the back seat Broady can see the man becoming more irritated. "It's ok, honey," he calls out, extending out onto his tiptoes to make eye contact with her.

"Everyone is going to be just fine," he says, staring back toward the man.

The man groans loudly at the sound.

As Broady slowly steps closer he gets a better glimpse of the man's face, looking somewhat familiar.

"The car is yours, ok," Broady says, anxious to get Charlotte out.

"Just let me take my daughter and you can go." Broady circles around the man, moving closer to the rear door. Broady's heart feels like it is exploding out of his chest.

"I'm just opening the back door, ok, no need to panic," Broady says, commentating his every move. The man doesn't respond, yet he doesn't argue, either.

Allison remains completely still not wanting to aggravate the man as Broady opens the back door, careful not to make any sudden movements. He leans in pushing bags of supplies and belongings onto the floor clearing a path, he unbuckles her seatbelt lifting her from her seat.

"Hurry up!" the man yells impatiently, bending down, desperate to get moving.

As Broady turns to carry Charlotte from the vehicle, he sees a tattoo drawn around the man's navel as he stands upright. In that moment Broady pieces it together, he pauses briefly reflecting, the familiar car left of the side road; taken by the man who fled from the service station, the tattoo was on the man who held Allison down. Broady's anxiety turns to rage, angry having not killed the man along with the others, he briefly makes eye contact with the rifle still nestled in the front seat. He momentarily contemplates reaching for it, deciding it too risky.

"Get your brat and get the fuck out!" the man rages, fed up with waiting.

"Ok, ok, ok, I'm coming out," Broady says, concealing his inner rage. As Broady exits the rear door the man bends down checking inside the car. Tension runs high as Broady stares at the man watching his every move.

The man pauses dumbfounded as he peers into the front seat, tensions explode and within a split second the man removes the knife from Allison's throat, pushing her to the side as he lunges into the car. In a state of panic Broady flings Charlotte toward Allison who catches her midair before cuddling her tight, turning away as she shields her. Broady launches into the back seat of the car, leaning over into the front. The man reaches down, grabbing hold of the rifle with his right arm. In dire straits, Broady leans over into the front seat pulling the man's right shoulder back. Letting go of the rifle, the man swings back his elbow, connecting hard on Broady's nose.

The force pushes Broady into the back seat, the painful blow instantly waters up his eyes. With little time to recover he leaps out of the back seat, slamming the door. As the man resumes reaching for the rifle, his knees and left hand holding him up across the front seat, Broady bounds in, pouncing on the man's back, the force pulling him down onto his stomach. Broady manages to acquire the upper hand, his weight bearing down on the man's back. Broady reaches down with both arms onto the floor forcefully prying the rifle from the man's grip. Unable to move his body, the man's left arm pinned under his body, the man squirms. Turning his head, he bites down hard with all his might on the back of Broady's left arm, loosening his grip.

Broady screams in pain as he shakes his arm wildly. The man's teeth sink deep into his tricep, breaking through the skin. Broady lets go of the rifle and pulls his arm up, ripping it from the man's mouth. Taking advantage of the moment, the man rolls onto his back and with Broady's weight now off him, he pushes Broady back as he attempts to regain his position. Broady hits his back hard against the roof, with the man lifting his leg he kicks Broady in the stomach, launching him out of the car onto the road. Broady falls hard onto his back thumping his head on the hard surface and knocking the wind out of him.

The road is scorching; Broady gasps desperately for air as the midday sun beams into his eyes. With little chance for surrender and all their lives on the line, Broady jumps up, his body raging with adrenaline. By the time Broady has regained his footing, the man has hold of the rifle. Picking it up off the floor the man awkwardly manoeuvres the rifle in the tight space attempting to point the muzzle at Broady. Broady's gut drops as an intense fear washes over him as the man raises the rifle up. In a desperate, almost foolish attempt, Broady leans into the car grabbing hold of the muzzle with both hands. Placing a foothold on the side skirt of the car, Broady pulls hard on the rifle pushing with all his weight away from the car. As Broady pulls the rifle off to the side of his body the rifle discharges as it slips from the man's clutches. Flying backward out of the car, Broady lands onto his back again still holding the barrel of the rifle. Broady rolls quickly onto his side, springing up onto his feet. Making eye contact with the man as he lifts himself up, Broady can see the same look of surprise and fear in the man's face having been beaten yet again. Wasting no time, the cowardly man pulls himself up by the steering wheel as Broady grabs a proper hold of the rifle. Pulling down on the steering column he plants his foot on the accelerator. The door slams as the car accelerates off. Taking no second chance, Broady pulls the butt of the rifle into his shoulder raising it up to his eye. His heart still races from adrenaline, his vision still blurry. Broady screams out with rage as he fires mercilessly toward the vehicle. Each consecutive shot echoing out, reverberating off the sugar cane. Bullets rain down randomly on the car hitting the boot and shooting through the rear windshield smashing the glass. The man ducks down as he swerves the vehicle all over the road. Broady walks down the centre of the roads as he continues to fire, each shot tings as it hits its target.

Lost without thought he becomes unsure about what he's hoping to achieve. Panting heavily, he lowers the rifle as the car heads farther away. He bends over, taking in deep breaths. As he stands back up looking back toward the fleeing car, he sees it slowly veer off the side of the road, falling down an embankment and begin to roll over repeatedly kicking up dust and dirt into the air. Broady is stunned, mesmerised by the crash.

"DADDY!" the sickening scream of Charlotte's voice cries out. The intensity of her scream piercing his ears down to his core, knowing instantly that something is gravely wrong. He turns back; Charlotte stands in hysterics holding her teddy with one hand as it hangs down onto the road, her golden blond hair streaked with the bright red colour of blood. She's pointing toward Allison, who sits in the centre of the road hunched over on her knees. Her head hangs slumped down as she wraps both of her arms around her. From the side profile of her face, Broady can see her face is long, her gaze is fixated on the ground. Unsure at first, Broady slowly walks around toward her. As he moves closer, he sees her white shirt begin to turn red.

"Oh shit!" Broady yells, dropping the rifle and running over to her.

As Allison slowly begins to fall to one side, Broady drops down, cradling her as she slumps, her back against the road.

"Is Charlotte alright?" she musters out, her voice quivering.

Broady begins to weep as he looks down at her white shirt now soaking wet with blood.

"No, no, no, no, no!" he mutters, his voice crackling as he places his hands down over her wound.

"Shh Shhh," Broady says as she begins to speak.

"You're going to be alright," he says, attempting to convince himself as much as her.

"Daddy!" Charlotte calls, standing a few feet beside him.

"It's ok, honey, just stay back there, ok?" he calls back out to her, holding up his hand, now covered in Allison's blood. He moves his body around, attempting to shield her from the awful situation. Allison's arms shake uncontrollably as Broady lifts her shirt. Blood pours out from the exit wound in her stomach as she lifts her head, quivering in pain.

"Don't look," Broady says, placing her head back on the ground as he covers the wound with his hands, holding down pressure on it. Allison wriggles in pain. Despite the pressure, blood still trickles down the side of her body escaping through his fingertips. Blood on the road beneath her pools, the bullet having entered from her back.

Overwhelmed and completely powerless, Broady screams out

around him hopelessly for help. With the echoes of his screams going unanswered he notices Allison's body begins to soften as her moving slows.

"I don't know what to do; I don't know what to do!" he sobs helplessly, looking down. Allison's hand reaches up gently touching the tears streaming down Broady's face.

"I've never seen you cry," she says softly. Broady brings his face up in line with hers as she looks at the teardrops trickling down her hand. The colour rapidly drains from her face, partially delirious from blood loss, she whispers out.

"You never answered my question?" Speaking faintly her body begins to go limp. Broady grabs hold of her hand as tight as he can as it begins to sway, weakened.

Broady blurts out a laugh in the midst of his despair. "You didn't have to go and get shot for me to answer you," he says back to her as he continues to weep.

He holds her hand up to his mouth, he begins to break down, he gasps for air as he tries to hold it back, unable to gather his words he nods his head up and down. She softly smiles as a tear runs down the corner of each eye before she sighs, before closing her eyes.

Her hand welters in his as the life leaves her body.

Broady gasps heavily for air as his mind races, unable comprehend her passing. The tightness in his chest suffocates him until the sadness becomes too overwhelming to hold back. He lets out a blood-curdling scream, all the air passing out of his lungs drawing right down to the pit of his stomach, he rests his forehead on her body.

He weeps uncontrollably with grief and guilt.

"Daddy," Charlottes cries as she stands scared and confused.

Broady is so stricken that he doesn't hear her at first as he wheezes air back into his lungs.

"Daddy!" she cries out again, Broady's ears prick up. Lifting his head, Charlotte's bottom jaw is shaking as she holds up her hand, a finger resting on her tooth. Her cry reverberating from the shaking of her jaw as she exhales. Broken and distraught, he is unable to pick himself up. He crawls along the ground on his hands and knees the few feet along the road wrapping his arms around her. His head aches, the feeling like his mind has cracked, struggling to comprehend what's unfolded. Becoming light-headed and dizzy he slumps down onto his legs as he kneels.

He stares aimlessly down the road from whence they came running his fingers through the back of Charlotte's hair. Several minutes pass before Broady is able to speak.

"We have to keep going," he manages to muster, pulling back and holding Charlotte's terrified face in his hands.

Chapter 15

Broady stands, focusing on nothing but his breath he concentrates his thoughts onto what comes next. He turns around walking off toward Allison he notices Charlotte's apprehension and holds out his hand.

"Come here, honey, it's ok," he says. She quickly runs up close to him staring down at Allison's body as it lays in the middle of the road.

Charlotte stands beside Broady blankly staring down at Allison. Broady bends down, gently places his arms under Allison's, and lifts her upper body off the ground.

"What are you doing to her!?" Charlotte yells, sobbing and confused. Now faced with horrible fact he can no longer cover things up he attempts to explain.

"We can't just leave her like this," he says, grunting as he pulls her dead weight across the bitumen. She becomes lighter as he backs carefully down the side of the embankment. He rests her gently down, parallel to the road, placing her arms over her body, and kneels beside her. Sick with the guilt of her passing, he sobs intensely, but with little other choice he stands up, holding back the tears and composing himself. He climbs up the embankment and back beside Charlotte, she grips on tight to his leg as the two stand looking down.

"We're not going to just leave her, are we, Daddy?" she softly mutters.

"No, honey," he says, rubbing his hand over her head.

"I'll come back for you, I promise," he says, whispering to Allison, determined to make good. A single tear breaks free, rolling down his face onto the road.

Wiping away the tear he buries his emotions along with it.

"Come on, sweetheart, let's go," he says, beginning to walk off.

Charlotte lets go of her dad's pants, standing still her hand slips through his fingers.

Broady turns, seeing her still in shock. He steps back, bending down to her. "It's just goodbye for now. Daddy will come back for her," he says, reassuring her. Grabbing her hand, she reluctantly follows him looking back until Allison's body lay out of sight.

As they continue on, Broady sees the rifle sitting in the middle of the road, flooded with mixed thoughts, the bullets from the rifle having at one point both saved and killed his beloved friend and neighbour accompanied by the very real danger that may lie ahead. Struggling for a few moments he kneels, scooping the rifle up and placing it over his back.

Powering on, Broady doesn't want to spend another night in unfamiliar territory, with only a short distance to go he believes they will make it before sunset.

Farther down the road the two pass the turned-over vehicle;

steam billows out from the engine bay. Broady moves closer to the side of the road slowing down as he looks down at the vehicle. He hears the man groaning. As he peers over the edge of the embankment, he sees the top half of the man's body laying midway out of the driver's window on the ground surrounded by shattered glass. The man's torso is heavily soaked in his own blood.

Let him suffer, Broady thinks, snarling as he looks down.

"Come on, let's keep going," Broady says, ushering Charlotte along. Within a few feet of them walking away the man makes a cry for help. At first ignoring the man he bellows out much louder and sicklier, startling Charlotte as she jumps gripping to Broady's leg. His blood boils with the audacity of the man's plea, turning his head seeing the man's hand wave up in the air.

"I'm going to check for supplies, ok honey?" he says, bending down to Charlotte.

"I need you to cover your ears and look over toward the horizon, can you do that for me?" he says. Scared but appearing strong, she listens to her father, covering her ears as she looks north toward the horizon.

Broady walks to the edge of the embankment peering down at the wreckage. The man has managed to crawl from the driver's window, his arms are gashed and bloody from crawling through broken glass. Noticing only the man's arms pulls him along, his legs lay as dead weight behind him. Unhinging the rifle from his back he holds on tightly as he steps down the grassy embankment, a look of pure disgust on his face, as the man desperately crawls away. To where? Broady wonders, as he walks up to the man, kicking him over with his foot. The man rolls over onto his back; cartilage is poking through the top of his nose which has been split badly. The man sobs and quivers as he holds up his hand.

"Please," the man begs.

Cold and filled with rage, Broady will have none of it; he doesn't hesitate as he holds up the rifle, pressing it against his shoulder. Wasting no time, he looks down the barrel at the man, firing into the man's skull. His head jerks back, bouncing to the ground as his arm drops.

Charlotte jumps, startled by the single round as it echoes through the fields, crows on a nearby tree caw loudly as they take flight into the air, startled by the loud crack.

Broady believed he would feel better having taken the man's life. Instead he feels nothing. Irritated, he walks back to the wreck, reaching down through the smashed window in the back, he pulls out the rucksack that lay against the roof. He walks back up, hoisting the pack and rifle over onto his back.

Approaching Charlotte, he gently places his hands over hers, still pressed firmly against her ears lowering them slowly back down.

Kneeling, he whispers in her ear. "Everything's ok, we can go now."

The two walk silently for more than two hours. As Charlotte's pace slows, he bends down, scooping her up into his arms, making no attempt to entertain her. He continues on, silently replaying the traumatic events over and over in his mind, zoning out completely. Pushing on harder and harder his eyes well up with the suppressed emotions, unable to wipe them he continues walking aimlessly along the road, not even noticing the sound of his feet as they drag along the ground with every step before collapsing down onto his knees.

"What's wrong, Daddy?" Charlotte says, holding her hands against his cheeks.

"I'm fine, honey, I just need to rest," he says, struggling to unlock his fingers; his hands having gone completely numb. Sharp pains shoot up his arms as the blood flow pours back into his extremities.

Tired and severely dehydrated, he presses against the hot road with his hand managing to fight the increasingly difficult effects that gravity is now having on his body. Grabbing out their last bottle of water he cracks the top handing it down to Charlotte who vigorously chugs at the bottle, leaving less than a third.

"Good girl," he says, kissing her on the forehead before swallowing the rest in one gulp.

Noticing the afternoon sun beginning its descent over the horizon he looks down at his watch. 5:15 pm.

Broady wipes his blurry eyes in disbelief, startled the two have been walking for more than four hours. Still disorientated, he pulls out a chocolate bar from the pack, breaking it in half and handing some to Charlotte. He's quick to finish, his brain starved of nutrients. The two sit exhausted by the side of the road, watching the sun as it begins to hug the distant hills. A cool breeze blows over Broady's sweat-soaked shirt; he closes his eyes revelling in the cool tingling feeling, licking the chocolate off his dry, chapped lips.

The fog clouding Broady's mind lifts slightly as the sugary packed chocolate bar reignites his focus.

Broady reaches over, extending his neck out and pretends to

take a bite of Charlotte's bar.

"Hey!" she says, pulling away as Broady laughs.

"You tell me not to snatch, Daddy!" she says, displeased.

"I'm only playing." Broady laughs and pulls her in a loving embrace.

As he holds her tight looking over the top of his head his surroundings become clearer. Noticing a lonely street sign in the distance, slightly bent as if it's been bumped slightly—too far to read. Broady stands back up, his aches and pains pushed to the back of his mind. With the sudden realisation of where they are, he shouts, "That's Nanna and Pop's street!"

"Quick, up you get!" he says excited, barely giving Charlotte a chance to finish he quickly pulls her back up onto her feet, before picking up his rifle and bag.

"Come on, it's not far. You can walk from here," he says.

With a strong second wind, he pulls Charlotte along by her arm as he jogs as fast as his aching body can move, dragging his feet as he goes, in a state of excitement and desperation.

He blinks long and hard as they approach the street sign, hoping he's not hallucinating. He touches the cold steel pole reassuring himself he that he isn't.

A sense of relief trickles down over him. Charlotte looks oddly at him, not quite understanding the significance.

"Come on, let's keep going," he says, letting go of the pole and hurrying along. Charlotte races to catch up to him, his mind again drifting into tunnel vision toward their driveway, Charlotte puffs and pants heavily and she takes hold of Broady's hand staying close in tow. He slows down as they reach the old rusted letterbox. The flag is up. Instinctively Broady opens the back hatch, the door squeaks loudly. There's no mail, closing it again he presses on the flag, propping it down it springs straight back up.

"Must be busted!" Charlotte says, catching her breath.

"Hmmm, yeah," Broady replies, still lightly pressing the flag down. Worry starts to creep in, Broady's Dad is always so meticulous with their family's property, having rubbed a similar trait onto him. Broady's excitement has dwindled, gripping the rifle tight in his hands while he surveys the surroundings partly paranoid.

Fear, doubt and worry take hold. After Allison's death, he's now relentlessly questioning his decisions and not trusting his judgment.

"Come on, Dad, we're here!" Charlotte says, still excited, oblivious to his woes. She bounds over the steel cattle grid.

"Hang close, honey!" he calls to her. The slightly elevated dirt driveway is long. Large old wooden poles line either side, barbed wire strung between them, grassy paddocks where the cattle feed and wander on the other side.

The afternoon light fades quickly as thunderstorm clouds brew from the south. As they walk over a hilly mound the house comes into full view. The tin roof is as grey as the sky, no lights are visible inside or around the large wooden veranda that surrounds the old Queenslander home.

"Wait there, Charlotte," Broady says sternly, his quad muscles ache with every step on the slight elevation, energy spent as he catches up holding her hand tightly.

Weary, the two continue up, Broady fixated on the house.

Nearing a hundred metres from the house, the front fly screen door creaks open, his father walking out onto the deck, he bends over, fiddling with the gate at the top of the stairs not noticing the two. Even from a distance Broady can see his old man's bald spot on the top on his head. They step loudly as their feet drag along rocks and dirt. Toast, his dad's cattle dog barks viciously; his paws up on top of the gate, alerting his father as he looks up to see what Toast's commotion is about. Broady pauses as the two stare toward one another, neither moving a muscle. Emotions run high as tears begin well up in Broady's eyes, moments pass before Broady's mum appears behind the flyscreen door holding a plate she is drying with a hand towel, curious as to what's got her husband stunned. Looking down in their direction she sees Broady and Charlotte standing midway up the driveway, shocked she drops the plate smashing loudly on the floor, visibly shaking she opens the door, dropping down to her knees as her legs give way, overwhelmed by their surprise arrival.

"NANNA!" Charlotte yells breaking free from Broady's grip. Beginning to sprint up the driveway, the blond ringlets in her hair bounce as she sprints toward the house.

Toast breaks free, jumping over the fence and bounding toward her.

Broady looks up toward the sky as cold drops of light rain begin to fall onto his face.

"We're home," he whispers.

The END